GRAVE
SECRETS

GRAVE
SECRETS

A NOVEL

Mercedes King

Mercedes King
Visit my website at www.MercedesKing.com

Printed in the United States of America

First Printing: September 2020
Triumph Productions

ISBN-978-1-7343927-2-2

For Tina and Marlene

CHAPTER ONE

*T*he creak of my bedroom door and the familiar silhouette of my father as he slipped into my room at night made my stomach clench.

"Delilah…Daddy wants to lay in your lap and play. I brought our candy pretty girl."

Even in the dark, he'd hold up the plastic bag of orange slices, those gummy, sugar-coated candies that stuck to your teeth as you chewed. The plastic made a soft crunch as he swung the bag back and forth, as if it was an enticement.

I rolled to my side and squeezed every inch of my tiny body together. Crouched under my covers and clinging to my favorite doll, I knew it wouldn't save me from what was about to happen, but I squeezed anyway. At least I didn't cry anymore. Crying, fighting against him always made it last longer.

He stood at the edge of my bed and dropped the bag on top of my cover. His routine kicked in. He took off his flannel shirt. Then came the jingle from his belt buckle, and that sickening zip as he removed his pants. The soft flop of his underwear topped off the pile of clothes.

He pulled back the false safety of my blanket cocoon and crept in behind me. I never turned my head toward him, never faced him. His bare flesh touched my pajamas, but I knew not to flinch. He pawed my hair with his hand as he whispered into my ear. His breath, rotten with the stench of alcohol and cigarettes, snaked into my nose.

"Daddy just wants to play a while with his favorite girl."

He reached for the candies and fingered the bag as he took one out. I tried focusing on the faded wallpaper in my room. Those bunches of big pink flowers...someplace happy...where little girls were safe....

He lay his cheek against mine. His stubble like tiny needles to the side of my face.

"Got your special treat. I know it's your favorite."

I never ate orange slices outside of my room, in the daylight, apart from my father. As far as I knew, he didn't either.

He rubbed the candy against my mouth. Little grains of sugar stuck to my lips or crumbled to my chin. Back and forth he'd rub. Until I opened my mouth and let him slide the candy inside. I began to chew. Sloppy, loud chews.

"Daddy's gonna be real nice now. Real nice."

I bit the orange goo between my teeth, so I wouldn't scream....

I squinted, shuddered away the too-vivid memory. Wiped my sweaty palms on the side of my shorts and refocused on my driving. This always happened when I went back home. Dark memories from my childhood threatened to surface and engulf me. I powered down the window and breathed in the wind whipping on my face. Thankfulness washed over me. I didn't live in that pit of despair anymore. Helplessness had no hold on me. That broken nine-year-old girl grew up, built a life. Conquered those deep-rooted insecurities. Waylaid the false comfort of resentment.

As for my father, he was the one crouching—for the last fifteen years—in a cell at the Blackburn Correctional Complex.

Oscar, my orange cat, gave a purr-growl from his cage on the passenger's seat. He loathed road trips as much as being trapped in the plastic blue carrier. His disgruntlement was expected and probably neared wrath, since he'd been cooped up for three hours.

"It won't be much longer." I picked a piece of hotdog from the plastic baggie and poked it through the metal door. Oscar sniffed but didn't eat it. Still mad at me for the cage. Thanks to my former roommate offering hotdogs as treats, the cat developed an unhealthy obsession. Earned him a cute name though.

Oscar and I drove past the *Welcome to Venice* sign, purple prairie bluestems swaying at its base. Home. Agitation gripped me. I couldn't call Venice, Kentucky, home anymore. More like the tattered emotional wastelands I'd deserted. Venice sat about a hundred and fifty miles from my campus apartment at The Ohio State University. I'd finished my master's in psychology and had a job waiting for me with Franklin County Children's Services come September. Before devoting my life to helping kids in crisis, as an occupational therapist, I knew I needed to return home. Clean up that wasteland. Prove I was done being careless with my family's feelings. That I'd shed that skin of teen angst and bitterness.

My grandma knew I was coming, but I hadn't touched base with my brother Donnie. Hadn't mentioned to Grandma that I planned to stay for the summer. Part of me wanted to leave that open, in case being here was a mistake.

As soon as I turned into the driveway, Grandma came out the door, hands waving. Her gray curls bounced with her step while her poodle barked from inside the house. The creases on her face had deepened, probably from the years of worry I put her through.

"Delilah, I'm so glad you're here!" That Kentucky twang ever-present in her voice. Glasses that looked the same as the day Donnie and I came to live with her and Grandpa. She wrapped her arms around me and pressed her feather-soft cheek into mine.

It was the first time I'd let her hug me—really hug me—in ages. I'd done a good job pushing her and my grandpa away. Grandma could've told me not to come, could've said she was too tired or too busy or not up for company. She had reason enough.

"Let me look at you." She stood back and held me at arms' length. "Blonde hair now?"

I nodded and touched my messy bun.

"So thin, child."

"I get a lot of exercise, Grandma."

"Still teaching that Kung Fu?"

"Jiu Jitsu."

"I guess it keeps you…fit. Though I don't know why a pretty girl like you would want to jump around and punch people."

"It's self-defense."

She nodded somberly and pressed her lips together, right as I was about to say something about how I'd never let another man touch me the way Bill Ramsey had. Maybe she understood. She used to talk about how horrible she and Grandpa felt, not being able to help us or protect us from that situation. They had suspected Bill was abusing my mom but didn't know about the sexual abuse Donnie and I lived through until later. *I just didn't know what to do,* she'd said.

I used to get upset dwelling on it, because I wondered if there *was* something she could've done, like maybe bust into the house with Grandpa and his 12-gauge to get us out of there. But I'd learned to let that type of thinking go.

"Well, grab your bags and let's get you settled."

"Sure." I took my caged cat out of the car, along with a smaller suitcase.

"Is that a cat?"

Oscar's fur was fluffed. He grumbled, ready for battle.

4

"Yep, this is my baby, Oscar. Don't worry, he'll warm up to you after a while."

"I don't think I can have a cat in the house, not with Princess."

"Oh, I thought I could use the apartment above the garage."

Grandma ran her fingertips across her forehead. Whether she was thinking over my suggestion or simply sweat-speckled from the humidity, I couldn't say. "I'm ashamed to say it, Delilah, but the apartment is a mess like you wouldn't believe. Looks like a tornado hit it. I've been using it for storage, especially since your grandpa passed, and I hardly go up there anymore."

My plans were beginning to crumble. There was no way I could stay inside Grandma's house like a roommate for a whole summer, not with her yapping poodle and chain smoking. And sharing a bathroom with her? Not happening.

"Could we take a quick look?"

"Well, I'll have to find the key…" Another swipe at her brow.

I left Oscar on the front porch, still-caged for his own safety, while Grandma and I searched for the key. Princess greeted me with her twirly dance and flittering tail.

We found several potential keys and headed out back to the garage-apartment. Grandma took her time shuffling up the wooden stairs, which looked as though they needed repairs. The fourth key she tried opened the door.

I flipped a switch and lit up the darkened space. Dust and bugs fluttered. She wasn't kidding about the mess. An assortment of furniture was scattered about. Boxes sat on top of the kitchen counter and were also stacked on the floor. Growing up, my grandparents always had someone living there, either a relative needing a place to stay or a renter. The space had an open layout for the kitchen and living area, with barely enough room for a table and a couch. The bedroom was closed off and had a closet. A small and tight bathroom meant that all basic needs were met.

"Grandma, what's that reek?" I slapped my hand over my mouth and nose, glad I hadn't eaten since early that morning.

"Probably from the fridge. I bet it needs cleaning out."

"Shouldn't we open a window?" I didn't mean it as a question. It took some thumping and budging to get one half-open. The afternoon breeze crawled in, reminding me that the space didn't have air conditioning.

"Worse than I recall." Grandma planted her hands on her hips and shook her head as she surveyed the room. "I might have to get someone out here to clean this."

"I could do it."

A timid smile appeared on her face. "Why, you meaning to stay a while?"

I suddenly felt like a little kid in her presence, aching for love and approval with pinches of regret mixed in. I should've asked her first, thought this through.

"Well, that's up to you, but yeah." I dug my nails into the pads of my fingers. "I was hoping we could spend some time together, maybe talk about a few things."

Glee faded from her smile, and I knew I'd said the wrong thing.

"I mean I wouldn't mind helping you out around here," I clenched my hands tighter, "and maybe we could get to know each other again. That sort of thing." I didn't want her worried that I had expectations—or that I was there to get something from her.

"Now, that sounds like the best news I've heard in ages." She cupped my face with one hand and squeezed both my cheeks, just like she used to when I was little. "Let's head back to the house and get supper started."

As I followed her down the stairs, I hoped I wasn't being a jerk. Because I did want something. Repairing relationships wasn't the only reason I'd returned to Venice. I was finally ready to find out the truth about my mother's disappearance.

Sloan Ramsey had vanished nearly twenty years ago. Most people believed my father had killed her and disposed of her body. *Most people* included me.

I'd decided the rumors and stories from my childhood were no longer good enough. I wanted the truth. The internet only featured four articles on Sloan's disappearance. My aching heart and yammering curiosity only had four articles to feast on. Each one echoed the others: *Young mother vanishes. Husband claims desertion. Foul play suspected but authorities find no proof.*

Proof. The one thing separating me from the truth.

For years, I suspected there was plenty Grandma never said, never told me. Maybe she was worried I was too young or couldn't handle it. I wanted to prove to her I was ready, that I was mature and strong enough for total honesty. How I was going to do that, I didn't know. The mention of Sloan usually caused Grandma to change the subject or drove her to tears.

Some people said Sloan Ramsey had her issues, and that it came as no surprise that she ran off. Maybe that was true. No one walks through life without struggles or weaknesses, knowing pain or making big mistakes. Even if there was the slightest possibility that my mother had abandoned me and Donnie, left us with that monster we called Daddy, I had to find out why.

CHAPTER TWO

G round beef sizzled angrily under my spatula, and the dead-animal odor assaulted my nostrils. Now probably wasn't the time to tell Grandma I didn't eat meat. Becoming a Jiu Jitsu competitor and trainer had required a diet overhaul. At first, I hated the restrictions, until my body changed, my strength increased. Then it became a happy obsession. Most of the staples I grew up on, including sloppy joes, didn't touch my plate these days. But I couldn't tell Grandma. We were already off to a shaky start.

I'd brought in some of my things and put them in the guest bedroom, Oscar included. Staying one night in the house would be fine, I told myself. That was before I'd been assigned the task of cooking the meat.

"So, what's been going on, Grandma?" I went to the fridge, foraged for salad ingredients.

"Since you've been gone?"

Old me would've bristled at her remark. Hearing only, *Since you ran away and ruined the family?* I took off at sixteen, shacked up with a series of questionable people and their destructive habits. Shame lashed at me as I remembered how I used to call, tell her I was fine—I wasn't—and not to send the cops after me. Grandma sobbed during those calls. Grandpa ranted uselessly in the background. None of it moved me backed then.

Even after I turned my life around, got back in school, I nourished the divide I'd created. Being polite strangers was easier, less costly, than working toward redemption. My visits to Venice were short, sporadic—and I always made it clear I needed no one.

"Or do you mean since our last phone call?" Grandma flopped a bag of buns onto the kitchen table, snapping me from my memories.

The fridge had a few tomatoes and a chunk of lettuce on the verge of dying. With enough shredded carrots, it might work, but I dreaded those buns. Bread was now my sworn enemy, so this dinner promised to be an exercise in torture.

"I was just wondering what you've been up to, how you've been keeping busy." Tearing apart that lettuce distracted my anxiety.

"The usuals. Volunteering at church, helping in the nursery with the babies. Still kayaking and working part-time."

"Really?" Were most sixty-nine-year-olds still punching a clock? I gave her credit.

"Gives me a reason to get going most days."

I caught a hitch of sadness in her voice. Probably because she missed Grandpa. My eyes avoided looking at the corner by the front door, where he used to keep his fishing pole. Ignored the nakedness of the peg that had held his waders.

"Do you see Donnie much?" I kept my head down as I sliced the tomatoes.

"He was real good about coming over on Sundays for supper, but he's been slacking. Things is always complicated with him. He gets cranky if I say too much, so I let him come around when he wants."

Donnie had stayed in Venice. While I mastered being an uncontrollable juvenile delinquent and a runaway, Donnie mastered the art of self-destruction. He bounced around jobs and had been picked up for drunk driving.

"Does he bring Emery over?"

Grandma smiled. "Yes, but not nearly enough. That girl is just as precious as she can be. Pure as sunshine and sweet as wild honey." She pointed to a picture I'd missed on the fridge. Emery was sitting on Donnie's shoulders. His hands wrapped around hers. Both wore big smiles.

It was still hard for me imagining Donnie in the role of daddy. Emery became Donnie's saving grace, the same way academics and Jiu Jitsu had been mine. Even though Donnie and Monica never married, and their relationship didn't work out, they stayed on good terms for Emery's sake.

"He still at that restaurant?"

Grandma nodded. "He's manager now. Last time I talked to him he said the hours were about to eat him alive, but that's probably best for him."

"I'll have to stop in for a visit."

Visit. That's what acquaintances did. Maybe that was too hopeful, defining our relationship as acquaintances these days. We were far from the inseparable kids we'd been when our stepmother Rita delivered us to Paul and Wanda Baker's doorstep. Donnie had squeezed my hand, sending me that silent promise he'd still look out for me. I had kept my eyes on our grandparents. Strangers to us, thanks to my father. My knees had quaked as I clutched my favorite doll—one of the few things I brought with me—as I wondered if Donnie and I would be safe inside the new house. Grandma had won us over with a fresh batch of chocolate chip cookies. The aroma greeting us when we walked in.

We adjusted to the comforts of a normal life. Home-cooked meals. School on a regular basis. Therapy sessions. Sleep—when nightmares didn't intrude. But Donnie and I never talked about Bill and what he'd done to us. Even so, I always knew Donnie had it worse than me. Especially when Donnie irritated Bill, stoked his anger, just so Bill would head into Donnie's room at night instead of mine. *I'll teach you to mess with me, boy.*

And there were the bruises. I only glimpsed them a few times. Violet-colored welts on his back, his shoulders. Somehow, I knew not to say anything about it. Same way I knew they were from Bill. I wondered if my mom saw those bruises too. Maybe it didn't matter, but I wanted to believe Sloan would've done something if she'd suspected what was happening to us in the middle of the night.

By running away, I'd let my brother down—I'd let go of his hand.

Despite the regret now building in my chest, I tamped down the tears. An outburst wouldn't pair well with the singed meat. I sighed. Not enough that Grandma would notice. Or so I thought. She glanced at me, then did a double-take. I focused on setting the table.

A few minutes after we sat down to eat, my phone chirped, signaling a new text message.

"It's Britney," I said through a bite of salad.

"She knows you're in town?"

"I told her before I drove down and asked if she wanted to get together." Didn't know it would be the day I arrived.

"You mean this evening? Why, you just got in."

Grandma wasn't crazy about my cousin, probably because she was from Bill's side of the family. Maybe she associated Britney with my troubled teen years, since we were caught together doing plenty of things we had no business doing.

I seized the moment. Eager to abandon that seeping orange-brown sandwich on my plate.

"Yeah. Says she's working the next few days and has some free time tonight. I should stop in and see her." I stood and put my dishes into the sink before Grandma could protest. After giving her a peck on the cheek and promising not to be late, I was out the door.

Part of me knew this wasn't a good idea. A couple hours in Venice and I was sliding back into my old ways, dashing off and doing as I pleased. But when I plopped into my car, I knew it was too late to go back in, apologize and eat that stupid burger. Plus, I was running out on Oscar. No telling what he was doing in the bedroom, alone in a strange place and possibly still traumatized from the caged car ride.

I went to Britney's anyway.

My jaw dropped when I walked into Britney's cottage-style home. I knew nothing about home design, but I doubted any of her furniture belonged to a previous renter, like my couch and side tables back in Columbus. Only a few steps in and I could tell the place was worthy of the Wanda Baker seal of clean. The immaculate feel unnerved me a bit. Based on her house, Britney had her life together. A stark contrast to mine.

"I mean, where do I start?" I said breathlessly, as she released me from our hug. "You told me things were going well, but—wow! And you look amazing!" I hated that I wore my yoga pants, accessorized with cat hair, and still had my hair in a bun. More jabs to my self-confidence, a game I no longer played. I fought back in my head, reminded myself I'd traded lanky limbs for defined deltoids and cut triceps.

"Same goes for you, gorgeous." Britney ran her fingers through her silky chocolate waves and matched her home with head to toe perfection. "It's good to see you in person. FaceTime is great, but I've been waiting for the day we could be in the same room."

She gave me a tour, and no room lacked order or beautiful furnishings. Maybe it shouldn't have been a surprise. Britney had opened her own beauty salon after cosmetology school, which she'd talked about doing since we were little. As we settled in the living room, against perfectly-puffed throw pillows on her couch, drinks in hand, something unfamiliar pinched me. Envy? Britney had made her dreams a reality.

"You've come a long way from the girl who used to shop at thrift stores." I toasted her with the bottled water she gave me.

"And you've come a long way from the girl who used to shoplift at thrift stores." She held up her glass of wine.

We both winced and drank to better days.

Her remark had the same effect as a thorn in my side. A sharp reminder that I couldn't trust Britney, not fully. Growing up, we'd had a strange relationship. Always quick to get into trouble, we blamed the other if we got caught. Bickering and name-calling followed. After a day or two of *I'm never playing with you again!* we became inseparable once more and the cycle repeated. I hoped we were past those exhausting, immature days, but her comment put me on alert.

"Seen Donnie yet?" Britney asked.

"No. Wanda was a little cautious when I asked about him."

"He's doing better. Been clean for a year or so, I think. But he's trying to get primary custody of Emery."

"Wait. He's battling Monica for custody?"

Britney nodded. "He wants the kid all to himself, but he probably won't win, not with his record and the hours he's putting in at work. He's pretty stressed."

"Sounds like you see him a lot."

"I'm in his restaurant once a week or so. It's close to the salon."

I bit my lip from the inside. Maybe it was petty, but it kinda hurt, hearing how Britney and Donnie had maintained a relationship. She knew what was going on in his life, meaning he talked to her, trusted her. I felt demoted—discarded—as his sister, but it's what I deserved for moving away.

"Let me know when you're going to stop in," Britney said, "I'll go with you."

I gave one of those slow, non-committal nods. Was I competing against my cousin for my brother's attention? No, I was not. I was not that shallow.

We talked about guys, failed relationships, her hot yoga classes, my blue belt in Jiu Jitsu, what establishments were still around that we had to visit. I warned her that I might use her as my means of escape from Wanda on an as-needed basis.

"How long you staying?"

"That might depend on Wanda's cooking."

Back at the house, Grandma sat watching the news with Princess in her lap and cigarette smoke surrounding her like dense fog. She asked about Britney and our visit. I gave her the basics and asked why she hadn't mentioned Donnie's custody battle.

She had to stretch to look at me from her recliner. "I didn't know about it."

Glad I wasn't the only one.

"I'll get some cleaning supplies in the morning and start on the apartment," I said, figuring it was best to leave Donnie's legal troubles alone.

"We could work on it together, after church."

"I think I'll skip church for now."

A fierce Baptist, Grandma loved her church family. Once Donnie and I moved in with her and grandpa, there was no such thing as Sunday without church. Wasn't that I didn't like church—I used to live for summer camp—but I wasn't ready to jump into the Venice social scene just yet.

"Well," she sighed, "it's a shame, but I can still help when I get home."

"Sure." I hadn't mentioned needing help, but it was her stuff.

After kissing her goodnight, I headed to the guest room. When I opened the door, I found Oscar, sitting on my bed like he owned it, and licking his paw. He ignored me at first, pretending he didn't want my attention. That lasted .4 seconds after I slid onto the bed. He rubbed his head against my cheek and along my jaw.

I plugged my phone in to charge and sent Donnie a text, telling him I was in town and wanted to see him tomorrow. He surprised me by responding quickly.

I'll be at the restaurant by 9. Come in before we open. Use the side door entrance. We can hang and grab a bite.

That was it. I'd hoped for something like *Can't wait to see you!!!* followed by hearts and happy faces, that sort of thing. Did he respond so plainly to Britney? I couldn't tell if he was glad I was here or if he was merely doing his brotherly duty by agreeing to see me. My nerves amped up. How hard was I going to have to work at mending our relationship?

Whether it's bluegrass music, whiskey, tobacco, horse racing, or college basketball, Kentucky is robust with bragging rights. Pride runs through the state like the Red River Gorge. Venice was no exception. Local businesses drew on the state's heritage for their names, with the Derby ranking high among favorites. I entered the Jockey Club restaurant from the side entrance. I hadn't seen my brother for a couple years, not since Emery was toddling around, learning to walk. It pained me to think about that too, the fact I'd missed a couple of her birthdays.

Donnie sat at the bar, surrounded by paperwork, but got off his stool when he saw me. "Hey, little sister."

I didn't realize how much I wanted that hug until he was holding me tight. What made it even better was taking a good look at him and seeing his eyes were clear, his complexion wasn't haggard— no obvious signs of drugs or alcohol. Thankfulness poured over me, and I wondered if he noticed my happy sigh of relief.

We went through the usual run-downs about how good we both looked, which was mostly true. I'd showered and straightened my hair for the occasion. Donnie still had that boyish grin and kept his sandy-colored hair short and spiky. His stubble enhanced his ruggedly handsome features.

"How's Emery?"

Donnie took out his phone and slid through a slew of pictures. My heart ached when I saw that I'd missed a lot more than birthdays. There were trips to the zoo, naps, videos of her splashing in a baby pool, eating ice cream as it melted everywhere, and a few pictures where she'd gotten into lipstick. Her giggle and her squeaky little voice in a couple videos were the cutest sounds ever.

"I can't believe she's so big." I playfully swatted him on the shoulder. "You're really lazy about sending me pics."

"Maybe you should come around more."

If it was meant as a jab, I deserved it, but I didn't detect any malice in his voice. Same as Wanda, he was just stating the truth. Maybe it sounded weird, but I thought Donnie and Wanda would both punish me for doing my own thing, working on me, and giving them scraps of attention.

"Yeah, I wanna change that. I'll be here all summer."

"For real?" Donnie put his phone aside and looked at me with disbelief.

I nodded. "Hoping to spend a lot of time with everybody. You, Wanda, Emery…"

"You'll love Emery. She's the cutest girl ever. Super sweet too." He called to one of the employees in the back and asked for an appetizer and some waters. "Have you seen Britney yet?"

"Last night. She told me you were going through some things with Monica."

"Mmm. It's been rough." Donnie swallowed hard.

"Are things that bad between you two?"

He shrugged a shoulder. "We were doing fine, until she started seeing this guy Rob. He seems all right, but he's moved in with Monica."

"That was bound to happen."

"Sure. I want her happy, but I have to protect my daughter."

I nodded, understanding the firmness in his tone. "Can't you do a background check on the guy? Or get to know him better? Anything besides going to court?"

A half-hearted smile appeared. "Yeah. Maybe. I just…needed Monica to know I was serious about looking out for my little girl."

I kept from flinching as a shudder ran through me. What was it like to be loved like that—by your father? "Did you tell Monica what happened, growing up?"

"I gave her the big picture, told her Bill was pretty abusive and got locked up."

Our food and drinks arrived. A bit early for appetizers but I didn't turn them away. We picked at the corn dip with zucchini slices and relived a few memories, like the time I chased him into the house with the garden hose. Grandpa Paul had a fit—until he grabbed the hose and turned it on us. Britney and Wanda also came up.

"You know, I was worried about you," I said tentatively, finishing my water. "I didn't think you'd be in such a good place, not after…everything." *Maybe it's why I stopped coming down here, I was afraid of watching you destroy yourself.*

"The drinking?"

I nodded.

"I wasted a lot of years blaming Bill for how crappy my life was. Probably wasn't until Emery came along that I finally quit hating myself, had something else to live for—had someone who needed me to get my head on straight. Spending a few weeks in the county jail was another wake-up call. Made me realize some people don't get second chances." Donnie shifted on his stool.

It was the first time we'd been so candid about our past mistakes.

"I guess I had to get away and make it on my own."

Donnie smiled. "Looks like you did, little sister."

"We both did." I reached over and hugged him by the neck.

"You picked a strange time to come back though. Nothing like being tested by fire, I suppose."

"What do you mean?"

"Bill. He's getting released from prison."

"What? How could that be? I thought he had more time added to his sentence for fighting with another inmate."

"He claimed self-defense, only got another year or so. Didn't Wanda tell you he was getting out and heading back here?"

A sudden memory took me back to the day Bill was arrested. He tried dodging the police officers. A weak, cowardly attempt at escape. The police officer snatched him, shoved him face-first against a wall and handcuffed him. Bill, his mouth an awkward wrinkle, forced a smile my way.

*Don't you worry, Delilah. Ain't no one keeping me from my sweet girl...*Bill's words echoed in my head and tore through me like a jagged knife.

"Does Wanda know?"

"Everybody knows. He's Campbell County's most famous criminal."

18

"And he's coming back here? How's that possible?" I rubbed my temples, trying to hush Bill's voice and stop the onslaught of images crowding my mind. I'd worked hard at purging Bill and his damage, but now my progress felt threatened.

"This is home for him," Donnie said. "He's going to stay at our old house, out on Milt's property." Donnie spoke with a resignation I didn't understand. How could he sit there, eating dip and laughing about Grandpa Paul with the hose like everything was okay?

I feared I might be sick all over the bar top. "I can't believe this. I never thought he'd get out."

"Welcome home, little sister."

CHAPTER THREE

B ill didn't deserve to be released from prison. Fifteen years wasn't enough for what he'd done to me and Donnie. For what he'd taken. For what he'd left behind. And not a single second of those years accounted for Sloan.

I left the restaurant so Donnie could get to work. My brain in a fog as I drove back to Wanda's. When I pulled into her driveway, I sat there, trembling with fury. Bombarded with a dozen angry thoughts. Struck by sorrow. Could I stay here knowing Bill might show up any day? Walk the Streets of Venice a free man?

I texted Britney. Why didn't you tell me Bill was getting out??

Humidity swelled inside my car, matching the heat from my frustrations. Worry struck. What if Bill wanted revenge? Donnie had been the one to speak up, told his teacher about the nightmare we were living at home...

A tap on my car window startled me.

"Oh, Grandma!" I got out of the car.

"Sorry, Delilah, but I saw you just sitting there. Wanted to make sure you was all right. A bit early for the heat to be getting to you but—"

"I saw Donnie this morning, and he told me about Bill."

Her face took on a defeated expression, one that said she had no way of denying it.

"Why didn't you tell me he was coming back?"

"I was afraid you wouldn't come. That man kept you and Donnie from me and Grandpa when you was little, and I didn't want him keeping you from me again." There was a growing resolve in her voice. "He's already done enough harm…caused more hurt than a person should."

We were both in tears, and I felt like that broken, scared little girl again.

"Please, Delilah, don't run off on account of him."

I pulled her in to me. "I won't, Grandma. And you're right. We're not going to let him hurt us anymore."

Armed with rubber gloves, masks, and bleach—and still-simmering anger at the thought of seeing Bill again—we started emptying and scrubbing the fridge in the garage apartment. After cleaning and disinfecting every surface, we assaulted the space with air fresheners and fans on high. We ditched the masks and gloves.

Sorting through the boxes came next. Many of them held clothes, trinkets, and fishing tackle belonging to Grandpa.

"I guess I stashed a lot of things in here for safe keeping," Grandma said.

Grandpa put up a fight, best he could, but cancer took him six years ago. Back then, my selfish side prevailed. Kept me from Grandpa's bedside, holding his hand as his life drained away. Back then, I had no qualms about letting Grandma endure the burden of caregiver. Gave no thought to her weariness and heartache. Insulating myself from grief proved most important.

"I'm sorry I wasn't there for you, Grandma. It was pathetic, the way I acted, like I couldn't be bothered." The last part came out weakly, as though I didn't have the breath or strength to finish the words. Choking on my disgrace.

Even after he passed, I hadn't cried with abandon for Grandpa. Not like he deserved for all he'd done for me and the ways he loved me.

"No sense in looking back or getting upset over things we can't change." Grandma ran the back of her fingers over my cheek. Her gentle touch erasing tears. A subtle tremble in her chin. "I never gave it a thought. Death is hard on everyone. We all handle it in our own way. You were here at the funeral, and that's all that mattered. All I cared about."

I smeared away more tears. Grandma often described herself as a peacemaker, preferring harmony over strife. Forgiveness over grudges. I understood that now—and knew I didn't deserve her gentle ways.

"He was a fine man and loved you dearly," Grandma said. "Remember how you two used to watch *Scrubs* and *House*?"

"I'd forgotten about those shows."

"He loved medical shows but—"

"Hated going to the doctor," we said in unison.

"And he loved taking Donnie to the Reds' games and teaching him to fish while we kayaked in the creeks and rivers." She elbowed me. "Those were good times."

With each box we opened we became wrapped in memories. Clumsy artwork pieces from school. Random pictures that preserved our bad fashion and *what we were thinking* hair. Holidays, birthdays, summer days revisited. We started piles of what to keep, donate, and throw away. Having a purpose helped us get through more.

I started on the boxes in the bedroom closet. One felt particularly feeble as I took it down from the top shelf. I held it against me, which was dumb, because dust sprinkled onto my face. I opened the flaps with my free hand—and gasped. There was a picture staring back at me, one featuring my parents and me and Donnie. I'd never seen it before.

Still cradling the box, I sank to the floor and studied every detail of that portrait. Beaming with pride, my mom was the focus of the picture. She held me in her lap. I looked about a year old, which made Donnie around five. His smile said he wasn't into it. Bill wore a smug expression that suggested he was too good for a Sears family photo session.

My eyes kept going back to my mom. Sloan. Youthful and radiant, the way I'd immortalized her in my dreams. I searched her eyes, traced my finger along the curve of her face. No way did she look like the kind of person who would walk out on her family. Leave her babies. She was too happy, too convincing in her smile that life was anything less than perfect at that moment.

I set the photograph aside and reached back into the box. Inside I found ladies' clothes, jewelry, and a handful of blue pills. My hand dug to the bottom and scratched something. It was a cover, maybe to a book. I fished it out slowly—and then I saw it, the word *Diary* on the front.

My body suddenly pulsed with nervous anticipation.

"What'cha got there?" Grandma asked from behind me.

I turned to her, the diary still in my hand. "I found this box."

Grandma blanched. Her shoulders sank. "Oh, I'd forgotten about that." She seemed to swallow a lump of emotion that jumped in her throat.

"Your father, he dropped that off one day. He was mad as a hornet, almost pounded the door off its hinges. He shoved that box at me when I opened the door, said, *Here, take this. She's gone and left me and I ain't having nothing of hers in my house.* I don't know if he was drunk, might've been. No telling now, but he got in his car and tore off down the road." She paused, then shook her head ever-so slightly. "All those years ago. That day, when he gave me that box, I knew right then, something awful had happened to your mother."

Wanda helped herself to the picture. As she stared at it, a parade of emotions marched across her face. Then tears welled up. She placed the picture beside me on the floor, her lower lip trembling, and walked out of the room. I knew what that was like, having deep-rooted pain swell up on the inside and demand a way out.

"We've been at this for hours," Grandma said from the living room-kitchen area. The soft sound of sniffles followed. "I'd better get something whipped up for lunch."

I stayed where I was, feeling crippled by awkwardness. Said nothing in response. I heard the door close, and a sense of emptiness filled the space. Wanda was as strong as they come—until the topic of Sloan arose. Watching Grandma become emotional over the family portrait made me ache for her. The scars on my own heart also felt picked at.

Alone with the diary, I didn't know what to do. It felt like a holy relic, containing history and maybe secrets. But relics are often cursed. Inside the pages, I'd discover a private side of Sloan, one meant for no one to see. My memories of her were sparse and foggy at best, probably influenced by stories Donnie and Grandma had told me. Now, I could get to know Sloan from her own words.

But what if I didn't like what I found? Grandma clearly recognized the diary. Almost seemed traumatized. She must have read it. Was there something Sloan shared that Grandma didn't like?

My mind could reel and speculate forever. I wiped the cover with a damp rag, then took a deep, deep breath.

On the first page, I found an array of doodles. Rainbows, unicorns, flowers, and the name Sloan Ramsey in a fancy script. I went to the back of the book and the last entry.

I can't write those words, and I'm ashamed to say what I walked into. The unicorns might hear, the bad ones!! Blue and Yellow. It was so obvious what was going on. I slapped Bill and pulled Donnie to me. I wanted to bury his face in my chest, hoping to smother the horrible picture from his mind. I yelled at Bill and told him never to touch me again. Donnie was crying. I took him into my bedroom and locked the door. I sat him on my lap and rocked him. I pressed his head against me and told him it would be all right. The unicorns must not hear! Bill kept yelling and beating on the door. I don't know how long we stayed like that. Donnie crying, me rocking and whispering to him, Bill yelling and screaming. The unicorns must not hear!!!

The noises stopped, because Bill had to go to work, I didn't know what to do. After Bill was gone, I put Donnie in the bathtub and let him clean up. The unicorns must not see!! I was crying now but not in the way he might notice and get scared again. I wiped away tears as they came. There were bruises on my boy. The unicorns…

I'd seen things or thought I did. Things that didn't make sense, because they were so ugly. I knew something wasn't right with Donnie, but Bill kept saying it was school, that Donnie was probably getting picked on and that's why his grades were so bad and the teachers sent home reports about his bad temper. I didn't know how to sort it out or what to believe.

While Donnie was in the tub, I called Glenn. He didn't know about the unicorns like I did. It was time for us to go away. Glenn said he needed time to think about things. I didn't want to think. I wanted to go.

She knew? My mom knew what Bill was doing to Donnie and let it go on? The date of the entry was April 2001. There were no more entries after that. My mom went missing in June.

And what was with the unicorns?

I flipped back to the beginning of the diary and read it straight through. Took an hour. Over the two years that were covered, a distinct progression occurred in my mother. Early entries were adorned with drawings, hearts, and a sense of happiness. It captured the free-spirit, child-like personality of my mom. But as time with Bill wore on, the playfulness tapered off. She stopped writing about picnics, catching bugs and fireflies, and camping in the living room. There were fights with Bill. Nights where Bill locked her out of the house and she slept in her car. Regret became her new theme—along with an increasing desire to leave Bill.

That is, as long as I ignored the mention of unicorns and trolls. Some entries dipped into a fantasy realm, detailing how there were good and bad of each, how she alone knew this—and knew the unicorns and trolls were trying to use me and Donnie to increase their powers. Other entries included her desire to move to Los Angeles and become a famous actress, like she'd always wanted.

She also mentioned Glenn, the man she had an affair with. Everybody knew about Glenn, including me and Donnie. When he came to our house, my mom would tell us to go play outside while she and Glenn had *grown-up time*. I didn't know what that meant. Donnie wouldn't tell me. He climbed one of our trees out back and stayed there for hours. My mom would come out after Glenn left and tell Donnie to come down, but he ignored her. That told me Glenn coming over wasn't a good thing. It was an odd memory to harbor.

I closed the diary. Part of me didn't want to think about it anymore. Nausea gripped my stomach. A headache threatened.

I repacked the box of my mom's things. Questions churned inside me. Too many to sort through. I made my way back to the house, unsure how to face Grandma. Unsure how to ask the question chewing on my mind the hardest—What the hell was wrong with Sloan Ramsey?

Entering the kitchen felt like stepping onto a field of emotional land mines. Grandma's lack of eye contact and busy-bee movements told me she didn't want to talk about the diary. Whatever puffed-up courage I had to bombard her with questions suddenly fled. Now that I thought about it, maybe she never meant for me to find that box.

My stomach clenched. Not only from the idea of Grandma keeping secrets but also from the sight of her carving slices of bologna for sandwiches. I chopped up ingredients and made a quinoa bowl, having picked up a few items earlier from the store. Our lunch prep filled the silence between us.

We settled at the table. Both casting dubious looks towards the other's plate.

"I think the apartment is ready for me and Oscar." A heavy sigh accompanied my words. Like a breath I'd held in. I rambled about giving the fridge another scrub down and how Oscar would enjoy the space. Mentioned that I could buy a small a/c unit and drop off the stuff she'd decided to donate. Grandma nodded.

Bottling up emotions was no longer my go-to defense mechanism. Apparently, that wasn't true for Grandma. Sustaining a one-sided conversation felt like chipping away at a rock wall. Not that I was upset with her. I just didn't know how to ease the impasse.

"I was thinking we could have company tonight for dinner," Grandma finally said.

"Who did you have in mind?"

"Donnie and Emery."

That eased my tension. "Let's do it, but how about I make dinner?" I resisted another glance at her sandwich.

Grandma tilted her head down and looked at me over her glasses. "You're not gonna make one of them healthy dishes, are you? All twigs and leaves?"

"You can at least try it."

She held up her hands and shook her head.

"Don't worry," I said. "I'll make chicken for you and Donnie and Emery, but promise me you'll eat a bite of the tofu?"

"I don't know. That might get my bowels out of whack."

We burst out laughing. Genuine, ab-crunching laughter. I couldn't remember the last time we'd laughed that hard together. It was the refresher we both needed.

My phone jingled. A text from Britney, which made me realize she hadn't answered me earlier about Bill's release from prison. Apparently, Britney also had an innate sense of when to punctuate our meals. Judging by the frown on Grandma's face, she didn't appreciate Britney's talent as I checked my phone.

Sorry!!! I thought you knew! Thought that was why you were here, to help Wanda with it. Hope you're not mad.

Then came another text. We should go and check on gpa Milt.

I paused, not sure what I should say to her. Grandpa Milt was Bill's dad. Britney and I, along with our other cousins, always acted like wild savages at Milt's place. I hadn't been there since Granny Ginny had passed, which was a good eight years or so. Last I'd heard, his health was declining.

My gut reaction was *No thanks!* Milt and Ginny had been strict and coarse, as far as grandparents went. As kids, we learned every cuss word thanks to their epic yelling matches at each other, and were kept in line with their perfected whack to the back of our heads. Neither one of them was ever far from a foul mood. I wasn't afraid of them, since they were all I knew as grandparents for a while, but I lacked a desire to be around them. There was no way I would visit Milt on my own, so Britney would serve as a good buffer.

Can we go tomorrow? I asked.

She replied with a yes and we set up a time for her to pick me up. I hadn't treated Milt any better than Wanda, so I owed him a visit and an apology—but there was no telling if he'd remember me or be happy to see me. Didn't matter. I'd do my part, then forget ever setting foot on that property again. Especially with Bill on the verge of returning.

I had plenty to do before Grandma's dinner party. After I helped her clean up from lunch—and apologized for not being in the mood for bologna—I set off on errands. It was the first time since I'd been back that I drove around town, checked out what had changed, what remained. After emptying my trunk-load of donations at Goodwill, I stopped in a martial arts studio and chatted with the owner. Then, on a whim and with my nerves in a bunch, I headed to the one place where I knew there wouldn't be a cheery welcome.

CHAPTER FOUR

Bill

Venice, KY
Spring 2001

B ill couldn't say when he'd decided to kill his wife, but lately the thought wouldn't leave him alone. He also couldn't say when he found out about Sloan's affair with that wimpy Glenn Rodgers. Didn't matter. Bill was done with Sloan. Rather than waste time and money on a divorce, he aimed to get rid of her on his own.

He smashed up the pills with the back of a spoon. Tonight there were six. Plenty, he figured. Enough to do the deed—not enough to make him a suspect. *She was always mixin' things up. Never was right in the head, you know.* As he made a step toward the refrigerator, Bill tripped slightly from the cat coiled around his feet.

"Scraggs, what am I gonna do with your worthless hide?"

The cat replied with purrs deep enough to be confused for growls, especially when Bill reached down and scratched underneath his chin.

"Them kids catch you in the house I ain't never hearing the end of it. They're already begging for a dog—which they aint gettin'."

Scraggs laid his head heavily in Bill's palm.

"I ain't got time for this." Bill stepped away from the cat and got a can of tuna from the cabinet. He dumped in onto a paper plate while Scraggs watched attentively; his tail swishing sharply from side to side. Bill made kissy-noises and led the cat out the back door. "Here."

He put the plate on the top step as Scraggs mewed with delight.

"Keep out of trouble now." Bill ran his hand along Scraggs' tail before he went back inside and closed the door.

He sighed and listened for a moment. Sloan was upstairs, getting the kids ready for bed. Feet padding on the floor, a thump here and there told him everything was the usual. Once Sloan was gone, he'd move in Rita. They'd been involved for a while. Long enough that Rita complained about Sloan. *Just make her leave so we can be together, Bill.* She was no real prize in the looks department—not like Sloan—but she'd do for the childrearing.

Bill took two beers from the fridge and cracked one opened. He downed a couple swigs, then carefully swiped the little mound of blue powder from the counter and onto the top of the beer can. Using his fingertips, he brushed the chalky crumbs into the liquid.

Sloan didn't drink beer much on account of the medicines she took. *The doctor said I'm not supposed to have alcohol.* Bill would tell her one beer wouldn't hurt a thing. That it might make her feel better—make the medicine work stronger. If she gave one of her stupid excuses about it mixing up her head, he'd insist—and make sure she drank every drop.

Because a man couldn't live with a woman who disrespected him and whored around with another man. He would make her pay for that—and for choosing Glenn over him. Bill grinned to himself as he carefully swirled the opened can of beer and climbed the stairs.

CHAPTER FIVE

I sat there, parked in the lot of the Campbell County Sheriff's Office, and reconsidered my bright idea of going inside. If any place held possible leads or answers to my mom's disappearance, it was here. My plan was simple. Explain who I was, demand to see the case files. Saw it on a show once.

As I paced my stride into the sheriff's office, my nerves amped up. Two reasons. I didn't know if I had any business making demands. Probably should've Googled *rights of a victim's family member*. Plus, they might consider me an outsider now. A girl who left her hometown for something better in the big city. Combine that with my questions about an unsolved case—which might not be well-received—and you had a recipe for a chilly reception.

I stepped up to the reception desk, choked back my doubts.

"Afternoon," the officer said. "How can I help you?"

"Hi, there. My name is Delilah Baker." I almost couldn't hear myself over the pounding in my chest and the throbbing in my ears. My unrehearsed speech rolled out. "Back in 2001, my mom, Sloan Baker Ramsey went missing. She was never found." No way I could say *her body* was never found. "I was wondering if I might be able to look at the case file."

Dalton, according to his name plate, gave me a deadpan stare. "So you want access to a cold case file?"

"Yes. Please." With my fingers laced together, I stood with my shoulders tight and hoped I looked like a good citizen. Whatever that meant.

Dalton seemed to give it consideration, then he squinted his eyes at me for a moment and said, "Did you say your name is Delilah Baker? Are you that same girl who vandalized the Beauty Bar Salon over on Main Street?"

I could've melted under the weight of the shame. "Yeah, but that was...long ago..." Was it worth explaining to him? I'd thrown a rock through the plate glass window of Tonya Ramsey's salon back when I was fourteen. Bill's sister and Britney's mom, Tonya had a flair for spreading gossip to her customers. She told anyone who'd listen that Sloan never deserved a man like Bill, that Bill had to put up with a lot of crazy, and that Sloan was an unfit mother, always running around with that low-life Glenn Rodgers. Through the years, the chatter often got back to Wanda. When I found her crying bitterly over the phone to one of her church friends one afternoon, I decided to do something about it.

Dalton snapped his fingers. "So you must be related to Bill Ramsey, the guy who's getting out of prison. Right?"

Every inch of my skin burned with embarrassment as I nodded and looked away.

"Huh." Some sort of pleased expression struck Dalton's face, as if he was proud of himself for recalling pieces of my past and making me relive the disgrace. "Tell you what, let me talk to one of my supervisors, see what he says about you checking out the case file." He patted the desktop before excusing himself.

At least I was alone in the reception area and didn't have an audience for Dalton's steel-trap of a memory and the brief rehashing of my history. The police station's scent of paper and stale coffee did nothing to calm my nerves.

When Dalton returned, another man followed him. Taller and with a dusting of gray hair at his temples, the officer wore a stern face. Unlike Dalton, the new officer had an air of wisdom and intimidation.

"Delilah Ramsey." He stood ramrod straight, smiled warmly. "Been a while. How are you?"

I squeaked out a feeble reply of fine, or something. No one had called me by my given name in years. Hearing it now startled me.

"You don't remember me, do you?"

"No, sir."

"That's all right. Can't say I blame you. I'm Lieutenant Mark Snyder. I was in court for Bill's trial. Escorted him in and out every day, then helped transfer him to Blackburn."

"Oh." I wasn't sure how he expected me to remember him. After Bill's arrest, I didn't see him again. My grandparents insulated me and Donnie from the legal proceedings as best they could, which included them changing our last name from Ramsey to Baker, hoping they could save us some grief of being associated with Bill.

"You, uh, settled back in Venice or just visiting?"

"I'm here for a while."

By the way Lieutenant Snyder narrowed his eyes at me, I guessed he didn't like my vague answer.

"You've heard about your father, right?"

I nodded.

So did Snyder. "Have you two, uh, mended fences?"

Was he serious? *Why, yes, officer, we're planning a big party for father's return...* "No, I haven't seen him or spoken to him since he was taken to jail."

"Can't blame you there after what he put you through. It's interesting, though, you showing up here in town, right when Bill's getting released. And you say you want to review the case file on your mother?"

34

I nodded. The bizarre circumstances weren't lost on me, and I hated that these guys weren't making this easy. My mother was gone and hadn't been proven dead. Coming here and seeing what information the police had was a reasonable place to start searching for answers.

Snyder glanced at Dalton, then looked back at me. "I hope you're not planning on causing any trouble. If I recall, you had quite the mean-streak going. Your brother wasn't much better."

"I'm not trying to stir anything up, Lieutenant. I don't care about Bill and plan to avoid him." I could've been honest, told him I didn't know about Bill's impending return until recently. But what good would it do? I already felt like I was in quicksand. "I wanted to see if there's anything in the file that could help me find out the truth about my mother."

Snyder chuckled. "So you're gonna run around, acting like Nancy Drew?"

Dalton snickered.

That didn't sound like a bad thing to me, but I knew this was their way of belittling my hopes. They wanted me to know that no one was smarter than the cops in this department.

"Tell you what I'll do." Snyder slid open a drawer, rifled through files, then plucked out a sheet of paper, which he handed to me over the counter. "I'm gonna have you fill out this form. Bring it back in and we'll see what we can do about getting you access."

I filled out the form right then and there and handed it back to Snyder. He didn't seem impressed. What could I do to assure him my intentions were genuine, that I didn't view him or any officer who'd worked on my mom's case as incompetent? Finding the truth meant solidifying my identity, complete healing from my past. Couldn't they understand that?

"Thank you." I shook hands with both of them, kept my chin up, but not enough to seem arrogant. As I turned to leave, I felt their stares bore into the back of me. Based on that brief encounter, I was fairly certain that Lieutenant Snyder would do his best at stonewalling me and making sure I never got a peek at Sloan's case file.

"Can you believe it?" Wanda asked. "All these years and it still works!" She pressed the PLAY button and *"Coal Miner's Daughter"* started twanging out of the CD player's speakers. Grandma's devotion to Loretta Lynn ran bone-deep. If she wasn't wiggling her derrière to Loretta while she cleaned or made dinner, then it was George Jones or Hank Williams. As a side effect, I won most *classic country* karaoke battles among my college friends.

We unpacked the groceries I'd brought back, and I schooled Grandma on how to make orange tofu. As I expected, she wasn't instantly won over. Cauliflower rice was brand new to her, but she taste-tested everything and gave it a shoulder-shrug of semi-approval. I gently informed her that meat, bread, and basically everything in her pantry didn't cross my lips any more.

"I figured you had weird eating habits, thin as you are," she said. "Doesn't bother me none, as long as I don't have to eat what you eat all the time."

"Fair enough."

Donnie and Emery arrived as we set the table and the timer for the barbequed chicken dinged. When he walked in, grabbed me in a hug, it felt like I was seeing my brother for the first time in years. Away from work and in full-on Dad-mode. There was an ease to him I hadn't seen before. A twinkle in his eyes—and when I looked at Emery, I knew why.

Emery took my breath away, both with her big brown eyes and her energy. She didn't remember me, but it didn't matter. Her questions came at me like Nerf darts. Being around a toddler was new to me, kind of scared me. In preparation for tonight, I'd bought Emery a toy and several books. Aunt DeeDee had a lot of time to make up for, and bribes never hurt when it came to winning favor with kids. Or so I'd read.

Emery provided plenty of dinner entertainment. She whipped her ponytail to the side for us to see and said Daddy fixed her hair but it wasn't good, that her mommy does a good job and doesn't pull hair. Donnie apologized, and she patted his back and said that was okay; Mommy would fix it later. She sang the newest song she learned in pre-school, counted to thirty-seven, and told us all about bats, complete with sounds they made.

My cheeks hurt from laughing so hard while happy tears escaped my eyes.

Grandma passed out plates for dessert, then set the chocolate cake down in the center of the table.

"Chocolate!" Emery clapped as her eyes bulged.

"I know it's your favorite, sweet pea." Grandma beamed as much as Emery. It reminded me of how Grandma always made dessert when Donnie and I were growing up. Cakes and pies were her specialty, with Derby Pie being Grandpa Paul's favorite. "Just remember, you get to help grandma clean up after we're done."

I looked at Donnie, who was already smiling, and like me, probably recalling how Grandma always made us do dishes after we ate. We were pretty sure the dessert worked as an enticement and a stimulant, creating ideal conditions for the clean-up crew.

There was a knock on the back door, making everyone but Emery pause. She was jumping in her chair with her hands flat on the table. Her tongue was out over her bottom lip, giving her a puppy-like expression. Princess barked from her bed in the corner but didn't bother getting up.

"Oh, must be our other guest for the evening." Grandma went to the back door and pushed it open. "Come on in, Glenn."

Inwardly, I gasped. Glenn Rodgers, my mother's old boyfriend, entered Grandma's kitchen. He wore a tentative grin and looked directly at me.

"Hey there, Donnie," he said with a wave. "Hello, Delilah. Nice to see you again."

"Nice to see you too, Glenn." I kept *What are you doing here?* from spilling out of my mouth. Glancing at Donnie and Grandma, their lack of reactions told me I was the only one who didn't know Glenn would be joining us.

"Get yourself a seat, Glenn." Grandma pulled out a chair. "We're just getting into dessert. Plenty for everybody." Grandma set him up with a plate and a generous slice while he and Donnie traded what's-new. Emery came with her plate and sat in my lap. Having someone to wrap my arms around and squeeze felt good—like having my Sally doll back. It helped with the troubled feel of not knowing what was going on.

"Heard you're back in town for a while, Delilah," Glenn said, after complimenting Grandma on the cake.

"Yes, sir. Some family time was long overdue."

"Your turn!" Emery did her best to feed me a too-big bite. Crumbs sprinkled down the front of my shirt and icing collided with my nose. Laughter filled the kitchen.

As the cake dwindled, we talked about my life at Ohio State, my studies, and how I'd spent the last four years in a hard-core cycle of work, school, and Jiu Jitsu. Then we shifted to Glenn, learned that he'd married, had three girls, and started a lawncare business.

He was no longer the Glenn of my memories, having added thirty pounds and heavy bags under his eyes. His presence had thrown a damper on our family dinner. At least for me. Just like when he came to visit my mom, I had that feeling that he didn't belong here.

After we moved in with our grandparents, Glenn came around on occasion. He used to bring bags of candy, until the time I cried. It had reminded me of the orange slices Bill used to bring into my room. Maybe that was another reason I didn't like him—I couldn't keep from associating him with Bill.

I tried reading Donnie's face for a sign—something—as to what was going on. How was he this comfortable around Glenn? Donnie gave me nothing.

"I'm so glad you made it over tonight," Grandma said. "Glad I could give you a proper thank-you after you installed my new hot water tank last week."

"Happy I could help out. Been nice visiting with y'all. I'd best be goin'." He thanked Grandma again and stood to leave.

"I'll see you out." Maybe it was a strange thing for me to say. Donnie and Grandma gave me curious looks. I popped Emery off my lap and encouraged her to help Grandma with the dishes.

Once Glenn and I were outside, walking toward his car, I said, "You've been keeping an eye on Wanda all this time?"

He stuffed his hands into his jean pockets and nodded. "Yeah, I take care of the yardwork for her and things that need fixing around the house. I know she doesn't have much family around anymore, now that her kids are grown and moved away. Plus, all the things Donnie's been through haven't been easy on her."

"I think you mean all the things Donnie and I *put* her through." Usually, it took more than sharing a round of dessert for me to grow so bold. Truth was, I couldn't suppress my irritation any longer. Glenn had earned a handyman-hero badge from Grandma, which was great. Comforting to know he'd looked after her. But why hadn't Glenn rescued Sloan? According to the diary, he knew Bill was a maniac, that Sloan wanted out of the marriage. Sloan had written that Glenn had to *think about it*. Think about helping her?

"There's that, but it's good you both came around."

I stopped as we reached the sidewalk. "Why are you really here tonight?"

"Wanda called, told me you were back and curious about Sloan. She said you might wanna talk about things."

"So?" I said it without sounding defensive.

"She's afraid, Delilah. She'll be gettin' up in years soon, and...well, doesn't know if she can go through all them memories again. You and your brother might not remember, but Wanda had a hard time, losing Sloan. We all did. But for a mother not knowing what's happened to her child, well, it tore her up inside, and she couldn't let you kids know it."

"I know it was horrible for her, and I don't want to upset Wanda. But one way or another, there must be some proof out there about what happened to my mom. Don't you want to know the truth?"

He hesitated, then shrugged. "Maybe, but not if it means good people gettin' hurt."

His remark caught me off guard. *Maybe?*

"Were you in love with her?" I asked.

"That was a long time ago. You know some would say your mom was scatter-brained and flighty. She was a good woman but hard to understand at times. It'd be awful watchin' your grandma get upset again, especially after all she's done for you."

Not exactly an answer to my question.

"I need to get home." Glenn's keys jingled when he took them from his pocket. "You take care—and be good to your grandma, okay?" Without waiting for a reply, he got into his car and drove away.

I wasn't sure what to think. Had Grandma really called and asked him to come over to pacify my interest in Sloan's disappearance?

One rumor around town after my mom disappeared had been that Glenn had ended their relationship. He refused to leave Venice with her, the story went, because he was afraid Bill would hunt them down and kill them both. People said she took off anyway.

Glenn had good reason to fear Bill though. We all did.

But what if there was more to that story? What if Glenn broke it off but still couldn't get rid of my mom? I envisioned her as the clingy-type, always needing a man. The diary made no mention of a break-up, so anything was possible—the biggest problem with a case almost twenty years cold.

Like Lieutenant Snyder had suggested, I was no Nancy Drew, but what if trouble was brewing in Sloan and Glenn's relationship? I'd never thought of anyone else capable of hurting my mom besides Bill, but Glenn had been part of her life too. Maybe I was getting desperate for answers, because I let the thought run through my mind: What if Glenn was involved with Sloan's disappearance?

The idea made me feel as though my skin was covered with creepy-crawlies. Especially when I pictured him at Wanda's...mowing the lawn, helping her around the house. Was he bound to her—looking out for her—because of guilt? Was Glenn the *good people* who could end up getting hurt if the truth was discovered?

Back inside, I pretended to shake off a chill from the night air. A lame ruse, considering the evening temps had yet to fall below seventy-five. Grandma and Donnie pinned me under their curious gaze. I was having a hard time blocking images of Glenn hurting my mom and couldn't let on, so I relieved Grandma from dish duty. She took Princess and a pack of cigarettes outside. Standing on a chair by the sink, Emery was up to her elbows in soap suds. We took turns, making shapes with the bubbles and blowing them in each other's direction. In between we cleaned the dishes. Donnie scrolled his phone.

After we finished, Emery said she needed to go potty. I dried her hands and helped her down from the chair.

"You knew about Glenn coming over tonight?" I asked Donnie after Emery took off for the bathroom.

He gave me that knowing smile of his, the one I used to get when he knew something I didn't. He milked those moments for all he could.

"Grandma mentioned she asked him to stop in, wondered if I minded."

"I guess you didn't," I said, my snarky tone unleashed, "since you two seemed like old pals catching up."

"You got something against the guy?"

"Just that he was having an affair with our mother." Leaning my back into the counter, I crossed my arms in front of my chest.

"Come on, you're a big girl now. You know as well as I do there was nothing between her and Bill for a long time." Donnie shrugged, didn't look up from his phone. "What could she do?"

"Do you ever wonder if the rumors about Glenn are true, that maybe he had something to do with her disappearance?" I might have been making that last part up. Far as I could recall, no one had accused Glenn of anything other than having an affair with Sloan.

"Oh, so that's what you're ruffled about. No, I don't think Glenn had anything to do with it. You saw him tonight. He's as soft as they come. Why would he still care about Grandma if he hurt her daughter?"

"Could be guilt."

Donnie laughed, but I didn't join him. My silence caused him to look my way. "Is that what you're going to do while you're here, blame people for what happened over fifteen years ago?"

I turned from him, put away a few dishes for a beat. Then, "I went to the police station."

"For what?" The bite in Donnie's tone surprised me.

"To get a look at the case file." I gave up on the dishes, faced my brother and his hardened expression.

"Are you serious?" Donnie sprang to my side. "You're really nosing around?"

"She was our mother, Donnie. There are people in this town who think she abandoned us and left us with Bill." I thought about the diary, the part that suggested my mom had walked in on Bill abusing Donnie. If that were true, Donnie never mentioned it. What must that have done to him, keeping that secret inside?

"I don't care what anyone thinks. Not about me or things that happened a lifetime ago."

A sudden realization began to crawl over me. One I hadn't considered until that moment.

"You think she walked out on us, don't you?"

We glared at each other, and for a thick moment, I didn't know who we were. Me, ripe with accusations; Donnie, flashing his temper.

Emery came storming out of the bathroom, bursting our stand-off. "Can we go now, Daddy?"

"Yeah, baby." Donnie looked down at her, ran his hand over the top of her head. "Get the toys Aunt DeeDee got you." He turned back to me. "Whatever happened to Sloan makes no difference to me now. There's no going back to change any of it."

"You mean that?"

"It's over, D. Leave it alone. Focus on Wanda and time with her. Help keep her mind off Bill. You really have no idea how happy she is that you're here. Don't mess this up and make her miserable. She deserves better from you."

His words hit like a kick in the gut, but I forced a smile as I held and kissed Emery bye. She thanked me for her gifts, after Donnie reminded her.

Holding the door open for his daughter, Donnie looked at me, like he wanted to add one final remark before he walked off, as if he was about to warn me—or threaten me—but he said nothing and let the screen door slam shut.

I didn't reveal much about my conversations with Glenn and Donnie, even though Grandma kept asking questions. Maybe she heard Donnie's elevated tone from outside. As we finished cleaning the kitchen to her standards, I gave her Mmmhmms and minimal answers. No doubt she was fishing for an indication that I'd gotten the message from Glenn about leaving Sloan's disappearance alone. I didn't want to give her that satisfaction. It felt like our relationship was moving backwards, back to the days when I was irritable and proficient with the silent treatment; Grandma was a pillar of patience and long-suffering. Not what I wanted for us.

Back in the garage apartment, Oscar greeted me with a series of mews.

"I know, you're pissed at me too."

I took care of his bowls and fed him half a hot dog, my pathetic attempt to get on his good side. It worked, as the rubs and nuzzles came.

Energized by frustration from my chats with Donnie and Glenn, I wiped down the kitchen area again and casually wondered how many more times it would take for it to feel clean. The rancid aroma had been replaced with a sea breeze scent from the plug-ins. The bedroom needed the most attention as far as cleaning and clearing out boxes went, but there was enough room for me to crash-land on the bed.

I stretched out, texted Jason, my boyfriend. Told him I'd call later. He asked how it was going. *Great*, I sugarcoated. Even included a smiley face. Less than proud of my fib, I said I was off to bed, would call tomorrow. He sent back kisses.

A moan escaped me. I took Sloan's diary from the nightstand and went through the entries, starting from the beginning. Oscar joined me, mainly for more scratches under his chin. Maybe I'd tell Donnie about the diary later, but right now, I wanted it all to myself. Was it ridiculous, how it made me feel close to my mom? I'd propped the family portrait on the nightstand, after covering Bill with Post-its.

Sloan's diary had the therapist in me suspicious. My backpack, next to the bed on the floor, held the textbooks I brought with me. I bent over and reached for my DSM. Short for Diagnostic and Statistical Manual of Mental Disorders, it's the bible for identifying conditions. I flipped to the pages detailing schizophrenia. No one had mentioned Sloan having a disorder, and maybe my inklings were premature. Reading through the lengthy list of symptoms, though, failed to water down my concerns. I bookmarked the page and closed the book with a heavy sigh. Once again, more questions than answers.

Oscar pawed his way across my torso as I sank back onto the bed.

"Yeah, don't mind me."

I closed my eyes and replayed the evening. The push-back from Donnie unnerved me. He was usually easy-going, rarely had a strong opinion to share on a matter. There had been two times when we were teens that he played the big brother card and inserted himself into my life. He refused to let me go out with Griffin Keel. I told Donnie who I dated was none of his business, but Donnie threatened the guy. That was all it took for Griffin to treat me like I was infected with a contagious flesh-eating bacteria. Later, Griffin and his new girlfriend were arrested for drug trafficking. The other time, Donnie wouldn't let me go to a club in Cincinnati. Legally, I was too young to get in, too young to drink, but that wasn't stopping me. Donnie sabotaged Britney's car so we didn't have a way there. Turned out that a couple college guys had been spiking drinks with the date-rape drug at that particular club, until they were busted.

How Donnie knew the potential dangers of each situation, I don't know. He never told me how he got his inside info or if both incidents were a fluke. Despite those times when Donnie saved me, I still got into plenty of trouble.

I couldn't dismiss Donnie's reaction though. If looking into Sloan's disappearance meant stirring up bad memories for him—and meant torment for Grandma—maybe he, and Glenn, had a point about letting it be.

I took the family portrait from its spot on the nightstand and held my mother's jubilant stare.

"I can't let it go, Mom. I have to know what happened to you."

CHAPTER SIX

When I rolled out of bed the next morning, I wasn't fully prepared to spend time with Britney, but there was no getting out of it. As I expected, she showed up looking like she was ready for a board meeting at nine and a concert at six. She had the energy to match.

"Got your tea, just like you asked." She handed me the cup as I slid into her car.

I'd fixed my hair and put on a little make-up in a feeble attempt to downplay my role as the ugly cousin. My brand-name activewear, bought at a discount, paled next to her heels and designer jeans though. It was okay. I could bring an attacker to his knees and do a hundred pull-ups in a row.

"Thanks." I texted Grandma, told her I was off to see Grandpa Milt with Britney, and that I'd left the key to the apartment under the mat so she could peek in on Oscar, since the two had yet to get acquainted.

"Does Grandpa know we're coming?" I took greedy-slurpy sips of the tea. No need to mask my desperation for caffeine.

"Grampy, remember? I called him yesterday. Don't be mad, but I think he's more excited about the groceries than about seeing us."

A case of beer sat behind Britney's seat, along with a shopping bag loaded with Slim Jims.

"That's what you're taking him?"

Britney shrugged. "It's what he wants. Not like he's going to live forever."

"Isn't his health already in rough shape?"

"Yeah, he's got the tube under his nose."

"Oxygen support?"

"Yeah, and he rides in that scooter thing to get around."

"He's that bad off?"

"I think he can walk, but it doesn't take much to wear him out. The scooter makes it easier for him to get around. My mom and I set up his house a few years back so he wouldn't run into things. Then people pitched in, cause he's a Veteran, and redid his bathroom."

"Oh. How is your mom?" I wasn't sure that sounded as genuine as I wanted, which was probably why Britney shot me a side glance before answering.

"The same, still runs the salon." Britney touched her hair, as if showing off her mother's handiwork. Few duos were as much alike as Britney and her mother. Both owned salons and both put a lot of work into their appearance. Some would consider them shallow and self-absorbed, but I knew them better. Personal experience had taught me how crafty and cruel they could be.

"That's...good." I hadn't decided if I owed Tonya an apology for breaking the window. That was one incident Britney and I didn't discuss. Maybe she held that against me—but I doubted she considered how her mom's gossiping had hurt Wanda.

We turned off the main road and onto a gravel drive that served as the entrance to Milt's property. Grampy owned forty acres, which had been great for us grandkids to play on and explore growing up. The first thing I noticed was the sign. Ramsey Salvage greeted customers who were on the hunt for anything old and rusty. Inside the warehouse, Grampy kept a bounty of old cars, motorcycles, and building scraps. A red neon OPEN sign still hung above the door to the office. It hadn't been lit in years, far as I knew, primarily because

Grampy hadn't been able to run the business. Maybe it didn't work anymore.

I couldn't believe the building hadn't been condemned and declared unfit for humans. Sure, it was a salvage shop, so rust covered every piece of metal in sight, but patches of four-foot weeds, mud, mud puddles, and trash made the rust look good.

Farther back sat a separate garage where Milt used to restore motorcycles, and a large shed Bill had used for his own projects. A three-bedroom house, where I lived with Donnie and our parents, sat elsewhere on the land and was accessible by another road. It couldn't be seen from Grampy's section of the property. All I remembered about that place was the hazardous set of stairs leading to the basement and how the windows rattled when the wind breathed. I hated that house.

Across from the salvage shop, roughly a couple hundred feet, was my grandparents' trailer. Life at Grampy and Granny's provided a small escape when I was younger. Playing hide-and-seek in the warehouse, climbing trees, and gorging on strawberry Pop-Tarts were sweet reprieves from my father. With kids coming and going, there was usually someone around to play with.

Two dogs trotted up to the car and barked when we parked and got out. Britney called them off. She used her key to Milt's double-wide and walked in. The two dogs pushed their way past me and entered behind her.

Memories assaulted me. I took a deep, deep breath in, both to clear my head and to calm my racing heartbeat.

"Grampy?"

Slumped in his recliner in front of the TV, Milt dozed quietly. His scooter was parked beside him. Judge Judy droned from the old tube-style television set. Stale, dust-laden air—now bolstered with smelly-dog aroma—welcomed us in. It didn't seem right, that a man who'd served in the Korean and Vietnam Wars, and had once shaken hands with General MacArthur, spent his days deteriorating in a worn chair.

Britney touched his shoulder, right before one of the dogs nudged his hands. Milt blinked awake.

"Hey, Grampy. I brought you some stuff—and some company. Do you remember Delilah?" She kissed our grandpa on the cheek and shooed off the dogs, who obeyed.

His consciousness registered slowly, like a diver making a careful ascent to the water's surface. He stared at me, his jaw slack, and his eyes opaque. For a long moment, embarrassment clawed me from the inside. Was I supposed to remind him I was Bill's daughter? *You know, that son of yours who's getting out of prison soon, the one that raped me and my brother for, oh, most of our childhood.*

"Little DeeDee?" He croaked over dry lips.

"It's me." I hugged him, gently and quickly. A whiff of chemicals and plastics greeted me, along with body odor and the fading scent of detergent.

"Delilah Cascade. Bill's youngest. Got a brother. Dante Valentino."

The rush of heat to my cheeks knocked me silent for a beat. "Yeah. Amazing you remember that." How Donnie and I loathed our mother's penchant for unique names. I switched Cascade for Cassidy years ago. Not legally, but who wants to be named after dishwasher soap?

Britney helped take care of Milt's latest round of medication, and I perched on the couch. Milt hadn't bothered redecorating since Granny's passing. Either he didn't care, or he preferred the yellowing walls that way, lined with photographs that had been there when I was growing up. I glimpsed a snapshot of a younger Bill. My discomfort ratcheted. His fixed stare like the hot breath of a ghost against the back of my neck.

50

"You know about that no-account father of yours?" Milt's speech gurgled, and a coughing fit struck. Britney patted his back and readjusted his oxygen tube after he settled.

Watching her tend to him was endearing, but I didn't want to spend the morning discussing Bill. Having him seep back into my life, even inadvertently, strained my emotions.

"Yes, I heard he's coming back." I tried sounding neutral and petted one of the dogs.

"I got all kinds of letters, phone calls, and visits from people at the Department of Corrections, making sure he could live here after he got out. He's called me about every week, saying he's coming back and going to run the shop. Wasn't my idea, but I can't exactly tell him no. He's kin. But I ain't never forgiven him for what he done to you kids and your mother." He pointed his finger, at no one in particular, when he said the last part.

When people realized I was Bill's daughter, their natural reaction was to slather me with pity. *Always felt so bad for you and your brother,* they said. Their intentions were kind, well-meaning, but such reminders stung and induced flashbacks to Bill's hands on my skin, to the sound of him chewing the orange slices, and the cries I muffled with my pillow. Another reason I'd left Venice—to escape the *You poor thing* mantra from the locals.

"You know, I always loved that woman," Milt continued, "but that Bill...what he done. Shameful. They shoulda locked him up for good. Ever'abody in town know'd what he done."

I nodded. Mainly to myself. A confirmation that my gut-instinct proved right—coming to Milt's was a bad idea. Britney probably enjoyed watching me squirm from Milt's musings. Not that I could see her. The dog, panting heavily and enjoying my attention, sat on my feet.

"Shoulda sent him to the chair."

"They don't use the electric chair anymore, Grampy." Britney made sure her voice carried over Milt's increasingly-loud tone.

"Well, he deserved to be fried. Hurtin' you kids…then what he done to Sloan."

I stopped petting the dog. He left me. "What do you mean?"

Milt's eyes met mine. A glazed expression on his face. "He bragged about it. We were a-sittin' right there on the back porch. Drinkin' kamikazes like we always did on Fourth of July. He said he was getting ready to shack up with that Rita woman, that he'd gotten rid of Sloan."

Rita, my stepmom, flashed through my mind. Donnie and I often found her passed out on the couch, on the days we made it to school. She feared Bill as much as we did and rarely made a meal more complicated than PB&J sandwiches. The day Bill was arrested, though, she swatted, jabbed, and yelled at him as he was led to the police cruiser.

"Did he kick Sloan out of the house?" I had to focus on Milt and his story.

"I asked him, I said, What do you mean rid of her? And he said, Just what I mean. Ain't no one gonna find her and if they do, they ain't no proving it's her." Milt gripped the armrests on his recliner. Breathed a little faster. "I said, How's that? And Bill said, I know from TV that they need a body and they use the teeth; I took care o' that. Sunk 'em all."

"Sunk…Like he dumped her body in water?"

Milt answered with a shrug-nod combo.

I stood, started pacing. "Maybe a river—the Ohio River? Oh, my God! He dumped her in the river? That has to be it, right?" My mind went there—pictured Bill holding Sloan's limp body, wading into water up to his knees, then dropping her like a sack of garbage. "It's no wonder she was never found."

"Delilah, calm down." Britney darted a glance from me to Milt.

She was right. I sat back down, realizing I couldn't let my hysteria overwhelm me and possibly upset Milt. No one had ever told me anything concrete about Sloan's disappearance. Or even the days leading up to it. To hear Milt say that Bill had confessed to getting rid of her…it was the same as hearing Bill confessed to murdering her. I didn't know how to process the info. In my mind, I always knew Bill was guilty, but I never figured out how he got away with it.

"Grampy," I said, nearly gulping the air, "did you ever tell the police about this?"

He shook his head. "It would've been my word against his, and there was no way of proving what he said."

"Do you think Bill was drunk and just making up a story?"

"No. Theys two things that don't lie—kids and a drunk. You get a good buzz going, that'll loosen your tongue."

I looked to Britney. "We should go to the police."

"No!" Milt yelled, surprising Britney and me. "It's too late for that now. Your mother's resting in her grave, wherever that may be. Bill will be here tomorrow or the next day, and…" his hands started shaking, "I don't know what it'll be like, the two of us here again. Prison changes a man." Milt looked to me, his eyes glossy. "And with Bill, knowin' the evil that's in him, there ain't no hope it's made him a better man."

When we piled back into Britney's car, she slammed her door shut and turned to me.

"What is wrong with you? How could you treat him like that? He's just an old man."

It took a moment for the reproach to sink in. Having been gone for a while, I had forgotten about Britney's talent for distorting a situation. "I didn't do anything wrong. You're acting like I badgered him for information. He's the one who brought up Bill. And didn't you hear what he said? Bill killed my mother!"

"And you believed him? He forgets to take his meds and shower. You think he remembers a conversation from years ago—where he and Bill were hammered? Please tell me you're not *that* stupid." Her eyes were so wide that her false lashes touched her eyebrows. If I wasn't fuming on the inside, it might have seemed funny. And if Wanda's house wasn't ten miles out, I would've walked—or crawled—my way back. Anything to get away from Britney at that moment.

Not for a second did I think Milt was wrong. Drunk, traumatized, whatever, there are moments in life and snippets of conversations that stood out, that youth and old age can't smother. Plus, according to Milt, Bill had sunk Sloan's body. No way that detail was random.

"Grampy's right," Britney went on, "whatever happened back then doesn't matter now. How can you be so selfish? Couldn't you see how terrified he is of Bill?"

"Then why aren't you and your mom doing something about it if you're so concerned?"

Britney slumped in her seat as if she were considering my remark. Then, she faced forward and started the car.

"Bill insisted on staying at Grampy's." Her voice was calmer. "Mom has a boyfriend, and Bill didn't want to be around that."

"So Bill gets his way."

"You know what he's like."

Her words sliced into me like a medieval hatchet. She accused me of being selfish—wanting to know how my mother was murdered—but it was okay for her to be insensitive to what I'd been through at the hand of my father. Her reactions reminded me of Tonya and how she used to tell people that Bill didn't abuse me and Donnie, that it was a misunderstanding. *Overactive imagination*, she called it. *Probably got it from their mother.* She always jumped to Bill's defense and was the only person in the family to have anything to do with him, far as I knew. Apparently, that tainted thinking had leeched into Britney's head too.

Britney's phone vibrated from the depths of her purse. She dug it out, read the message, and sighed.

"It's my mom. She needs me to swing by her shop."

"Now? Can't you drop me off at Wanda's first?"

"You can stay in the car while I run in."

We rode in silence, which was best. Britney had the windows down. The air was cooler than it had been yesterday, a storm approaching. The wind streaking across my face brought a welcome relief. My head contained a circus of hurt and rage and thousands of questions all vying for my attention. I played with my phone hoping Britney would take it as a cue that I didn't want to talk or argue or let her cut any deeper into my wounds. Topping this morning off with a stop at Tonya's salon was perfect.

Tonya came out of her shop as we pulled up to the curb. She carried a box, which presumably contained whatever she texted Britney about picking up. Britney popped the trunk of her car and hopped out. Tonya smiled at me, big and bright like I was a favorite customer and she'd touched up my roots last month. She was a slightly-older-looking version of Britney with hair and make-up for days. But underneath the layers of contouring and moisturizer, I detected a sneer in her eyes.

Britney and Tonya chatted as they put the box in the back. I made a point of not listening. The sooner the trunk thumped shut and we were off, the better.

"Hey, Delilah," Tonya said. Her unexpected greeting startled me. She practically framed herself in the driver's side window, which was still down. That power-watt smile she displayed probably endeared her to every client. I bet they lapped up the phony charm she exuded and paid her handsomely so they could look as attractive as she did. Too bad she wasn't as beautiful on the inside.

"Hi, Tonya." That was it. My conversation well had dried up. I didn't know where to go from there. Jump to a half-hearted apology? Forget all the angst that had passed between us? I shifted in my seat, tried to look comfortable.

"Heard you were coming back." The breeze caught Tonya's hair, whipped it around her cheek. "Awful nice of you to check on Milt. He won't admit it, but he gets lonely out there. A visit from you probably did him good."

Tonya lavishing compliments, being cordial threw me. We didn't do civil.

"Yeah, I hadn't seen him in a while." No telling how long my grin would last. If Tonya knew I had rattled Milt with my questions about Sloan, her cheeriness would disintegrate.

"Since you were in the mood for visiting, I thought you might want to catch up with someone else you hadn't seen in a while." A corner of her mouth curled deviously as she nodded toward her shop.

I looked past Tonya. The door to the salon thwapped closed. Bill Ramsey clopped heavily down the steps.

CHAPTER SEVEN

I never thought I'd see that man again—not alive. There he was, leaving The Beauty Bar with the loose swagger of a man with no cares. No burdens or regrets hampering him. I slouched in my seat, wished hard for a trap door that would slide me into another dimension.

Tonya stepped aside, called out to him. Bill stopped, bent over a little and shot a squinty-stare my way. Recognition bloomed on his face. So did a smear of slyness.

Fury uncapped inside me. Along with determination to remain in control. I got out of the car, stepped onto the sidewalk. No way I was facing my father sitting down. The rest of the world melted away. Bill ran his hand over his head, looking like he had a fresh haircut, then took another step toward me.

"Don't!" I didn't yell, but I was firm. My entire body pulsed. He was right there. The man who shattered my sleep, robbed me of feeling safe in my own home. The man who had put every inch of himself on my body.

With his hands on his hips and a sloppy posture, he looked me over, then slid his tongue across his lips. A thick paunch insulated his middle. His dark hair now streaked with gray.

"My girl ain't little no more." He lifted his chin, gave me a pathetic wink. Proving in an instant he had no remorse. Milt had been right—prison hadn't fazed Bill.

"I'm not your girl. You're nothing to me and never will be." Words formed like freshly-pulled taffy in my mouth. My tongue swelled. All the things I'd said to Bill, when he'd crept into my nightmares, wouldn't come.

"About what I expected," Bill said. "That's all right. Ain't nothing gonna undo the memories we got together."

The salon door opened, and Lieutenant Mark Snyder stepped out.

"Time to break this up, Bill." Snyder's voice was steady, harsh even, and joggled something in my brain.

Bill kept his eyes one me, probably hoping his casual stare would make me cower or cry. I wasn't about to let him have a drop of satisfaction. Instead, I matched his gaze, walked up to him, armed with courage. I never realized what a small man he was. Barely two inches taller than me, grizzled with deep creases in his face, sagging jowls on the horizon, he was anything but intimidating.

For the first time in my life, I wasn't afraid of him. He would never knock on my bedroom door again. Never wiggle that bag of candy in front of me again.

A half-grin cracked on his face and he spoke in a low tone. "Bet plenty of boys been in that sweet lap of yours by now."

I rocketed a jab to his face, striking his mouth.

Bill moaned and hit the ground. Blood dripped onto the pavement.

"That one hit is all you get, Ms. Ramsey," Snyder said.

"Stay away from me and my family," I said to the top of Bill's head. Then to Snyder, "It's Ms. Baker, Lieutenant."

I started walking toward Wanda's, not caring if I was headed the right direction, and not caring that a small audience had watched me punch my father. Because I was free. A thousand jabs to the face couldn't take away what Bill had done to me, but that was okay. Those scars were the patchwork of who I was. There was no more little girl, trembling and hiding under the covers, hoping to be saved; there was a strong woman, facing and taking down whatever monster stood in her way.

When I was far enough away from Bill and Tonya and everyone else near the salon, I started running. So did the tears. Not because I was upset over Bill, but because of Sloan. She never learned how to be a fighter, how to free herself from Bill and the abuse.

Gray clouds rolled in, suffocating and surrounding me. A chill swept through the air. Thunder gave a low rumble. The scent of rain hung pleasant and heavy. I ran maybe two miles before my lungs threatened to explode. Much of town was behind me. Panting, I looked around. Nothing was familiar but an auto parts store was up ahead.

I called Donnie, not having the patience to trade texts.

He answered with, "Where are you?"

"I saw Bill."

"Yeah, I know. Let me come get you."

I scarfed deep breaths to clear my head and told him where I was.

"Be there in five."

I nodded absentmindedly as he ended the call. The rain came. I stuffed my phone into my pocket and walked the short distance to the auto parts store. Before I got there, the summer storm had me soaked. Not that I could feel it.

When Donnie arrived, he got out of the car, left it running with the door open, and came to me. He smashed me into those big brother arms and buried his face in my neck. I don't know how long we stood there, holding and gripping each other, but long enough for my anger to melt under the raindrops.

"Come on." Donnie led me to his car and opened the passenger-side door.

I collapsed into the seat, numbness crawling over me.

"Thanks for coming," I told Donnie when he joined me.

"I should've known something like this would happen."

Maybe we both should have been more alert, better prepared to face Bill. I was mad at myself for not unleashing and saying everything I'd said and screamed at his picture in some of my therapy sessions. Mad for not confronting him about his confession to Milt.

"Sorry about your car." We had saturated Donnie's leather interior. I glanced around for a shirt or something to help stop the dripping but saw nothing.

Donnie sat motionless, clenching the steering wheel and staring straight ahead.

"What's wrong?" As the words came out, my stomach scrunched.

"Bill."

I put my hand on his shoulder, worried that buried memories were creeping up on him.

"You don't understand," Donnie said, still gazing out the windshield. "I saw him when he was in prison."

My hand withdrew as if Donnie became too hot to touch. "You went to visit him?"

He nodded. "Years ago. Not long after I turned eighteen."

"Why?"

"Because I'm not like you. I wasn't going to hide from him forever. I had to see him, and have him look me in the eye when I told him what I thought of him and what he did."

I tried imagining them together. Donnie, young and anger filled, sitting across from Bill, wearing prison fatigues and crowned with satisfaction.

"Lot of good it did you," I whispered, thinking about how Donnie had struggled with drinking until recent years.

He snapped his head in my direction. "You're the expert, right? The know-it-all because of that degree of yours?"

I didn't know why he was lashing out, trying to hurt me. Arguing wasn't in me at the moment. I turned away, regretting that I'd called him.

"When you saw him, just now, did he say anything about me?" Donnie asked.

It seemed like a strange question. "You think we sat down, chatted like long-lost Army buddies?"

Donnie sighed heavily.

This was stupid. I honestly didn't want to talk or think about Bill, not when Milt had just revealed the truth about Sloan's disappearance. Every fiber of my being wanted to bleed out the story Milt had shared, but an odd feeling gnawed at me, told me Donnie wouldn't listen.

"No," I said, "he didn't mention you."

"He's probably going to say things about me, spread it around town."

"Like what?"

Donnie was silent a few beats, then, "I don't know, but whatever you hear, don't believe a word of it. He's going to start trouble, because that's what he does, and that's all he's good for."

Donnie dropped me off at Wanda's but didn't come in, which aggravated me. He said he was picking Emery up from preschool and had to work, but I wondered if that was his convenient excuse. By now, I figured Grandma had heard about my encounter with Bill. The grapevine system in Venice was bar none.

My body felt tense, wiry even, when I thought about re-telling Grandma what happened. I dashed up to the apartment, needing out of my wet clothes anyway. Expecting Grandma to peck on the door at any second, I changed quickly. No knocking came, which surprised me. I combed my hair into a damp ponytail and went back down to the house.

The screen door slammed behind me when I walked in. Princess barked and trotted into the kitchen, her nails clicking on the linoleum. Grandma came too, shushing the dog and holding envelopes in her hands.

"You doing okay, baby?"

I nodded my soggy, scatter-brained head. She hugged me, warm and solid like she always did, and passed me a handful of envelopes.

"Here. You should have these."

Kentucky Department of Corrections stared back at me.

"Them's the notices about Bill's release. I got the same ones. They didn't have your address for Ohio."

Another nod from me.

"If you were thinking about leaving, I couldn't blame you," Grandma said. "Venice is small, and there ain't nothing that can keep you from running into Bill around town."

"I'm not leaving." No way, because Bill would get too much satisfaction from that. He would think I was too weak and rattled to face him. No way—especially since I knew, thanks to Milt, that Bill had killed my mother.

I couldn't tell Grandma what Milt had shared. For one, I couldn't imagine repeating those words to her. Second, I didn't know if Grandma was strong enough to endure such revelation. Maybe a person's heart had a limit, especially when it came to the death of her child. And today, with Bill's return, she was probably already dealing with a tornado of emotions.

My phone rang. Looking at the screen, I didn't recognize the number, but it was local. Could it be Bill, already starting to harass me? One way to find out. I answered.

"Ms. Baker? This is Lieutenant Snyder, over at the sheriff's office."

My eyebrows jumped. "Yes, Lieutenant, what can I do for you?"

"I need you to come down to the station as soon as possible."

"Something wrong?"

"It's best if we address the matter in person."

"All right," I said slowly, taking my damp appearance into account. "An hour okay?"

"That'll be fine."

We hung up. Grandma looked at me expectantly.

"I have to go to the police station." Quickly, I rummaged for a conceivable reason the lieutenant had summoned me. "I could be in trouble."

"What for?"

"I punched Bill in the face when I saw him. There's a chance he could be pressing charges." It sounded absurd as I said it, but I wouldn't put it past that snake—and the possibility that Snyder was taking Bill's side.

"I'll go with you."

"No, it's okay, Grandma." If Bill—and his new buddy Snyder—were set on being a thorn in my side, I wasn't about to back down. "Probably best if I do this on my own."

I swung the door open to the Campbell County Sheriff's Office, convinced that my confident strut would settle the pounding in my chest. It didn't happen. When I stepped up to the counter where Snyder was waiting, I made sure he could see nothing but self-assurance on my face.

"Thanks for coming down, Ms. Baker."

I appreciated his emphasis on the Ms. Baker. It almost served as an apology for his earlier behavior.

"Am I under arrest?"

Snyder's face scrunched. "Arrest? What for?"

"Is Bill pressing charges for what happened earlier?" It was late afternoon, but the day seemed to be lasting forever. Had it only been a few hours since I'd jabbed my father?

Snyder chuckled. "You think I called you down here to lock you up? Let me put you at ease, then. No charges are being brought."

I kept from looking over-relieved as best I could.

Snyder pressed a button that unlocked the door to my right. "Care to follow me?"

Intrigued and hesitant, I stepped through and followed his lead. We made our way into the building's interior, which was a tight maze of cubicles and doorways. Snyder opened a door labeled Private and motioned for me to enter. He came in behind me and closed the door. The room was bare concrete walls that had been painted white, a table with two chairs, and a cardboard banker's box sitting on the tabletop.

"You requested a viewing of your mother's case file," Snyder said. "Permission granted."

"What?" I was taken aback.

"I can make copies of reports. You're free to ask questions on items you may not understand. But I stay in the room while you go through everything."

I peered inside the unlidded box that had RAMSEY written on the side. Files and papers stared back. I took them out, then sank into a seat at the table. Was it real? Was there no longer anything separating me from the what the police had stored about my mother? No one had given me any insight into what had happened when my mother disappeared. Aside from those internet articles I'd read, the nitty-gritty details of the investigation were a blank landscape in my life.

Like an archeologist on a dig, I handled the items from the box with reverence and care. Photos of Mom, a copy of her driver's license, copies of Bill and Sloan's bank statements, and a Missing Person's report—filed by Wanda. Then there were interviews. The police had spoken to Wanda, Paul, Bill, Glenn, Milt, Ginny, various family members, neighbors, and friends. Next came reports of the searches: Milt's property, including a scouring by bloodhounds, a grid search of the acreage, and dragging the pond. Milt's double-wide and Bill's house were searched. So were the shop, garages, and Bill's workspace. *No evidence was catalogued*; *No evidence of foul play* concluded the reports.

After I finished reading every piece of paper dedicated to finding Sloan Ramsey, I rubbed the kink out of my neck and fatigue from my eyes.

"I'm really impressed," I said to Snyder. He had ordered lunch for us from a nearby deli. I open the bottled water he handed me and soothed my dry throat. "I had no idea this much effort had been put into finding her."

Snyder swigged from his own bottle, then said, "That's what I figured. You thought nothing had been done. Most people watch too much TV, get the wrong idea about how an investigation works. They think every case has forensic evidence sitting around and is solved within a week. Takes a lot of hours and manpower."

"I grew up on rumors and stories about my mom."

"Now you know why." Snyder referred to the pile of reports. "There wasn't any evidence that told us otherwise. No signs of blood at any of the properties. No indication of foul play. No witnesses. Nothing."

At the mention of witnesses, I winced inwardly. Milt's admission ran through my head. Why hadn't he told the police when they interviewed him? Had Granny Ginny known too?

Hesitation rose up in me and cautioned me about divulging Milt's story. That was quickly suppressed by the rising hopefulness that once Snyder knew about the confession, he could arrest Bill immediately. I'd pace myself though.

"Were any other bodies of water searched?" I asked.

Snyder flipped through the reports. "Besides the pond on Milt's property? I don't think so."

"I saw Milt this morning, and he told me that Bill confessed to killing Sloan." I relayed what Milt had shared, even included Britney's opinion that Milt was confused and unable to remember that far back. Snyder listened carefully and jotted notes.

He shook his head when I finished. "Poor Milt. Man's been through it. Your cousin might have a point. Time, medication, alcohol through the years, those can do a number on a person's memory."

"But the way he described the conversation and remembered Bill saying he *sunk it*—sunk the body—that was so clear." My insides shuddered, repeating that statement. "It's too specific. It *has* to mean something."

"Maybe. Milt's on edge over Bill's return. This recollection of his could be a way of getting your attention. Fact is, he's afraid Bill's going to kill him, make it look like an accident."

My eyes went wide. "You've got to arrest him then if he's been threatening Milt."

"Hold on there. Didn't say Bill outright threatened him, only that Milt's been anxious."

I shrank back in my seat feeling ashamed. I'd worried that Bill would harass me and Donnie but had given no thought to Milt. Hearing that he feared for his life made me want to help, but I didn't know what I could do.

"This might surprise you, Ms. Baker, but I'm on your side. What you're telling me about Milt, all of it could be true. Maybe Bill did dispose of Sloan's body in water. If there's a chance we can find evidence, put Bill Ramsey behind bars for good, I'm all for it."

I kept my jaw from hitting the floor.

"First thing I did this morning," Snyder continued, "once I heard Bill was in town, was head to that beauty shop and confront him. I made sure he knew I was keeping an eye on him—and that nothing had better happen to Milt. After your little episode on the sidewalk, I escorted him to the Probation and Parole office in Newport—which is where we also had him checked out after you decked him. His nose isn't broken."

Because I decked him in the mouth—trying to permanently remove that stupid smirk of his.

"Bill has to report and check-in regularly. He's under what they call Mandatory Reentry Supervision. Means we're making sure he behaves, does what he's supposed to."

Maybe it should've given me a bit of relief, hearing Bill was being watched. It didn't. If anything, that might inspire him to see what he could get away with. That was my guess.

"I took him out to your old place on Bevelhymer Road," Snyder continued, "Told him it'd be best if he settled in and laid low a while. Folks 'round here ain't too happy about his release. We'll monitor the situation. No telling what kind of welcoming he might get tonight and in the coming weeks."

The look Lieutenant Snyder gave me could've been interpreted as part warning. I held my hands up in surrender.

"I have no desire to throw dead skunks in his yard or spray paint his house or whatever it is kids do these days to try and scare people."

"Dead skunks?"

"Hey, I don't know." Yes, I did know from past experience. I dropped a dead chicken through the sun roof of Mr. Sabin's car after he gave me a D on my Spanish midterm in tenth grade. Much later, of course, I realized I earned that D from being a poor student. But that did nothing to make up for Mr. Sabin having to reupholster his car.

Lieutenant Snyder let me pick which documents I wanted copies of to take with me, then we packed the file back as it had been. A sense of hopelessness tried perching on my shoulder. Sloan's file had information but nothing particularly useful. No clues jumped out at me and there were no signs of a lackadaisical investigation. The Campbell County Sheriff's Office had done its job thoroughly.

"So I'll look into bodies of water, see if searches were done elsewhere and reports didn't get filed correctly. That sort of thing. Will let you know what I find out." Snyder handed me my copies of the reports.

"Thank you. I really appreciate this." I stood to leave and noticed Snyder grinning. "Did I miss something?"

"You still don't remember me."

Hadn't we been through this? "Yeah, you said you escorted Bill to court during the trial."

"That's right, but I thought I'd wait and see if anything triggered for you. Any memories."

He waited. For what, I wasn't sure.

"I was the one who slapped the cuffs on Bill and arrested him. You were just a little thing, squeezing that doll. Never will forget that look in your eyes or watching them tears hit your shirt."

My breath caught, and my brain rocketed back to the memory of that day. *He won't hurt you again.*

"That was you." And that's what my brain had been searching for earlier today, when Snyder came out of the salon and was harsh with Bill.

He gave a curt nod. "My first year with the department. Still here serving the citizens of Venice." He extended his hand for me to shake, which I did readily. "Now, I'm not making any promises that we'll find a thing. I want you aware of that going in. There's not a shred to go on. I'm willing to give this case a fresh look, but don't get your hopes up. Can you accept that, Ms. Baker?"

"Please, call me Delilah."

CHAPTER EIGHT

Growing up without a mother left a constant ache in my heart. Most people didn't know what it was like. Those that did had lost their mothers to disease or accident. Sloan's strange, unexplained disappearance put me in an exclusive club. But in the last couple days, listening to Milt, finding the family photo and diary, and now going through the case file with Snyder, made the loss feel fresh and raw. At the same time, there was a sense of relief. Because there had been days when I felt so far from Sloan, so empty and numb, I didn't know if she really existed. Now, I reeled from the awkward high and a pinch of hope that I could find out what happened to her.

Before Lieutenant Snyder and I started going through Sloan's file, I'd sent Wanda a text telling her things were okay, then I'd silenced my phone. In the hours I'd spent combing over the pages of reports and interviews, my phone had racked up an impressive amount of missed calls and messages. Impressive for me.

Donnie, Britney, Wanda, and a few others had reached out. Donnie was sorry for this afternoon, wanted to talk, call him later. Britney was sorry and had no idea her mother was staging an ambush with Bill. Wanda was worried, wanted me to call asap.

Driving back to Grandma's was a blur.

"What happened?" Grandma asked. Princess stood behind her, barking as I walked in.

"Long story, but I didn't get arrested." My chest was heavy.

"How 'bout I make tea?"

"Grandma, you don't have any tea. You're a Dr. Pepper addict."

"True, but I thought you mentioned drinking tea, so I picked up a few boxes."

That made me smile. Grandma was always one to keep track of things I did and didn't like. A peacemaker and a pleaser.

I sat at the kitchen table and Princess jumped onto my lap.

"Not sure what Oscar would say about this." I rubbed the back of her ear, which she nuzzled into.

"I went up and checked on him, made sure his bowls were full. He always make that much noise?"

"He's high maintenance and a bit of a drama queen."

She laughed and shot a glare at Princess. "They all are." Since she didn't have a kettle, Grandma set a pot of water on the stove to boil, then joined me.

"Do you know Lieutenant Mark Snyder?"

"Sure do. He comes in the Cracker Barrel all the time." Grandma worked there, tending the items in the gift shop and helping in the kitchen when they were short staffed. She had been a server but said it was too much work and people were too grumpy for her now. "He's a good man. Been an officer his whole adult life."

"Did you know he was the one who arrested Bill?"

She didn't but remembered he was at the trial. I told her about my conversations with Snyder and why he called me in to the station.

"What did you find out?" A mix of curiosity and apprehension showed on her face. "Is there new evidence?"

She listened as I went over the items that had been housed in the RAMSEY box for over fifteen years. With the water now boiling, I took over the tea, managing to pour the piping hot liquid into the mugs without splashing it on me. An accomplishment, considering the build of tension. Sloan's diary and the strange entries came to mind. I sat our mugs on the table and made the impromptu decision to venture into delicate territory.

"Grandma, why didn't you tell the police about Sloan's diary?" I felt guilty, not bringing it up with Snyder. Having looked through the file, I doubted the diary had an impact on the case. It wasn't my call to make, though, and I wondered if Grandma would be considered guilty of withholding evidence.

She stared at her tea and stirred mindlessly. "Afraid to, I guess. No telling what they would've made of it, with all her drawings and chatter about them damn unicorns and such."

"Was something wrong with her? Had she been diagnosed with a disorder?"

The stirring stopped. "It's one of those things I didn't want you kids to know about your mother. Couldn't change what happened to her, and I wanted you to keep the memories intact, what little you had of her. Didn't want none of that tainted."

I understood that. Memories and stories were all we had, apart from the diary and photos.

"Doctors did what they could, said there wasn't a cure though. There was medicine, but she didn't always take the pills like she was supposed to. You'd notice when she ran out or missed doses. She'd have problems thinking straight."

"Was it schizophrenia?" The DSM's description still fresh in my head.

Grandma met my eyes and nodded. "Used to hear these wild stories about your great granddad, how he ran naked through the cornfields and ate grass. They say the disorder can run in a family. Sloan's the only one, besides your great granddad, who had anything like that."

"Did the police know about her condition?" This was the first I knew about great granddad. That's what happens when you run off, insulate yourself from family and the past.

"No."

"Were you worried they wouldn't look for her, if they knew?"

Grandma wiped away tears as she nodded. "People said the nastiest things about her. They didn't know her. What she went through. No one really understood what was going on, and there was already plenty stacked against her with Bill and the affair with Glenn. She couldn't help it, couldn't control the things in her head." Grandma covered her face. "I didn't know the right thing to do."

I set Princess on the floor and knelt to hug my grandmother.

"Nothing was more important to her than you and Donnie. She wanted to be the best mother in the world. She tried hard. She did…but I know…"

"It's okay, Grandma. Everything's okay."

She didn't need to say it. That Sloan had failed us. Because I already understood.

I wasn't worried that Bill would show up at Wanda's that night, but Oscar and I stayed in Grandma's house. She needed us close. We talked a while about Sloan and how the schizophrenia plagued her. She had a lengthy list of symptoms, from seeing things that weren't there to confusing fantasy with reality. I'd done two internships at OSU's psychiatry hospital and worked with similar patients. It was easy to understand Grandma's instinct to protect Sloan and to keep the diary a secret. From what Grandma said, I gathered they didn't have the resources needed to manage Sloan's condition.

Grandpa Paul was also the kind of man who shied away from doctors. *If there ain't no cure, what's the use in going*, was one thing he used to say. So it was easy to understand why Sloan may not have gotten the medical help she needed. Once Sloan married Bill, and he eventually cut Sloan off from her parents, her condition may have spiraled out of control.

Grandma was too worked up and distraught for me to tell her about Bill's confession to Milt. Hearing it might help her heal and lessen the guilt she carried. Maybe she would also forgive herself for thinking there was something she could've done to save Sloan's life.

Watching Grandma's pained expressions and tears as she told me about my mother was wrenching. She took the news about me going through Sloan's case file better than I expected. Instead of railing against me or chiding me for getting involved, she hung on every word, asked thoughtful questions; she wanted to know what was in that file as much as I did.

When he was interviewed by the police, Bill didn't bring up Sloan's diagnosis. He went on about what an unfit mother she was and said she probably took off—with Glenn. In his interview, Glenn said that he'd ended his relationship with Sloan months ago, but that she kept calling him, wanting him to come over. She even talked about running off, he said. Glenn didn't say Sloan suffered from schizophrenia, but he said she wasn't always *right in the head*.

Next time I saw Snyder, I would mention the schizophrenia, see what he thought about its impact on the case.

I managed some sleep and sprang out of bed at 5:30a.m. the next morning for a kickboxing class. Before my initial visit to the Campbell County Sheriff's Office, I'd stopped in a martial arts studio. I told the owner about my blue belt in Ju Jitsu and offered to teach in exchanging for taking classes. He agreed. My body craved the non-stop routine I kept up at home. Exercise, classes, portioned meals. My studies were complete, but I'd brought a healthy diet of textbooks for light reading. Food was still an issue. In Columbus, I helped prep and deliver healthy, portioned meals in exchange for my own. Here, overnight oats had become an entrée.

I took Oscar back to the apartment and changed before class. Yesterday's voicemails and texts went mostly unanswered. After a solid hour of exerting myself, I'd be ready to face them.

If it was possible to feel miserable and exhilarated at the same time, that was me afterwards. Maybe teaching and partaking in classes back-to-back wasn't the greatest idea. After a long shower and nuzzles with Oscar, I sat at the table, dressed in shorts and a tank, with my head wrapped in a towel. The a/c window unit hummed, but I was losing confidence in its ability to battle the summer heat.

I scrolled through my phone. Regret jabbed at me for not responding to everyone yesterday, including Donnie. He had texted again this morning, inviting me to join him and Emery at the Boone County Public Library in Florence. The library was hosting a carnival to kick off their summer reading program. He said Emery was excited and wanted to see me. And we could talk. I told him I'd meet them there that afternoon.

Snyder had also texted me that morning saying Bill had stayed put last night. He wrote that a group of kids had set a couch on fire in Bill's front yard, after the deputy on surveillance had dozed off, but no other incidents occurred. I replied with thanks and told him Wanda and I slept better knowing precautions were in place. He sent back *You're welcome* and said he was free late in the afternoon to share an idea he was tossing around about Sloan's case. *Great! See you then* was my response.

I finished getting ready and drove to Florence. Apparently, a library carnival was a big deal. I parked in a lot a couple blocks away and managed to find Donnie and Emery. We filled up the bag she was given with more books than it could hold from the book mobile. She got a butterfly painted on her cheek. We rode the merry-go-round, slide, and Scrambler, which made Emery's smile nearly wrap around her head.

It was a wonder my phone didn't explode from all the pictures I snapped. Selfies and social media weren't my thing, but I memorialized the day with Emery and Donnie like it was a regular habit. There was a sweet sense of normalness to it that I hadn't really known. I had moments, pictures—and family—I could show the world. If people looked at me and Donnie now, they wouldn't know what we'd been through and the things we'd done. We were survivors. And today, we were like everybody else.

I couldn't recall going on rides at Emery's age, but it was fun watching her light up. Donnie bought her a bag of cotton candy but told her she couldn't have any until after she ate. She crossed her arms and pouted.

"Nope, not having that," Donnie told her. "If you're going to get mad, then I'll throw it away. Let's clean up that pretty face and get ready for Mommy."

Her pout turned into tears, and I thought I was going to die of heartbreak. I wanted to scoop her up, buy her ten bags of cotton candy—not really—and tell her Daddy was being mean. Instead, I was awestruck at Donnie's parenting skills—and feared I'd never be able to handle stuff like that. Especially not on my own, single-parent style like Donnie. I'd told my boyfriend I might never want to get married or have kids. I didn't know if I could do those things without screwing them up.

Donnie picked up Emery and held her close. "You can't get what you want just because you get mad or start crying. That's not the way to behave. You've been a good girl, and we've had a lot of fun. It's time to go now. You don't want to be grumpy for Mommy. Bet she's been missing you."

Emery leaned in to him. I couldn't tell if she was listening to her dad, but her outburst tapered off. As Donnie held her, patted her back as those final sobs came out, I wondered who I could've become, how my life would've been different if I'd know that kind of love from my father.

We started making plans for lunch but got interrupted by a call from the restaurant. When he flashed me that apologetic expression, I knew we wouldn't get the chance to talk.

A Tilt-a-Whirl of emotions spun through me. It meant everything that Donnie wanted to share, to let me know what was on his heart. Now, I'd have to wait. There was no need to make Donnie feel bad about heading into work though. I returned a grin to show I understood, but I wished he could just tell me. Secrets were the worst, especially when you're the one in the dark.

After Emery showed me what a strong bear-hug she could give, I went to the police station to meet with Mark Snyder. When I stepped into the small conference room, with Mark behind me, I gasped. He had dedicated the small space as a command center, his words, for the Sloan Ramsey case. Maps of the Ohio River and Campbell County now covered one of the walls. Sitting on top of the table where we sat and rifled through the case file was a framed picture of Sloan. The brassy-gold border gave it the same effect as a halo, wrapped around my mother.

"Figured we might as well do this right," Snyder said. "Best to keep our findings and info in one space."

For the first time in my life, I had hope—real hope—that we'd discover what happened to my mom. I smeared away tears and thanked Snyder. He gave me that curt nod.

"Now, based on what Milt said, you're thinking we should concentrate on searching areas around the Ohio River, right?"

"Bill said he sunk her. That sounded like water to me. Since the river's not far, I figured that's where...." I swallowed, couldn't say it.

Mark nodded thoughtfully, which put me at ease.

"I'm with you. Now, the river is 981 miles long, runs from Pittsburgh to Cairo, Illinois, where it empties into the Mississippi. But the current is affected by a few things, like flood waters, depth, and width. Its widest point is just north of Louisville. Stretches out to a mile. For reference, from Cincinnati to Louisville is 132 river miles, but we probably can't tell for sure how fast a body would travel."

"Would the body float at some point?"

"That's right. Even if it was weighed down, tied to cinder blocks or what have you. Wouldn't matter. The decomposition gases would bring it to the surface. After a few days, though, the body would sink again. What was left of it."

"It's freshwater, so no sharks." Was I really talking about my mother's corpse? I detached myself as best I could. The same way I pretended Grandpa Paul was on an extended fishing trip.

"Right, but plenty of catfish and bugs that would...eat away..."

"Yeah, I get it. So if her body rose to the surface and wasn't found, then it probably sank to the bottom..."

"Somewhere, at some point."

"And she became fish food and there's no way we'd ever find a trace of her." Despite my childhood and my angry teen years, I wasn't a pessimist. In light of the facts Snyder had laid out, clinging to hope now seemed foolish.

"That's a real possibility. We ain't giving up though."

"Why? What's our next move?"

"I been thinking this through, best I can, not being no physicist or science whiz. I'm gonna contact cities between here and Cairo, see if any sheriff's departments have...unusual evidence in their property offices or at the ME's."

"Unusual. As in...?"

"Jewelry or clothing you might be able to identify as hers." He cleared his throat. "Hate to say it, maybe a thumb or tooth with a dental filling."

"You think a body part of Sloan Ramsey is sitting in storage in Cairo, Illinois?"

"Now, don't go getting your hopes up. Like I said, just me thinking. Kids find all sorts of things, take it to their parents."

I pictured Emery playing along the banks of the river, the water lapping at her bare feet. It was easy to imagine her throwing rocks and using a stick to poke at things along the river's edge. Then the image soured, thinking of her picking up something particularly odd and taking it to Donnie, only for him to realize it was a body part. I went cold, wishing I could protect that sweet girl from the horrors of this world.

"If something was found a few days after Sloan went missing," Snyder continued, breaking my daydream, "got to the authorities in a timely manner, was wrapped up properly, that could bust this case wide open."

"An awful lot of *ifs* in that statement."

"You ready to quit on this?"

He had a point. The fact there was no body, no blood trail, no smoking gun made it look as though Bill had gotten away with murder. What else was there for us to do but track down evidence? To sift through the river, the dirt, whatever it took to prove Bill was guilty.

"Never," I said.

"Good to hear. About the only things we got to go on are the timeline and the westward direction of the current. We know where to look and when Sloan disappeared. Could be a long shot of finding anything. Moving water is about the worst grave there is. Add in summer and warm temperatures, that speeds up decomposition. Not to mention fifteen years. But it's worth a try. If we find something, might be able to have it tested for DNA. That science has come a long ways. Darndest stuff."

"So all we need is a necklace or a pinky to get Bill arrested for murder." I had no idea how I managed to say those things, as if I wasn't talking about my own mother.

"A pinky? Like a finger?" The absurdity of my comment wasn't lost on him. Apparently, my tough-girl act, if that's what you'd call it, wasn't working. "That might be a bit of a stretch, but let's just see what pops up when we go sniffing around."

CHAPTER NINE

It should have bothered me more, the things I was holding back from Lieutenant Snyder. He'd been amazing with his help so far. Gone out of his way and probably beyond his duty. Even if we found nothing and couldn't prove Sloan was murdered, I'd be forever grateful for his efforts—and for keeping Bill under his thumb.

Yet I hadn't been totally honest with Snyder. Hadn't told him about the diary or Sloan's struggles with schizophrenia. Maybe the contents of the diary didn't matter; it only affirmed her confusion between fantasy and reality.

Grandma had beat me home and probably had swiped leftovers from the restaurant for dinner. If she wanted to scarf down country fried steak and biscuits with blackberry jelly, who was I—with my vegetable stir fry—to stop her?

Making my way up the wooden stairs, the aroma of fresh cut grass and clotheslined laundry on the breeze, I craved Oscar's affection. Then I heard an odd noise. A flapping sound. I looked to the top of the stairs and saw a doll propped against the door to the apartment. The closer I got, the more a familiar sensation slid over me. Blond hair fluttered, along with a note taped to the doll's naked chest. Dread suddenly beat my torso.

Once on the stoop, I bent and picked it up. An exact replica of my Sally Secrets Doll. The one I'd had and loved when I was younger. The one I'd taken with me to Grandma and Grandpa's when we moved in. Her 'secrets' were the stamps and stickers she came with.

A slot in her belly dispensed the stickers. The bottoms of her shoes hid an ink pad and roller. Her earrings and necklace held the stampers. Of course, as a kid, I lost those accessories.

"Sally?" I whispered, as if she could answer me.

Her face was dirty. Hair disheveled and in serious need of detangling.

I read the note. *For my sweet, sweet girl and our times together.*

The handwriting was terrible, showed the skill level of a toddler.

Sally wore an undergarment that didn't belong to her. White, ruffled underwear that were too big. The panties held something lumpy that filled out the shape. I pulled back the elastic waistband and peeked inside. The sight and the sweet, tangy smell put me into a panic. I screamed, dropped the doll.

Sally crashed to the stoop, as orange slices tumbled out of her panties.

Maybe I was still screaming when I scaled down the stairs. Was Bill in the apartment, waiting for me? I could still smell the orange slices when I bumped into Grandma.

"Delilah! What's wrong?"

"I don't know. Someone's been in the apartment. I think it was Bill." Tears were flowing. "Oh, I have to get Oscar!"

"No, he'll be fine." Grandma took me by the wrists and pulled me toward the house. "Bill could still be in there. Let's call the sheriff."

We scurried into her kitchen. I locked the door and closed the blinds. Grandma called the police. Her words were frantic.

"Hurry, please!"

Grandma stayed on the phone with the dispatcher. Princess barked incessantly. I peeked through the blinds. An equal mix of fear and anger galloped through me.

Within minutes, cars screeched to a halt outside. Grandma opened the door for Lieutenant Snyder and Officer Dalton.

"Wanda, Delilah, what's wrong?" Snyder asked.

"I got home and was heading up to the garage apartment. There was a doll, like one I used to have, and a note from Bill, saying," I swallowed the lump in my throat, not certain I could get the words out, "For my girl and our times together." My bottom lip trembled. I couldn't tell him about the orange slices.

Snyder looked to Dalton. "Let's check it out."

We waited while Snyder, Dalton, and two other officers walked the property.

Snyder returned first. "You have the key to the apartment? Door's locked."

"Yeah. Did you find the doll?" I asked.

"Not yet."

"It was right there by the door…Maybe it fell down the steps."

Snyder nodded. "We're still looking over everything. If you want, we can search the apartment. I can check it alone or you can come in with me."

"I'll go." A quiver tinted my voice.

Snyder was right. There was no sign of the doll. No strewn orange slices either. I paused at the bottom of the wooden stairs and glanced around.

"There was candy too," I said, "with the doll. Orange slices."

I was relieved Snyder only nodded, didn't ask why.

The stairs creaked under our weight as we went up. The heat of the day had lost its grip. The sun was still out but stretching toward twilight. My sweat-slicked palms patted my shorts for the key, but I'd left it under the mat for Grandma. I told Snyder. He gave a firm nod and lifted the mat. I snatched the dulled metal key and unlocked the door. Snyder rushed in.

"Police! Anyone in here?"

We heard a rustling from the bedroom. Snyder put his hand on his gun. My spine stiffened. And Oscar came strutting out of the room mewing loudly.

"He supposed to be here?" Snyder asked.

"Yes, he's mine." I picked him up, planted my face in his fur.

"I'll check that room if you don't mind." Snyder went in, poked his head around. He did the same for the bathroom. "All clear. Does it look like anything's been disturbed?"

I glanced around the space, almost too flustered for anything to register.

"No." I couldn't say what was worse, the idea of Bill in my apartment, touching my things, or the surge of embarrassment currently replacing the adrenalin in my system. How was it possible the doll was gone?

Snyder carefully looked the room over. "Doesn't look like anyone's been here, but that ain't much of a lock."

Meaning, Bill still could've been in here. Could've found the key. I squeezed Oscar tighter, trying to make the shudders go away.

"Why don't you go through exactly what happened." The dinette chair, which was from the 80s, creaked under Snyder's weight as he sat.

I sank to the floor with Oscar in my lap, then relayed how I found the doll on the stoop. Even mentioned the candy inside the doll's garment. Snyder listened thoughtfully. Of course, I was quick to accuse Bill.

"You sure it was Bill who did this?"

"Who else? Bill knew I had that doll, and he...used to bring home orange slices." My cheeks burned from the stirred memories. The sound of his gooey chewing. His tongue on my thigh.

84

"I'll make a point of talking with him." Snyder stood. "You still okay to stay here?"

"Yeah. I can sleep in Wanda's spare room if I need to."

"Might not be a bad idea tonight, until we get a few answers. Let me check and see if they've found the doll."

Snyder excused himself and joined the other officers outside. I got up and let Oscar stroll back into the bedroom. Grandma came in; Snyder passed her on his way out.

"Did they find anything?"

"Not yet."

When Bill abused me, I thought silence would serve me better than telling someone. That was a lie, of course. Even when it came time to share everything with authorities, I struggled with finding the words and having strangers know what my father had done. The adults were soothing, reassured me that it would be okay. Kids at school were different. Fear and shame became my cloaks.

This time around I was quick to call for help, but it was starting to look like a pathetic cry for attention. The officers' stares and side glances reminded me of the cruel kids at school.

Lieutenant Snyder returned, empty-handed.

"Nothing. Nothing in the yard, nothing in the surrounding area." He leveled his stare at me. "Are you sure you saw that doll? Wasn't any chance that after today and all we talked about that it brought back things from the past?"

"I promise you I had that doll and the note in my hands."

"Then I hate to say it, Delilah, but someone may be messing with you. Might be watching the house too. Could've planted the doll and waited for you to find it. Once you started screaming, they snatched the doll, picked up the candy, and ran."

I looked to Grandma. Worry wrinkled her features. "What can we do?"

"Not a whole lot. We can dust the place for prints, but I don't expect we'll find any."

Grandma and I agreed. If Bill did creep into the apartment, he knew to wear gloves.

"I'll post an officer out in front of the house for tonight."

Grandma sighed, nodded her appreciation.

"I radioed the officer keeping an eye on Bill. He told me Bill's kept to the house, the salvage shop, and Milt's. Hasn't strayed off the property yet. That doesn't necessarily mean he wasn't involved. He could've had someone place the doll on your doorstep." Snyder shrugged. "Could be someone else trying to rev your emotions. Can't say right now."

Snyder was well-meaning and doing his job. Grandma had been right about him, that he was a good guy. I nodded and went along with his scenarios, but I knew it was Bill. He wanted me scared, worried that knock on my bedroom door would come again. I had fallen for it. Seeing the Sally doll and the orange slices had taken me right back to my tortured childhood. If Bill wanted to play games, I'd have to beat him at it. That meant not letting my guard down and knowing to be ready for anything.

After the sheriffs left, I caved and decided to sleep at Grandma's again. She offered to make chocolate chip cookies. If there was anything that could cure the ugly sting from the evening's events, it was Grandma's homemade cookies. Just like the first time I stood on the porch, soothed by the smell wafting through the air, tonight was no different. My dietary restrictions were also going out the window for those cookies.

"Grandma, promise me you'll never teach me how to make these." Three cookies in, I worried an intervention would be needed to stop me. It struck me too, that the last time I enjoyed her cookies, Grandpa had been at the table with me.

"Never. That way, you'll always need me around."

I liked that.

We tried letting Oscar and Princess nose each other and stay in the same room of the house, but that lasted a few seconds. Princess was already riled from the officers popping in and out, and Oscar was too used to commanding all the attention. Sharing the spotlight with a dog wasn't in him. I felt bad Princess was sentenced to the cage in Grandma's bedroom.

Oscar had jumped on the kitchen counter, to Grandma's horror, in an attempt to help himself to the ingredients. He was known to do that back at my place and was put off by the fact Grandma scolded him and wasn't aware of his anything-I-want-I-get-privileges. She took him off the countertop and shooed him away with a dishtowel.

It was relaxing, eating warm cookies and talking about our pets.

Until a knock tapped on the back door. We both tensed. I insisted on answering, my fist clenched and at the ready. As I stepped to the door, I realized that the blinds were still down and the evening air wasn't floating in, like it always did at Grandma's on a summer night. The place felt like a bunker.

I checked the peephole before opening the door for Glenn.

"Glenn, what are you doing here?"

"Sorry to drop in so late without calling." He joined us in the kitchen, wearing the same outfit he had on the night he came to dinner. "I heard there was a ruckus out here tonight and wanted to make sure you ladies were all right."

"That's right sweet of you, Glenn. Come in and sit. I don't know if you'd call that a ruckus or what." Grandma fixed him a plate of cookies and poured him a glass of milk. The ease she displayed around him told me Glenn spent more time there than I liked.

I felt the urge to take control, not wanting Grandma to divulge everything. "Yeah, we thought we had an intruder. Kind of silly. Guess we overreacted, calling the sheriff. They were great. Showed up in a matter of minutes and searched the whole place."

Grandma stared at me as if she didn't know who I was.

"I was hoping it was something like that." Glenn settled at the table. "It's just with Bill getting out and all, well, I got worried, thinking he might try and bother you."

It startled me on the inside, hearing how close to home his suspicion turned out to be. I hadn't discussed it with Grandma, but I wasn't anxious for the rest of Venice to hear about our mishap that evening. Didn't want people thinking I was jumping at shadows, or rumors generating that I was seeing things. Giving Glenn a watered-down version of events suited me.

"That was awful nice of you to stop in," Grandma said.

"Yeah, you didn't have to go out of your way," I added.

"Wasn't no bother really. Had a few errands to run. Always needing gas and twine. And you know, I heard Bill's dangerous. Still don't seem right he's back here. Acting like nothing ever happened."

"The police are keeping an eye on him," I said.

"That so? Glad to hear it. Means we can sleep better at night."

"Yeah..." Although I wasn't sure how Glenn would sleep, not with the amount of cookies he was scarfing down. "I was actually thinking of you the other day, Glenn."

"Oh?" he said with a gooey mouthful.

"I was going through the case file for my mother"—he choked slightly but recovered—"and I read the transcript of your interview with the police. You said that you and Sloan broke up before her disappearance. That you had called it off, and you couldn't get Sloan to accept it, leave you alone."

"Is that what I said?"

"Do you ever think about that? Or what if you had given in, told her you'd run off with her? Do you ever think that might have saved her life?"

It was a good thing Grandma stood behind Glenn, so he couldn't see her face. She looked appalled. Had I been younger, I would've been on the verge of getting one of those *You're gettin' it when we get home* glares.

"So you think I shoulda run away with your mom, left you and Donnie here?"

"She never would've left us." I smiled. "Or didn't you know that about her? Was that what made you break it off with her, or was it something else?"

I didn't know what I was doing. My intention had been to get him out of the house before he ate all the cookies. Petty, but the way he'd shown up and helped himself irked me. Like he thought he belonged here. I might have to mow Grandma's yard from now on, but that was the price I'd pay.

"Guess I'd better be going." Glenn wiped his mouth with a napkin and dropped it onto his plate. "Thanks for the cookies, Wanda. I'm glad you two are all right and nothing bad happened."

It could've been just me, imagining things again, but Glenn gave the word *bad* a brooding emphasis—and looked at me when he said it.

CHAPTER TEN

After Glenn made an awkward exit, Grandma folded her arms and scolded me with a disapproving stare. Maybe I took it too far. An apology didn't surface within me though. Not with Grandma acting like Glenn's guardian. Before an argument erupted, I went to bed.

Five-thirty came early the next morning on the heels of fitful sleep. The thought of someone—no, not someone—Bill—watching and lurking around the house was unsettling. *Daddy wants to play in your lap. Brought the orange slices for my sweet girl. You know how I love that tangy taste on my tongue…and on my girl.*

Lieutenant Snyder had checked in with me late last night, assuring me Bill was home and still under surveillance. That was the only reason I got any sleep at all. Only Bill knew about the Sally Secrets doll and the orange slices. How had he skirted around the police? Had Tonya helped him out? Placed the doll on my doorstep and waited till I found it? She was possibly the only person in Venice on speaking terms with Bill. Would she go that far for him, and was it worth it for her to put me under that kind of stress? Accusing her without any proof was useless.

No way I would let yesterday make me miss my early morning class. Not that I gave a full-throttle performance, but I managed. Taking a shower at the studio wasn't an option for me, even back at my regular training center. I brought clothes to change into and planned to stop by Donnie's apartment. He knew I was coming since we traded texts late last night. I didn't share about the doll and Glenn's intrusive appetite but planned to.

I picked up breakfast from a drive-thru and was knocking on Donnie's apartment door before eight. Judging by the looks of my brother when he opened up, he had a rough night.

"Mornings still aren't your thing." I handed him a large coffee.

Wearing unbuttoned jeans and dull circles under his eyes, he nodded his thanks for the drink and led me to his kitchen.

"Nice place. You live with someone?"

He raked his fingers through his hair. "No, why?"

"I don't remember you being this clean."

A half-grin appeared while he surveyed my post-workout appearance. "You always leave the gym like that?"

"Yeah."

"Explains why you're single."

That would've been a solid brotherly zinger except for the fact it wasn't true. I hadn't mentioned Jason, my boyfriend, to anyone in Venice. Our relationship was complicated. For me, not him. Jason wanted us to move in together when I returned in the fall. I didn't know what I wanted yet.

My scarlet cheeks answered for me, but I hoped Donnie wasn't awake enough to realize it was a sign of me hiding something. Come to think of it, there was plenty I still hadn't told Donnie. Finding Sloan's diary, her schizophrenia, and Snyder's renewed interest in Sloan's case. Donnie's sausage cheese croissant and my egg white omelet weren't enough to get us through it all.

As we spread out and settled at his kitchen island, I dove into the story of Sally Secrets' visit and disappearance. Hearing the story out loud, even I had to admit, it sounded weird. Had someone really been watching me? Waiting for me? Or was Snyder right? Was there a chance I had *imagined* that doll?

When I finished, Donnie stopped chewing as if his croissant had lost its flavor.

"It's Bill."

I nodded. "Has to be."

"I told you he'd start trouble." He put his breakfast sandwich on the wrapper and wiped his hands like he was already finished. "I should go out there, have a talk with him."

He stood; I snapped to my feet, put my hand on his chest.

"Are you crazy? No!"

"I can't sit back while he traumatizes my sister again!"

"Talking to him is a waste of time. He can't be reasoned with. And he probably wants you to show up and do something stupid." Like punch him in the mouth.

Donnie sat back on his stool, ran his hands over his face. He looked worn, not just tired from work but burdened. We returned to our food. Crinkle noises from the wrappers filled the silence between us.

"What is it with you and Bill?" I asked after a few minutes. "What's going on?"

Donnie stared at the countertop. "I can't get into it now."

"You wanted to talk about it yesterday, after the carnival."

"Yeah, but it's not that easy. There's things you don't understand…and I could lose everything, including Emery."

My chest hurt at the thought of Donnie and Emery being kept apart. No way I wanted to imagine a world where he couldn't hold that little girl and take care of her.

"Be straight with me," I said, ignoring the rising panic inside me, "just tell me what it is. I can help you."

He snickered but there was no humor in it. "No one can fix what's happened."

"Why can't you trust me?"

"It's not that—"

"Does Britney know?" I hated myself the instant those biting words flew out.

Donnie glared at me but passed the chance to lash out. "No."

An apology probably wasn't enough at this point. Donnie had his walls up. Pushing or begging him to talk was worthless. I started cleaning up our mess, wiping crumbs from the counter. It was something to do. Meant I didn't have to look at him.

I went to put the trash in his bin, the silence still heavy between us, and saw the unthinkable. Two empty beer bottles. I dropped the paper bag of trash into the bin quickly, as if I didn't notice the bottles. Chances were good my flushed face gave me away. A special kind of misery and anger mixing inside me.

"I'm gonna head out." The mousiest words that ever came out of my mouth. I gathered my things and made a point of avoiding eye contact with my brother.

"Hey...don't..."

I knew what he meant. He didn't want me to make an issue of him not spilling his guts; he didn't want whatever this big thing was he couldn't tell me not to come between us. He wanted me to make it easy for him. Pretend I wasn't hurt.

"It's okay." Because that's what we say. Maybe it's a brother-sister thing, I don't know. That way you have of communicating without saying much. When you don't want the thing to become a fight. Especially when it's too hard. "I'll call you later or something."

Donnie stayed slumped on his stool. Before he could see my tears, I ducked out the door.

I couldn't get away fast enough. Tears stung and practically blinded me, but I drove anyway. No destination in mind. Just the need to get away.

Beer bottles in the trash were troubling. How many more were in there, resting at the bottom? What was going on with Donnie that had him drinking again? I believed him, that whatever he was hiding was dangerous enough to rip Emery from his life. Had to be. Whatever was gnawing at him had lured him back to his self-destructive ways. That shoved my concern into panic-mode.

An incoming call from Snyder stole me from my mental rantings.

"You doing okay?" he asked. "No problems last night?"

"We were fine." I kept my voice steady. "Thanks again for coming out and checking everything." A flash of embarrassment shot through me again.

"To be honest, I was glad you were there with Wanda. Don't know how she'd handle Bill's release if she was on her own."

More embarrassment hit me, posing a threat of an inner meltdown. I wasn't a hero. I didn't come back home to look out for my grandmother, not like I should have—not like a truly loving granddaughter would have. Being in Venice while Bill was freed was a fortunate accident at best. But Snyder didn't know that.

"Just wanted you to know I put together a press release about Sloan's case. I'm sending it out to all the departments on or near the Ohio River. Told them we're hoping to find evidence, no matter how small it might seem."

The weight of the things Snyder didn't know hit me. I couldn't keep withholding from him, not when there was a chance he might be able to use the diary or Sloan's diagnosis to move the investigation forward.

I asked if I could swing by the station later, and he said sure.

"Thanks, Lieutenant."

"Wouldn't be the end of the world if you called me Mark."

Not even ten a.m. and my cheeks were flaming red for the second time that day.

Oscar sat on the lid of the toilet while I showered and prepared what I would tell Snyder—Mark—about the diary and Sloan's disorder. Before heading up to the apartment, I searched around the yard, garage, and house. Nothing. At least nothing conspicuous. A pop can, cigarette butts. Nothing that said a stalker, peeping Tom, or Bill had staked out my place. But what could I expect? The police had combed the area, but I had to see it for myself.

There were no signs of Sally, either. Thankfully. Or maybe that wasn't a good thing. I didn't know. My head felt fuzzy. Uncertain.

I let Princess out for a bit since Grandma was at work, and walked through the yard one more time. I even practiced hiding behind a few trees and bushes. None of it felt plausible, as though someone would really crouch and hide and watch. Princess tilted her head as she stared at me.

"Yeah, I know. Silly, isn't it?"

Back in the apartment, I sat on my bed and went through Sloan's diary again. My nerves ramped up at the thought of handing it over as evidence. Maybe it was foolish, but I hoped Snyder wouldn't need to keep it.

Oscar sat mewing. He'd followed me into the bedroom. Next to him on the floor in the closet was the box that held the diary and family portrait. Just then, I remembered there had been pills in the box. I emptied the box and found four pills. Blue-speckled and oval-shaped, the letters LCI were stamped in the top curvature of only one of the pills. I'd taken a class on pharmacology in college. Met Jason there. No drug came immediately to mind.

My phone rang. When I checked the screen, the number came up as Venice, KY, but didn't include a name. Again, I suspected it was Bill—and answered.

"DeDe? That you?" The voice came in gasps.

"Who is this?"

"Milt. I need help." Dogs barked and whimpered in the background.

"What's wrong?"

"I'm stuck. Dresser fell on me. Can't get up."

For several seconds, I stood frozen. Except for blinking excessively. A strange attempt to organize my thoughts and process what I was hearing from Milt.

"Did you call Tonya or Britney?" Stupid question maybe. Getting involved with Milt made me uncomfortable, especially since he was close with Britney and Tonya. How had he thought to call me— and how did he get my number?

"Nobody answered. Please, DeDe. Help me. Can't breathe too good."

"Okay, I'm coming."

On my way out the door I called Snyder and left a voice mail. I told him I'd stop in later than expected, that a situation had come up at Milt's. I felt better knowing that a police officer knew where I'd be, because what was truly waiting for me at dear ol' Grampy's house, I had no idea.

The pit in my stomach grew as I drove to Milt's. Was he setting me up for another ambush? Too much had happened in the past few days for me to believe that this was exactly what it seemed—a cry for help.

I called Britney, got no answer, and left her a message. Then I tried Donnie, but he didn't pick up either. What was with people and their phones? I knew both of them were constantly checking their screens and texting.

I skidded to a stop outside Milt's double-wide and knocked on the door. A silly move. The dogs started barking but the knob didn't budge. Milt kept an old pair of work boots near the stoop that held an extra key. I searched them and found the spare.

The dogs surrounded me, their whimpers sounding anxious. Nothing else looked out of place in the house. No other cars were outside. Whether it was from the rush of getting there or in anticipation of the unknown, my chest thumped like I had a thoroughbred inside.

"Milt?" I called out.

"Here."

In the bedroom, I found Milt on the floor. Trapped under a toppled dresser with its drawers open to various depths. Six drawers tall and made of solid wood, it had dove-tail edges and no particle board. As kids, we could almost touch the ceiling if we stood on its top. It had been handcrafted by Granny's father, if I remembered the story correctly. I squatted and pushed the furniture piece upright as Milt rolled out from under it. Socks, shirts, and boxer shorts were scattered around.

"Are you hurt? Should I call for an ambulance?"

"No, just get me to my chair."

Moving Milt from the floor to his chair proved to be a struggle. He wasn't heavy, but he could hardly stand. Coordination wasn't his strength either. Like Britney had said, walking was difficult for him. He alternated between wincing and soothing the dogs as I dragged him, gently as I could, to the living room. Inwardly, I was grateful for incorporating tractor tire flips into my workouts. Once I got Milt seated and comfortable, I checked him over for injuries. The dogs kept nudging in between us and putting their heads in his lap.

"You should see a doctor," I said. "What if there's internal bleeding?"

"Naw. I'm all right. Just need to catch my breath."

I hooked him up to his oxygen tank and waited to see if his paleness would change. He explained how the dresser toppled when he yanked open the top drawer.

"Didn't know my own strength," he joked.

It made me smile too. As we sat there, I glanced out the window behind Milt's chair and saw Bill. My smile left and my insides went cold. Maybe I was as pale as Milt now.

"What is it?" Milt asked.

"Your son."

Bill walked across the gravel, smoking a cigarette, headed toward the salvage shop. I noticed a bruise above his lip, courtesy of the jab I landed on him in front of Tonya's salon. The morning sunlight gave it a deep purple glare.

"Told me yesterday he had a customer coming today." Milt's breathing became steadier. "Said he sold some scrap and the guy would be by to get it."

The idea of Bill making a living and transitioning back into a regular life irritated me. He didn't deserve such pleasures, as far as I was concerned.

He glanced at the trailer and did a double-take when he saw my car.

"No." Fear pulsed through me. I sprang to the door and slid the chain into place. Dialed the two deadbolts too. When I peeked between the blinds again, Bill had changed direction. He was heading toward Milt's.

I couldn't think. No way I was letting him in. But what could I do to get rid of him?

"You got company in there, old man?" Bill's bellow was heard easily through the mobile home's thin walls. Before he reached the metal stairs that led up to the trailer's door, a car pulled in frantically, spitting gravel everywhere. Britney popped out of her car.

"What you doing here?" Bill asked her.

At the sight of Britney, I could have sworn the walls of Milt's trailer were closing in on me. This was it. Their plan to gang up on me...to...I don't know, but I didn't like it.

"I got a message that Grampy was hurt." Britney brushed past Bill and made her way to the stoop.

"Oh, yeah? Who told you that?" Bill flicked away the remains of his cigarette.

"Your daughter." She spun around and practically spat the words at him. "So you'd better scoot. Bet she's already called the police."

"Delilah's here?" Bill shaded his eyes and looked toward the windows. "Where's my sweet girl?" His words filtered in like a sing-song taunt.

I pressed my back against the wall. Granny Ginny's old curtains, grime on the windows, and the yellowing blinds hampered Bill's attempt for a glance inside. Still, I took in a deep breath, hoping it would elongate my body and make me invisible. Only glass and thick cardboard separated me from my father.

"Open up, D," Britney said from the door. Her key now useless. "I'm not going to let Bill in."

I didn't know what to think, what to believe. What was happening? Was Britney here to help Bill drag me back to the house, so he could torture me again? Breathing didn't come easy.

"Git outta here, Bill." Milt croaked out the words with more gusto than I thought he could manage.

Another car approached. Bill left the window. A car door opened and shut. Bill greeted whoever got out. Voices muffled and trailed off.

"Delilah, please," Britney said. It sounded like a loud whisper, seeping in through the door jam.

I stepped away from the wall and looked outside. Bill was with a man, supposedly his customer, walking toward the warehouse. He glanced over his shoulder at the trailer and flashed that smug grin.

"You gonna let her in?" Milt asked.

I nodded slowly, though unlocking the door still didn't seem like the best idea. After I fumbled open the locks and Britney came in, I also fumbled through the story of finding Milt trapped. Britney listened and nodded. We both knew now wasn't the time to talk about Tonya's stunt.

Britney hugged Grampy and talked to the dogs while I stood back. Awkwardness practically set me ablaze. I hadn't thought to embrace Milt after getting him freed from the dresser and settled in his chair. Proving again I wasn't the ideal granddaughter. If Milt had any qualms about it, I couldn't tell. His face remained solemn, even with Britney fawning over him.

I took a minute to calm down. What was wrong with me, overreacting whenever Bill appeared? He was the one walking around with a bruised lip—from a punch I served up. There was nothing for me to fear from Bill anymore. I'd proven that to myself.

"I think Bill's a fixing to kill me," Milt said.

Britney and I exchanged glances.

"Has he threatened you, Grampy?"

Milt nodded. "He's been puttin' pressure on me to sign everything over to him. Wants the property in his name. Says it's easier if we do that now, while I'm alive. He thinks I could go at any minute—and he gets that look in his eye, like he's done thought of a few ways to do me in."

"Don't sign anything," I said. "Don't let him force you."

"What am I supposed to do? He told me he can make me do what he wants. Acted like he was gonna spill hot coffee in my lap when he said it. Said he can make it look like I had an accident, no one would ever know the difference—or care! Exactly what he said!"

"It's okay, Grampy." Britney rubbed his shoulder. "We won't let anything happen to you."

I wondered if Milt living alone was a good idea. Surely, Tonya knew how fearful Milt was of Bill, and that Bill posed a danger. I suspected something strange was simmering with this family, which is why I didn't bring it up.

Britney made Milt a salami sandwich, then situated him with his meds and the TV. I went to the bedroom and replaced the spilled contents back in the dresser. For good measure, I did a quick clean of his bathroom. The place was the epitome of old person smells, that stale, mothball scent that clings to every fiber, object, and surface more than twenty years old. Scrubbing it gone was hopeless, but the task took my mind off the fact that Bill was close by in the salvage warehouse.

I had to get a grip. When it came to Bill, I had two settings: sheer panic or volcanic anger. Neither worked well and both consumed me when they kicked in. Bill had no control or influence in my life—only the power I kept giving him in my weak moments.

Here I was now, strong and independent, no longer living in the shadow of an abusive childhood. I was an overcomer. Perfectly capable of taking care of myself. Why was I running to lock doors when I could deliver a jab, kick, or throat punch before he could blink? As I finished wiping down Milt's bathroom, I resolved to stop fueling Bill with power over me that he didn't deserve.

Back in the living room, Milt had dozed off. Both dogs were cozied up at his side. The earlier frenzy had been replaced with a soothing serenity. I wanted to soak it up, but Britney motioned for me to join her in the kitchen.

"So what happened here?" she asked.

I gave her the rundown, from Milt's call for help to Bill showing up right before she arrived.

"I got here as fast as I could," she said, checking her phone. "Not easy to leave a client in the middle of a balayage treatment though."

"Well, if Milt needs more attention than you can manage, maybe you should consider hiring help. Sounds like Bill is a danger to him."

"Bill's a nuisance, that's for sure."

We checked out the window for any signs of Bill. Apparently, he was still inside the warehouse with the customer.

"I'm sorry about the other day," Britney said. "I swear to you I didn't know Bill was at my mom's salon. I never would've gone there. The guy gives me the creeps. Mom knows I don't want anything to do with him."

Yes, Britney, let's make it about you. Maybe I couldn't resist being petty around her.

"It's done." I shrugged a shoulder to go with my nonchalant tone. "Running into him was bound to happen. At least around Venice."

"You sure put him in his place, busting his mouth the way you did. Think you can teach me to hit like that?"

Like you would ever risk breaking a nail. "Sure."

Just then, noises came from the salvage shop. We scrambled back to the window and saw Bill outside talking to his customer. They shook hands and parted ways. Bill stood on the gravel lot and lit into a new cigarette as the man drove away. After a drag, he turned his attention to the trailer. My blood ran cold when that smug grin of his appeared and he licked his lips.

"I can't stand him." Britney sent Bill a laser beam of a stare. Her disdain for the man was palpable. "I hope he ends up in jail again."

For a change, while staring at my father, I suppressed my own smile, because that *was* something to hope for. Thanks to Snyder's help, I felt like there was more than a good chance of finding evidence. It wouldn't take much, right? Just that one piece was all we needed to prove Bill was guilty of murdering Sloan. Then I could serve up my own smug grin, just for Bill.

CHAPTER ELEVEN

We watched as Bill locked up the shop then walked the worn path that led into the woods. Presumably heading back to his place. A good time for me to leave. Britney stayed with Milt, not wanting him to wake up alone after his traumatic morning. She slid the chain and deadbolts into place when I walked out. The metal on metal sound sent me scurrying to my car. Almost as if I were a deer shoved into an open meadow during gun season, and Bill could pop up and take a shot at me.

Britney's tenderness for Milt impressed me, but I wasn't over the stunt she pulled with Tonya. Maybe she didn't have a part in it, like she said. I wasn't sure what to think. At the moment, I was still flustered from my reaction to Bill showing up. How many times would it take before I didn't panic and become unraveled by my apprehensions?

I paused inside my locked car.

Was I experiencing signs of schizophrenia? Grandma mentioned that Sloan and my great-grandfather were the only family members who suffered from the disease, but what if...it was manifesting in me?

According to the DM3 manual, signs of schizophrenia usually began in the teen years. A diagnosis could be complicated, because the common symptoms mirrored other disorders: lack of interest in personal hygiene, depression, hostility, forgetfulness, inability to focus. And hallucinations. The list of symptoms was staggering, so were their combinations. Schizophrenia wasn't a textbook-style disease that affected each sufferer the same.

I wasn't taking any meds. Until my return to Venice, I hadn't experienced any episodes or signs that roused my concern. Not until the Sally doll appeared—then disappeared. What if I was a late bloomer when it came to the condition?

I shook my head to scatter the bombarding thoughts. There were bigger things to worry about. Namely, those two empty beer bottles in my brother's trash can. When I considered how our relationship had gone since my return—a whopping six days ago— frustration stewed within me. It was a series of progress and setbacks. Not what I hoped.

After I pulled into the driveway at Grandma's, I texted Donnie and asked if I could swing by his place for a bit. He replied he had just dropped Emery off at preschool and had a couple hours before he had to be at the restaurant.

Maybe I should've dwelled more on what I was about to do. Thought through to the possible consequences, but I didn't. A weakness I hadn't outgrown. I packed a few items into my tote and left, ignoring Oscar's mews as I locked the apartment door behind me.

On my way over to Donnie's, I became more convinced that I'd discovered how to repair the rift between us. Donnie had been cold and dismissive about Sloan and her disappearance because he didn't know about the schizophrenia. Once he read the diary, he would realize why she wasn't capable of a normal response to Bill abusing us. He would see that she'd been a victim too, of her own mental capacity.

It was one thing for townspeople to believe Sloan had abandoned us. Quite another for my brother believe it. If Donnie truly thought Sloan had walked out on us, knowing what was going on, then it made her as awful as Bill. I couldn't accept that.

I knocked lightly on his apartment door when I arrived.

"It's open," came from the other side.

Donnie was at the sink doing dishes. An array of pink kiddie cups lined up on a drying rack. Hard to say what made me smile, my brother's domestic skills or the sweet contrast of those cups against his stark bachelor pad.

"Didn't think you'd be back so soon…after this morning."

"Yeah, about that." Okay, I'd forgotten. It had been a busy morning since then, but Donnie was right, we hadn't parted on the best of terms. "Sorry for the way it ended. I really don't want any problems between us."

On the heels of that comment, my scalp prickled. What if I was making the wrong decision, heaping the info about Sloan on him?

"Same here, little sister. Unless it's a food fight, not worth the energy."

His good mood deepened my hesitation.

"Any update on the doll?" He rinsed off the last cup and placed it with the others.

The question caught me off guard me and distracted me from the warning bells going off in my head. I figured it was Donnie's way of asking, *Any signs of Bill?* Inwardly, I groaned, thinking about the encounter at Milt's trailer. No way I could rehash that now.

"Nothing new on that front." I tapped my fingers on the counter, needing a release for my nervous energy. "But there's something I wanted to show you."

I removed Sloan's diary from my bag and put it on the counter. A deep breath followed.

106

"What's this?"

"You should read it."

He gave me a squinty look and finished drying his hands. He sat at the island and opened the cover. My heart raced like a runaway train as I watched his eyes and waited for him to recognize Sloan's handwriting.

"Wait. Sloan kept a diary?" His head snapped up. "Where'd you get this?"

I told him about the garage apartment at Wanda's and finding the box during clean-up.

"Do you remember this?" I slid the family portrait from the bag.

Donnie took it. Same as Wanda, he became transfixed by the image.

"Man, that was a lifetime ago," he said.

"You were cute back then." I tried—unsuccessfully—to repress my smirk.

After mocking me, he laid the picture aside and went back to the diary. I kept quiet as he flipped through pages, taking his time. I watched him and waited. Anxiety spiked through me, making me fidget and bounce my leg. To lessen the sensation, I took turns making my hands into fists.

When he finished, he closed the diary and sat with a blank stare for a moment. After a deep breath he said, "I don't get it. What's with the trolls and unicorns and crap?"

"Wanda never told us, and we were too young to realize it, but Sloan was schizophrenic."

He sat frozen. "You're telling me she was crazy?"

"That wouldn't be the best way to put it. She had a mental disorder. Her reality wasn't the same as everyone else's. She had medications, but Wanda said she wasn't consistent with them. And there's no telling how Bill dealt with it."

"Why are you showing me this?" His face became haggard, his eyes red.

"I thought it would help you understand her."

"What good does that do me now?"

Not the reaction I hoped for. Not a total surprise either.

"Can't you see, Donnie? She had problems. She didn't know what to do, being married to a monster like Bill. Her mind didn't function properly." *That's why she didn't leave him after she caught him abusing you.*

"Fine. I get it. She was messed up. That doesn't undo what happened."

"Nothing will. It's not about that. I wanted you to read the diary so you could forgive her, Donnie. So you could let go of that pent up anger inside you."

"Now you're my therapist?"

It was a snide remark, but knowing I was going to spend a career working with a spectrum of troubled kids, I was bound to hear worse. A thick skin would be a necessary part of my daily wardrobe.

"I'm trying to help both of us," I said. "And I'm trying to figure you out. I know you're going through some tough situations right now. I just want to be there for you."

"This is how you do it? Dig up the worst memories of our lives?"

"If that's what it takes to prove Bill killed her, then yes."

"That again?" Donnie scoffed. "You've got no chance of that happening."

"Maybe, but I've got to try, and Lieutenant Snyder is working with me—"

"What? I thought I told you not to get the police stirred up? How can you do this to me?" He shoved the diary across the counter. I saved it from sailing to the floor. His brows furrowed and face flushed with rage.

108

"Donnie, what are you talking about? It's an unsolved case. Why are you so angry?"

"You should leave." He stood, stormed to the door and whipped it open. "Now!"

I grabbed the family photo and ducked out of his apartment. My legs couldn't move fast enough. Running down the stairs and out to my car, tears erupted.

Mark Snyder found me in my car at the police station parking lot, crying uncontrollably. How I managed to get there and how long I'd been wailing, I didn't know. Mark took me inside and held me as the ache poured out of me. He asked me a slew of questions. *Are you hurt? Is Wanda hurt? Was it Bill?* All I could do was shake my head.

Slowly, I managed to calm down. Mark got me water and a box of tissues. I was beyond tissues. A hose would've been better, but I appreciated his gesture.

"Can you talk about it?" Mark asked. We were sitting across from each other, our knees touching.

My face was swollen, almost to the point my eyes were shut. I couldn't recall another time in my adult life when I'd unleashed such hysterics. It was a mess, but I told him about Donnie. From the beer bottles in his trash to his yelling and throwing me out. Mark had a gift for listening patiently. At that moment, nothing could've meant more to me.

"Ain't always easy being family," he said, "especially with the history between you two."

"Wish I knew what's going on with him. How could he blow up like that?" My voice sounded as pathetic as I probably looked.

"Best thing you can do is give it time. Let him have the space he needs. He'll come around. When he does, I bet the first thing he says is that he didn't mean to upset you. He'd be tore up right now if he saw you like this."

I wanted to believe that. Donnie and I were used to being hurt, then we poured our angst into hurting ourselves and others. One thing we didn't do was hurt each other.

"Why don't you take a few minutes." Mark patted my knees. "Use the restroom. Clean up a bit. We've got some things to discuss, if you're up for it."

I nodded and scooted off to the bathroom. As I took in my reflection from the mirror, I thought I was staring at a stranger. How had I become victimized by my emotions? Ruled by every whim? Back home, in Columbus, I couldn't recall the last time I cried or lost my temper with anyone. Most of my emotions were reserved for therapy sessions. Jason had never seen me cry. None of my college friends would recognize me. Irrational and vulnerable weren't me. Maybe that was my overriding problem—I didn't know where home was anymore. Away from my hometown and my roots, I had become a healthier person—that independent, self-assured woman I wanted to be. Did I belong here in Venice, or was I better off in Columbus?

After splashing my face with cold water half a dozen times, I joined Snyder back in the command room. Sloan's picture caught my eye. What would she think if she could see me now?

"Better?" Snyder asked.

"Yeah." So far, the man was a better psychologist than me. I was amazed how tenderly he treated me. He could've been patronizing, self-serving, domineering. Any would've been understandable, given his position. But he kept going out of his way for me, took his time with me. When I thought of the feelings I had for him at first—anger, mostly—I was ashamed. Trusting him now came easily.

"Glad we worked that out. So what was this you mentioned about Sloan having a diary?"

By the time I left the station, it was dark outside, and one of my worst fears had not been realized. Snyder let me keep the diary, after he made a copy of the pages. Sloan's words were beside me, tucked into my bag. Snyder walked me to my car.

"Wish I could tell you the diary is gonna help," Snyder said, "but at first glance, doesn't look like there's anything we can use. Sure paints an ugly picture of Bill, which we already knew to be true. The good news is, you don't have to worry about Wanda. Not gonna be filing any charges against her for obstruction."

That was the bright spot of the day. As we reviewed the diary entries, I filled Mark in about Sloan's condition. As far as the investigation went, he said it wouldn't change anything.

Before we parted ways he gave my shoulder a rub and a squeeze.

Yet again, I found myself thinking about him outside the context of the lieutenant in charge of my mother's case. During our time together, he mentioned his boys casually, hated that he was divorced but was determined to make the best of it for his kids. His boys texted or called while we went over information, and it was nice knowing they were keeping tabs on one another. I could picture him cheering his boys on at their little league games and making sure they did their part when it came to chores and yard work.

I couldn't say where the fascination sprang from. Couldn't say why I pictured myself sitting on the couch with Mark, a pizza and drinks between us. It made zero sense, especially since I didn't eat pizza or drink alcohol.

"Maybe I am hallucinating."

I could add talking to myself to the list of concerns.

Grandma was home when I got there. I talked her into letting me make spinach-kale smoothies for us. We settled on the patio and took advantage of the cool, inviting evening before the bugs got feisty. I glanced up at the windows of the apartment to make sure Oscar didn't catch me with Princess on my lap.

When Grandma asked how my day went, I dove into the story about the mishap at Milt's. Including Bill's random appearance.

"They say he's up to no good out there," Grandma said. "Heard tell that he's selling drugs. Made plenty of connections in prison, supposedly."

I thought back to earlier, when I'd watched Bill with his customer at the shop. Neither Bill nor the man carried anything out from the warehouse, and nothing was loaded into the man's car. No old doors, scraps of iron, or old motorcycle parts.

My stomach fluttered, knowing I would need to tell Mark.

"That wouldn't surprise me." I told Grandma I had breakfast with Donnie but left out the part about our falling out. If that's what it was called. "I also showed him Sloan's diary and told him about her condition."

Grandma propped her feet up. She looked tired and achy. Smoking seemed to relax and ease her discomforts. She tilted her head back and exhaled a puff. "How'd he take that?"

"He gets bothered when I bring up Sloan, and he wasn't crazy about having her case reopened." She nodded while I sipped my mango-kale smoothie. Not my favorite flavors but couldn't let Grandma know. "Is there a reason why he gets grouchy about Sloan?"

"It's rough on a fella to lose his mamma, 'specially young as he was."

"He wasn't too interested in hearing about her disorder." I shrugged. "Maybe it's too hard to believe now." Or maybe Donnie had a point, *Doesn't do me any good now.*

I didn't want to dwell on the subject. It pained me, recalling how upset Donnie got over the situation. Shoving the diary at me, like he was disgusted by it. Plus, this wasn't the best topic to end Grandma's night after a long day.

She sipped her smoothie cautiously and her faced puckered. "Fresh mowed grass might taste better."

I figured sleep would steal me away easily that night, after a long, emotionally charged day. Wrong. My mind replayed and rehashed my squabble with Donnie. I tried blocking it out with images of Mark—and wondered why he came to mind so effortlessly. Was it because Jason had skipped texting me today? I didn't care. No, I cared…but not as much as I should've cared.

Being alone in the apartment was uncomfortable now. Sure, I had Oscar, but the sanctity had departed. A beloved childhood doll showing up and disappearing could do that. Two fans whirled at full blast, doing nothing to combat the heat.

Maybe staying in Grandma's guest room—and air conditioning—wasn't so bad.

Somewhere in the night, my body's need for rest must've taken over. Because I didn't hear him come in. I didn't creep out over his presence in my bedroom and startle awake. No. There was no warning. His hand was over my mouth and his face next to mine when he whispered, "Don't scream."

CHAPTER TWELVE

My body went rigid, my eyes wide. I tried to make sense of what was happening in the dim light. The stench of alcohol tore into my nostrils. He held me down with an unexpected force. His forearm laid across my chest; his fingers on my bare shoulder.

Oscar mewed. The split-second distraction was all I needed. I managed a short-range but solid right hook to the side of his head. His hold released. I pulled my legs up to my chest and kicked him in the chin. The impact sent him flying backwards and to the floor.

I sprang from the bed. His hands went to his face. I flipped him onto his stomach as he moaned, then stepped on the back of his leg. He yelped. I put my arms around his neck. A swift jerk and I could break his neck. He'd be dead.

"You're never coming into my room again." My anger swelled as I said it into his ear.

"Delilah, please." His words slurred, gasped. "Don't. I'm your brother."

I snapped from the trance of rage. I got off him and turned on the light. Donnie was crumpled on my bedroom floor.

I thought you were Bill came to my mouth, but I was too stunned to speak.

He continued groaning as he got to his feet. I helped him to a chair in the living room. Oscar followed us, then went and perched on the kitchen counter. His tail flopped like a metronome, which happened when he was mad or uncertain. Both probably applied.

"Donnie, what the hell are you doing here?" I turned on more lights. The clock read 4:42 a.m.

"Damn, little sister." He squinted, touched the side of his head. "That karate stuff works."

I didn't feel like correcting him. "Are you crazy, sneaking into my house in the middle of the night? And you're drunk!" I thought about punching him again just for that.

"Don't be mad. I had to talk to you."

"This is how you do it? Middle of the night, grabbing my face while I'm asleep."

"When did you get a stupid cat?" He glanced at Oscar, who was still agitated.

"You'd better start talking, Donnie." My hand throbbed from the blow to Donnie's head. Adrenaline surged through me and had my body doing a nervous-quake.

"Yeah, I know. You freaked me out yesterday with all that stuff about Sloan. I didn't know what to do. Seeing that picture, reading that diary, I could hear her voice again. When it comes to Sloan, I push her out of my mind. I don't want to think about her...and what happened."

"You scared me."

"I'm sorry about that. I didn't mean to lose it. That was dumb, me getting mad at you."

"Not as dumb as you getting drunk and showing up in my room. I thought you were Bill attacking me. I almost broke your neck."

His eyes widened. "You are one badass chick."

For a brief moment, I pictured Donnie sprawled on my floor. The thought of his lifeless eyes staring up at me made a wave of disgust shudder through me. Sweat beaded my skin.

"Go home, Donnie."

"No." He stood. "I need you to come with me. There's something I gotta show you."

The whack to my brother's head helped sober him up, which was a good thing, since he insisted on driving. He'd made tea while I changed. That also helped wake him up. I texted my friend at the martial arts studio, letting him know I wouldn't make it for the early morning workout. As we crept by Wanda's house to leave, there were no signs she'd heard anything or been disturbed.

We rode in silence. Donnie was back to brooding while I was on edge and ramped up. When I realized we were headed toward Milt's, anxiety set in.

"Did something happen to Milt?" I asked.

"He's fine. I guess he's fine. This isn't about him."

"Then where are we going?"

He hesitated before he said it. "Home."

"Home?" I didn't recognize that word. "Where we lived with Bill and Sloan?" *as a family?* I couldn't bring myself to say the last part, since it wasn't true. Not in the real sense of family.

Donnie nodded.

"I'm not going back there. That's where Bill lives. Why would you take us there?"

"Because I have to show you!" He said it loud enough to temper my growing hysterics.

Donnie focused his intensity on the road; I felt like I'd stepped on a steel trap of bewilderment. Pain and agony spiked through me. So did a desperation for survival. Could I force those jaws open, escape and limp away somehow? Donnie must have known how I'd feel. The main reason he chose to drive—and practically abduct me in the middle of the night.

As we drew closer to Milt's, Donnie turned off the main road and onto a path. It wouldn't be considered a road by any stretch and

116

was only noticeable if you knew what you were looking for. We bounced along. Tall grass and branches brushed and scraped against Donnie's car. He paid no attention.

We came to a small clearing after two or three miles. Donnie shut off the engine.

"Let's go."

"Where are we?"

"Back side of Milt's property. Milt, Bill, and Uncle Ron didn't like using the main roads to get around the property, remember? So they wore a path through here. If we cut through these woods, the house is about half a mile up ahead."

"Please, Donnie, tell me what's going on."

"I've never told you the truth about Sloan." He turned to me. His eyes held a mix of worry and apprehension. "It's best if you come with me. I'll show you and explain everything. You gotta come with me, and we have to wait for Bill to leave."

"What makes you think he's leaving?"

"He's checking in with his parole officer today. Tonya's picking him up. We wait till they're gone, then go inside."

"How do you know this?"

A weak grin appeared. "Keeping my own tabs on Bill."

We left the car. Donnie took my hand and led me into the trees. Daylight permeated the sky. Warblers and woodpeckers were already singing, and the morning dew quickly dampened my shoes. The familiar scent of pine and wet wood took me back to my childhood. A time when there was no fear of snakes or spiders, only poison ivy. Wild blackberries, climbing too high into the trees, and being out of ear-shot from our parents were our rewards. So was the solitude.

We'd been in this patch of woods dozens of times as kids. Made playhouses out of scrap metal from the shop. Tried making a tree house we could use to hide in, certain we could construct a place

Bill wouldn't find, but it never worked out. Never held together. We were too young to use the tools we needed or to get the right supplies. Didn't matter though. The fantasy of making a place where we couldn't be found sustained us some days. Other times, the lean-tos or shanties that we constructed were good enough places to hide and cry. Tears being our only medicine.

Now, the woods weren't a source of refuge. When we reached the other side, Bill would be there. So would the house. I didn't realize how much I hated that place until now.

We stayed inside the tree line and had plenty of foliage for coverage. Donnie still held my hand. I couldn't say whose palm was sweatier. We hunched low and stared at the back of the house in silence.

It was a late-1800s farmhouse. The original house for the property. How long it had been in the Ramsey family, I couldn't say for sure. Fields had once nourished tobacco and corn while the barns were stuffed with hay and potential thoroughbreds. Now, the outside suffered from emptiness and neglect. Termites had come and gone, leaving their rot. Once-glorious features—the wrap-around porch, slate-shingled roof, and Kelly-green shutters—suffered from decay and cried out for repairs. Shoddy additions were as much a part of the house as its crunchy-brown, patchy lawn.

I wanted to dart back into the woods and get away. No. On second thought, I wanted to do the same thing Jenny did to her childhood home in *Forrest Gump*—throw rocks at the place. But I knew it wouldn't do any good...'and sometimes there aren't enough rocks'.

A car pulled in. Moments later, Tonya got out and went up to the door. Bill appeared and followed her back to the car. He looked clean and ready for inspection. I knew it was useless to hope his parole officer could see through his façade. By now, Bill was probably a master at manipulating the system to suit him.

From where Donnie and I squatted, I didn't see a patrol car nearby. Had Snyder already pulled deputies from surveillance—or had they been there at all? Maybe it was a ploy to pacify me and Grandma.

As Tonya and Bill drove away, my uncertainty swelled.

"I don't know if I can do this."

"We have to." Donnie gripped my hand tighter and pulled me out into the open field.

"You better not be breaking in."

We stood on the stoop near the kitchen. I felt exposed—and positive Bill and Tonya would return to pick up something they'd forgotten. What if they caught us? I doubted Bill would pass on a second chance to see me arrested.

Donnie pulled a key from his pocket. "No one changes locks around here." He unlocked the back door and took me inside.

When we stepped into the kitchen, childhood memories came flooding back. I pictured my mom standing by the sink, singing quietly to herself as she sipped her morning coffee. Everything was still the same. The linoleum, countertops, cabinets. A layer of grime coated each surface. Maybe I was imagining it. I wasn't sure. Cigarettes and the lingering stench of marijuana clung to the air.

I let go of Donnie's hand. What propelled me, I couldn't say, but I went into the living room. A worn chair, beat up couch, and TV were the major items in the space. Carpet stains the accessory. I went down the hallway. Donnie's room had been across from mine. I slid the door to my old room open with my fingertips. My mind replayed the sound of Bill, tapping against the painted wood. His muffled whisper. *Delilah, Daddy wants to play in your lap.* The sound of the candy being shaken in its bag.

I crossed the threshold. A mattress sat on the floor, topped with wrinkled covers. An out of body experience took over. I saw myself, bunched and hidden under the covers. My stuffed animals were gone. No more unicorns or bears or dolls with their ever-watching, unblinking stares. The trembling started in my feet, then crawled up my legs and over my body like a swarm of hungry ants.

"Delilah?"

I spun at the sound of Donnie's voice. His hand on my shoulder rescued me from the memories. Had I not been with him for the last couple of hours, I would've assumed he'd been in a brawl. His eyes looked heavy and weary-worn. The lump on the side of his forehead, more swollen now, added to his beat-down appearance.

"Come on."

We went back into the kitchen, where Donnie opened the door to the basement.

"You know how many times I went down there?" I asked. "Maybe three."

"If you want to hear the whole story, you gotta come down with me." Donnie flicked the switch and started to descend.

I had no choice but to follow.

The stairs were as precarious as I remembered. One of the reasons I hated the basement. There was no railing. One side of the staircase was flanked by cinder blocks. The top part of the steps was secured into the risers with six nails. Two on each side, two in the middle. Each step looked brittle. Wide cracks trenched the wood grain. The steep angle made it feel more like a ladder than stairs. Except for the side with cinder blocks, the stairs were open and bordered all around by raw, worn edges. Every creek made me pause as I took them one at a time. Donnie reached up and held my hand so I made it to the bottom without breaking an ankle.

Cool air radiated from the concrete floor. The mildew smell, which reminded me of laundry that got left in the washer, hung heavy.

"Do you remember what Bill told us about Sloan?" Donnie asked.

"He said she couldn't handle us kids, that she took off, didn't leave a note, and didn't tell anyone where she was going." I ran my hands over my arms, uselessly fighting the chill.

Donnie nodded slowly. "He liked telling us that, but he lied. Sloan never ran off. She didn't have a chance."

My stomach knotted at every word, and part of me thought I knew what he was going to say. That he had seen Bill hurt her. That he was hiding—sleeping in his closet like he used to do—when he saw something he shouldn't have. Saw Bill kill her.

"Bill lied to protect me."

"What are you talking about?"

"I killed Sloan."

Donnie wasn't making sense. My mind couldn't process his words.

"No!...You couldn't have." Milt's story ran through my head, when he'd told me about Bill's confession and how he got rid of Sloan.

"It was an accident." Donnie was crying. "Partly. I didn't mean to, but I wanted to. I was so mad at her for not doing anything. You read the diary. You know that she walked in on Bill and what he was doing to me. Yeah, she snatched me away from him, but she did nothing. Nothing! We stayed in this house and she didn't do anything." He rubbed his hands over his face, as if trying to make the images go away.

"She was sick and needed help—"

"So did we!" The words erupted from him like a volcano.

I didn't know the right thing to do. I wanted to hold my brother but couldn't.

"I hated her! Hated her for not taking care of me! I left the door open. She never liked the door open to the basement. Said she didn't want the stairs looking at us. Remember that?"

I nodded weakly.

"So one day, I left it open. She was in one of her stupors, not talking much, said her head hurt. When she headed into the kitchen I followed her. She went straight to the door and mumbled something about letting the evil out. I was right behind her...and I pushed her down the stairs. And I stood there, and I watched and I heard every sound she made as she fell down."

CHAPTER THIRTEEN

Donnie

Venice, KY

Summer 2001

"What'd you do, boy?" Bill stood at the top of the stairs. A pack of cigarettes in the pocket of his faded-white t-shirt. Pieces of his dirty hair slipped from the slicked-backed style.

"Nothing!" Donnie said. "She fell." Donnie was by his mother's side at the bottom of the stairs. He was too afraid to touch her.

"You're a liar. Always been a liar, aint'cha? Little liar with no respect for his momma. That's a shame. She was a pretty good woman."

"It was an accident." His voice crackled as the tears came. "I didn't mean it."

Bill joined Donnie in the basement, the wooden stairs groaning with each move.

"She's bleeding," Donnie cried and pointed to a puddle of blood at the bottom of the stairs.

Sloan's body was face-down on the stairs. The top of her head touching the concrete floor. Bill hooked his fists under her arms and pulled her limp body up and over. He laid her on her back with a gentleness Donnie didn't know his father was capable of. Blood oozed from a gash in Sloan's forehead.

"Look what you done." Bill shook his head and looked at Sloan. "Don't know what they do with a nine-year-old that's killed his momma, but it can't be good."

Bill got to his knees. He put his ear next to her nose, then checked her wrist for a pulse.

"She's dead all right. Bet she cracked her skull on them stairs. A shame ol' Milt never done nothing to fix 'em all these years."

"No! She...she's not dead. She needs a doctor and the hospital. That's all." Donnie touched her hand. It was the first time in his life she didn't respond, didn't return his touch.

"Too late for that." Bill stood, put his hands on his hips. "I never told you this, for your own good, but your momma was scared of you. Yes, sir. Was afraid you were gonna do something awful to hurt her. Said she had nightmares about it. Woke up screaming a few times. I had to calm her down. Get her some sleeping pills so she could have some peace. I told her there wasn't nothing to be afraid of, that you's just a little boy. I done my best to protect you both. Your sister too." He shook his head again. "But look now."

Gripped by confusion and shame, Donnie couldn't speak. Couldn't picture his mother afraid of him.

"All them times she found you hiding or crying in your closet," Bill continued, "she thought you was up to something then. When you did that thing where you'd sit at the dinner table, not eat or talk or look at anyone. She done thought a demon moved inside you. Yeah, I reckon the signs were there, that we were bound to have trouble with you."

Had his mother really felt that way, said those things to Bill? Donnie couldn't believe it. His head was fuzzy. Too many thoughts were crashing inside him. He didn't hide from her; he hid from Bill. The episode during dinner had been a silent rebellion. Donnie was angry. Angry he couldn't make Bill leave him alone. Angry he couldn't protect DeDe. Angry his mother wouldn't listen when he tried to tell her.

We shouldn't talk about it, Donnie. We want it to stop and go away, right? We have to close our eyes really tight and wish really hard. Wish those bad trolls would come out of your father. That's the only way to make it stop.

He wanted to punish her for that—for not believing him—but he didn't mean to kill her.

"We're gonna have to get rid of her," Bill said, "not let anyone know what happened. Otherwise, you'll go to jail the rest of your life, son. You don't want that now, do you?"

"No!"

"Yep, never get to come home again, and the way little boys get treated in jail"—Bill whistled—"will make you wish you were here. With me. You get what I'm saying?"

Donnie understood. In that moment, he would've taken a thousand nights at the hand of his father over the unknown abuse from a stranger.

"I can help you out, but it's gonna take some doing. Can't make no promises, neither, cause you gotta keep your mouth shut, not tell another soul. You got that?"

Donnie nodded, the image of Bill distorted by his tears.

"And if I do this for you, well, you gotta be a good boy from now on. You know what that means, don't you?"

More nodding. More tears.

"I got some thinking to do first. Gotta do this the right way. You get on up to your room now." Bill grabbed him by the arm as he stepped past him. "When I come for you, be ready to do what I tell you, boy, no questions."

Donnie ran to his room and locked the door. He skidded across the worn gray carpet and sat with his back against the wall. His knees burned. So did the hot tears streaming down his face.

Donnie thought about sneaking into the kitchen and calling for help. He didn't want his mother dead. If the police came with an ambulance, they could save her. There had to be a chance. But just the thought of leaving his room made him tremble. He knew Bill would snatch the phone from him. A beating would follow.

Shame poured over Donnie, because he was afraid. More afraid of Bill than of not saving his mother. He didn't know how to be anything but afraid. Aches embraced him, like a lonely kid getting pelted with rocks in a school yard. He craved the refuge of his mother's arms. Not that it had done him much good or saved him from Bill's abuse. Donnie wanted to lean into her, feel the strumming of her heartbeat against his ear.

He cried. Cried alone. Cried over what he'd done. Cried over what he hadn't done.

Evening crept in, darkening Donnie's room. He'd dozed off on the floor, but a rumbling from downstairs woke him. Voice rose up. Yelling. He heard the back door bust open, the same sound it made when DeDe ran outside to play. She always forgot the closer was broken and let the door slam.

With his bedroom window open, Donnie heard people outside. What sounded like running across the patchy, pebbled yard. Then came a scream. At least Donnie thought it was a scream. Who could be screaming?

Then an explosion, like a firecracker, startled him.

Donnie peeked out his bedroom window. Sprawled on the ground was his mother, face down. Bill walked up to her. Stood above

126

her and stared down at her. He looked like he was catching his breath. Something was in his hand. He tucked it between his gut and his jeans. Donnie couldn't see what it was. Bill glanced around, and Donnie ducked below the window sill. Donnie waited a few seconds, then slowly dared to peek again. Bill had turned Sloan over, like he had in the basement. She lay face-up, with her eyes closed. Her arms and hands were above her head, as if in a display of surrender. The blood on her forehead had darkened. Looked crimson-brown.

Donnie didn't understand. Why was she on the ground like that? If Bill had carried her up from the basement, he wouldn't have dropped her at the side of the house.

Bill took Sloan by the ankles and started dragging her across the dirt-patched yard.

Donnie couldn't watch anymore. He sank down from the window and onto the floor in his room. He squeezed his eyes shut, wanting to make the pictures of his lifeless mom go away. Wanting to make all of it go away.

Please, God! he prayed. It was all he knew to say.

"Donnie?" said a squeaky voice on the other side of his door. The knob rattled but didn't turn. He had locked it.

"Go away!" His sister always came to him at the worst times. When his dad left his bedroom at night, or when all Donnie wanted was to be alone. Her with that doll. Always asking, *You okay, Donnie?* He just wanted to cry himself to sleep, and he didn't want her to see.

"Is Mommy in there?"

"No."

"Where's Mommy? I can't find her."

"I don't know. Now go away!"

"I heard a big noise."

She heard it too! Now Donnie knew he wasn't imagining things. It didn't explain how or why his mother's body ended up in the yard. His head hurt, not knowing what to think.

"I want a story."

"No! Just go to bed, DeDe."

She didn't listen. He could tell. She lied down outside of his door, the way she always did when she wanted to be by him but couldn't. Donnie knew it was mean, not letting her in. Sometimes he gave in, unlocked the door and let her stay in his bed. He caught her watching him sleep. There were times he did the same. Mostly, he liked DeDe being there.

He couldn't be around her tonight. Donnie worried he would say the wrong thing, that he would let it slip out that he had hurt Sloan. He wanted to keep DeDe safe. Like when he sometimes locked her bedroom door without DeDe knowing, because he wanted to keep Bill away from her. That meant Bill going into Donnie's room instead. Tears stung his eyes when he thought about it. Not that it made Bill stay away from her altogether, but Donnie knew there were nights he'd saved her from Bill. That's what brothers did, wasn't it? Now, he ached to keep DeDe away from the horrible thing he'd done, as best he could.

Bill would be coming. Another reason he had to push his sister away.

He didn't know how long he sat there. On the floor of his room, underneath the window. His knees pulled to his chest and his forehead against his legs. Holding tight. Crying.

Donnie was awakened by a nudging. His eyes popped opened. He realized he must have fallen asleep.

Bill stood over him. Sweat stains darkened his gray-white t-shirt. He wore his tan work boots. They were the chunky kind and usually had small metal pieces stuck to them. Donnie had never known the boots to be clean, and their smell reminded him of Bill's workspace. His mother never let him wear those boots in the house. An assurance she was gone.

"Better get up, boy." Bill tapped him with the toe of his boot. "We got work to do."

They got into his mother's car and drove off in the pitch-black night. The clock on the dash read 2:13 a.m. Donnie noticed his mother's purse on his side of the floorboard. They drove away from the house and down a tire-worn path that led to Grampy and Granny's.

"What about Dede?" Donnie asked, though he was afraid to say anything.

"She's sleeping." Bill lit into a cigarette, and that's when Donnie saw it—the discoloration on his hands. They were covered with reddish-brown smears.

Bill drove to the other side of his grandpa's property. The car crept slowly by the salvage shop and past Grampy and Granny's trailer. No lights were on inside, but the utility lights above the shop lit the way. Bill pulled up to his work shed and put the car in park.

"I'm gonna need your help, 'cause we're in this thing together. Right?" His cigarette flicked up and down as he spoke. Smoke curled around his head.

Donnie nodded.

"I'm helping you out, so you gotta help me out." Bill reached over, put his hand around Donnie's throat. "What you're not gonna do is make any noise. You hear me?"

Another nod, though it was compromised by Bill's firm hold.

Bill returned the nod, then got out of the car. He popped open the trunk, then motioned for Donnie to come. Mindful of his steps on the gravel, Donnie followed his father into the workspace. Bill flicked on the fluorescent lights. Their eerie hum and yellow-green glow filled the area that had once been a garage.

Donnie's body began to quake. From the nighttime chill or from the stale air in the work space, he couldn't tell. There was a strange smell he couldn't identify. It wasn't the scent of rotting wood mixed with metal he knew well. Glancing around, the space looked the way it always had—dirty. A workbench piled with tools, metal scraps and shavings on the dirt-packed floor, two windows that had never been cleaned, rusty tool boxes lining the walls, skeletons of motorcycles and their parts scattered throughout, a film of grease coating most surfaces.

Then Donnie saw the bundle on the ground. Blankets he recognized from home were rolled around something. Bare feet stuck out at one end. Every toenail was painted a different color, and he knew it was his mother's feet.

Donnie grabbed his stomach, certain he would be sick.

"Not a sound, remember?" Bill's warning came with a slap to the back of Donnie's head.

Bill opened the door to the work space wide.

"I'll get this end. You get the feet."

Donnie stood frozen. The thought of touching his dead mother repulsed and terrified him. He'd never been so close to anything dead. This was his mother. And he'd done this to her.

He took a step back and shook his head.

"Better do what I tell you, boy, or you're gonna end up just like her." Bill pulled a gun from his waistband and pointed it at Donnie.

He urinated, soaking his shorts, and shivered as the warmth streaked down his legs.

"You ain't never gonna be a man, are you?"

"I can't." Cries muffled Donnie's voice.

"You're gonna carry that end to the car, or I'll put a bullet in your head, son. This ain't no time for your sissy games. Now do it!"

Trapped in a fog of terror, Donnie bent and wrapped his arms around his mother's legs. He thought of DeDe and how she would run to their mother and wrap herself around her bare legs. He pictured his mother painting her toenails and wiggling them when they were done. That was gone now. Donnie wanted to unwrap that blanket, wake her up, and tell her he was sorry and didn't mean it, and he would do anything if she would come back. His throat felt tight and constricted as he held back every bit of emotion.

Bill stuck the gun back into the waistband of his jeans. Donnie lifted his end of the twisted blanket. He shook as they carried Sloan's body outside and rolled it into the trunk of her car.

Donnie vomited before he got back in the car beside his father. If Bill noticed, he said nothing. They pulled away from the salvage shop and turned onto the main road. The night as thick and black as the silence between them. Donnie recognized nothing in the darkness. He fisted his hands at his side, hating the dampness of his shorts against his legs. What would come next, he didn't know, but he was certain Bill would kill him when they got there.

He told himself that's what he wanted. What he deserved. He hoped it would be quick but feared Bill would make it slow. Bill would like that, Donnie figured, watching him suffer and die. Donnie didn't care. After tonight, he didn't want to live anymore. Not with what he'd done.

Donnie glimpsed a sign that read, *Do Not Enter. No Access* and *Keep Out* also flashed by. Donnie knew why. He had been there before. With his father.

Driving over the grassland proved bumpy. Bill went slow, cussed and complained that he couldn't see much. Donnie braced himself against the dash. After much rolling and churning, Bill put the car in park and cut the engine.

"All right," he said, "let's get this over with."

As they got out, Bill grabbed two flashlights from the backseat, handed one to Donnie.

"Gotta be careful out here. One wrong step and we're done for."

The flashlight was the only pin-prick of light in the darkness. Bill searched the area, scanning his light back and forth until he was satisfied. Donnie couldn't say how far ahead it was, but he saw yellow tape tied to stakes and fluttering on the breeze.

"We're gonna have to push the car. I know you're puny, but you gotta push and do your part." Bill put his flashlight on the ground, then positioned his hands on the trunk.

Donnie did the same and pushed. Two streaks of blood ran from the bottom of the trunk lid down the car. The beam of the flashlights lit the ground by their feet. As they pushed the car forward, they moved from the light's reach.

"Harder!" Bill strained, pumped his legs more.

Donnie was spent. It was all he could do not to fall flat on his face.

"Let go!" Bill kept pushing as Donnie released his hands. With a grunt and a yell, Bill gave a final shove before he took his hands off the car.

Bill bent at the waist. With his hands on his legs, he panted heavily. Donnie stood motionless. The car continued to roll, then tipped forward and dove over the edge of the Fitzmiller sinkhole.

CHAPTER FOURTEEN

"Took us the rest of the night to walk home," Donnie said, "and one of the flashlights gave out. I don't know how I moved at all. I was covered in dirt, my shorts were wet, and the taste of being sick was stuck in my mouth."

I didn't know what to say.

"That's why I went to see him in prison, Delilah. I had to know if he was going to tell what we'd done. Figured he'd like nothing more than seeing me in a cell beside him."

"What did he say?"

"Nothing. He would give me that stupid grin of his. Never answered one way or another. Probably enjoyed watching me squirm. Next best thing to coming into my room at night, knowing he could get in my head and still ruin my life."

I knew he was right. Knew that Bill probably relished the idea of slinking into our nightmares and randomly haunting our lives with the memories he'd scarred us with. Shudders jolted through me when I thought of Bill dangling that uncertainty over Donnie's head.

"Delilah, you have to put a stop to this investigation. If you don't, I could go to jail. Worse, I could lose Emery." Upon saying her name, he lost it. "Please don't let me lose my baby!"

I went to my brother. Sobs of grief overtook him. Tears streamed down his reddened cheeks. I held him tighter than I ever had before. Right there, at the bottom of those brutal, unforgiving stairs, where Sloan Ramsey had fallen to her death.

Something inside me said it was wrong though. All wrong. I believed what Donnie told me, that he had pushed our mother down the basement steps. That she had struck her head, was unconscious, and lay there bleeding. But I couldn't make that last hurdle. Couldn't accept that the fall was how she died. That *Donnie* was directly responsible for her death—and not Bill.

This was also the first time I'd heard Bill owned a gun. What had he done with it? Was there a chance it was still hidden in the house?

I also didn't know what to make about certain parts of Donnie's story. Voices or the sound of people yelling at one another. Bill dragging Sloan's body out to the yard. The explosion Donnie heard. They were fragmented pieces from a nine-year-old's memory. What did it all mean?

Donnie and I were still in the dank basement. Me holding him as the tide of emotions swept over him. Tears slid from my eyes too. It was unnerving, being right where my mother had died. If I looked hard enough, I'd find blood. Streaked and stained into the wood, it would be there. A silent witness verifying Donnie's recollection. My stomach twisted at the thought. I squeezed my eyes shut against the throbbing images of Sloan tumbling, of her head smashing, cracking into the splintered wood.

I don't know how long we stayed on the concrete floor, slumped together and crying. Long enough to make me panicky. What if Bill walked in and found us?

"We've got to get out of here." I wanted to clear my head and stop the trembling.

Donnie nodded, and we got to our feet.

"Promise me," he said, taking me by the shoulders, "promise me you'll get the police off Sloan's case." His eyes glistened with fresh tears.

"I'll do anything to protect you and Emery." Which was true. Except that I felt powerless and nauseous. I couldn't let Donnie feel my trepidation though. I cupped his face in my palms. "You've got to pull yourself together, Donnie. Promise me you won't touch another drink. No matter what."

He returned a nod, pain and shame evident on his face.

We made it up the stairs. A feat, considering my shaky legs and Donnie's racked condition. My brother just told me he accidentally killed our mother. I forced myself not to think about it. Getting out of the house demanded my focus—getting out before the monster came back.

Outside, we ran across the open meadow like our lives depended on it. Maybe they did. Or maybe we were fueled by the urge for distance from the past. Both of us convinced—or fooled—that such a thing could make a difference.

We got back to Donnie's car and hopped inside. My trembling had grown worse. Despite the morning's warmth, chills coated my skin.

"Who else knows?" I asked him, a quiver in my voice.

He didn't answer at first. Didn't look at me. Then he relented. "No one."

I replayed the events in my head, exactly as Donnie described. "It doesn't make sense."

"I was there, D. You think I'm lying about this?"

"No!" Sloan's bare feet and her rainbow-colored toenails flashed through my mind. Donnie had last seen them poking out the end of a rolled-up blanket. My chest clinched thinking how cold they must have felt against his skin. "It's just that..." I hadn't told Donnie about my first visit with Milt and the story he poured out about Bill. I had wanted to tell Donnie everything, especially that afternoon in the rain, when Bill had made his official return to Venice. I'd held back, because Donnie became abrasive whenever Sloan was mentioned. Now I knew why.

It wasn't the best time or setting, but I told Donnie what Milt had shared. Bill bragging to his father how he'd *sunk her*, referring to Sloan, her body.... How Bill bragged about ending her life—and getting away with her murder.

"According to Milt's story," I said, "Bill took full credit for murdering Sloan. There was no mention of you being involved."

Donnie gave a half shrug. "Doesn't mean much. Just that Bill wasn't stupid. Why play the ace up his sleeve? Wasn't like he was being interrogated. And if Milt ever went to the cops with that story, Bill could tell the police Milt was lying. He'd tell them I was the one who'd done it, and he'd kept quiet to protect me." He scoffed. "Can't you see it? Bill acting like he was *ever* a good father and avoiding a murder charge."

I rubbed my forehead and temples. Donnie made sense, but something was off. Bill was a sociopath, perfectly capable of murdering his wife. Donnie was a kid—an abused kid. There was no way he killed our mother...Or was this what denial felt like?

"Is that why you went to the police, started things up again?" Donnie asked. "Because Milt gave you some tale?"

Embarrassment flooded my grief-puffed face. "Part of the reason. I wanted to see the case file. See if I could find out why they never figured out what happened to Sloan. Lieutenant Snyder, well, he's been sweet." My cheeks burned at the mention of Snyder's kindness. "He took a new interest."

"Did you tell him what Milt said?"

I nodded. "Snyder believes it, thinks Bill is guilty, but he says Milt's admission probably wouldn't be enough to get Bill convicted. Too many ways a defense attorney could spin it, especially with

Sloan's illness and her affair with Glenn. Snyder's hoping to find new evidence." The words trailed out of my mouth. Now, I knew there was no evidence. And no hope of seeing Bill imprisoned for Sloan's death. Fresh tears threatened.

"Do you know if Snyder has talked to Bill?" Donnie asked. "Sometimes when they reexamine a case, they go back and interview everyone who was involved."

"I don't know."

"If Snyder goes to Bill, there's no telling what he might say." Donnie locked his eyes with mine. "You've gotta help distract Snyder. Maybe even convince him that there's no use opening the investigation again. Tell him it's been too long, or anything that will get him to lose interest."

His gaze, his words slammed into me like a brick wall.

How was I supposed to discourage Snyder—and keep the truth from him?

Silence roared between us as Donnie drove me back home. He wanted assurances I couldn't give. I had no control over Snyder or the investigation. But how could I walk back into that room and face Snyder—and the golden-framed picture of Sloan—hoping for evidence that didn't exist and knowing that my brother had pushed her down the stairs? What about the assurances I wanted, that Donnie would stay clean and sober?

"What are you going to do?" I cringed inwardly at how lame that sounded, but I had to punctuate the stillness.

"Probably crash until Emery comes over this afternoon."

That would be the best thing for him. Along with an icepack to the side of his forehead.

"What are you going to tell Monica about that?" I nodded, indicating his now-swollen lump.

He checked himself in the rearview mirror and winced when he touched it with his fingertips. "I slipped getting out of the shower, hit the corner of the vanity."

"That actually sounds pretty believable."

"Can't tell anyone my little sister about knocked me into next week." He gave me a pathetic wink. I smiled, just for an instant. That reprieve from the intensity of our early morning was refreshing. But fleeting.

I'd give anything to go back to Donnie sneaking into my apartment. Because that was the scariest moment of my adult life, until he took us back to our childhood home and admitted to the accident with Sloan. I would never look at Donnie the same, and I hated that.

What I hated even more was the fact Donnie had carried that story inside him for so long. He lived with and replayed that misery for nearly two decades. Alone. That trauma, combined with the abuse he'd suffered, explained why Donnie had turned to alcohol. Numbing that pain and dulling those memories had to be a priority. A survival tactic. Which I understood.

"I've been thinking." Donnie squirmed in his seat as he drove. "We've gotta do something. About Bill."

Hairs on the back of my neck stood at his unnerving tone.

"We need to stay away from Bill."

"No. I...I can't live like this, with Bill having a hold over me." Desperation flashed in his eyes. "I have to make sure Bill never tells anyone what happened that night."

"Donnie, no! You can't talk like this. And you can't...hurt someone. Not even Bill. Not even if he deserves it, because that's not you, Donnie. You're not a monster like him."

He focused on the road ahead.

"What happened with Sloan was an accident," I assured him. "You were a kid. Maybe we should just go straight to the police, tell them everything—"

"No! I can't risk losing Emery."

"You can't fix this by hurting Bill."

Donnie didn't look at me, didn't say any more. I worried he'd clamed up, like he did when we were young. That was his defense, slipping into that shell of quietness and blocking out the world. Only now, fear gripped me. What if Donnie was cooking up a scheme to end Bill's life?

Donnie's assertiveness left me speechless. So did his brooding. That told me there was nothing I could say to make him see things clearly. Nothing to make him realize that killing Bill—or whatever Donnie had in mind—wasn't the answer, that revenge provided its own kind of prison and entrapment.

I texted Britney and asked if she could stop by Donnie's later and maybe keep an eye on him. Despite my complicated and conflicted feelings towards Britney, I knew she cared about Donnie. Not that I could tell her what was really going on, but I'd think of something passable, with just enough truth to keep her concerned. She quickly replied that she would stop by his place in an hour or so.

When Donnie dropped me off at Grandma's, he seemed more himself. Even apologized for his crazy outburst. I told him to go home and get some sleep—and not to do anything stupid. He answered with a flimsy wave and drove off.

Part of me wanted to jump in my car and follow him. Maybe never leave his side, if that's what it took to ensure he would leave the booze—and Bill—alone. I had to find a way to convince Donnie to talk to Snyder. Finally revealing the truth was the only way for him to be free.

Oscar greeted me with a flurry of mews when I entered the apartment. I felt like a teenager getting caught while trying to sneak in past curfew. Even though it was now mid-morning. I scooped him up anyways, apologized for leaving him with empty bowls, and made it right.

Nuzzling Oscar gave me a brief escape from my thoughts. During the drive home, I replayed Donnie's story over and over in my head. There was one detail I couldn't let go of, and something I had to do. With Donnie teetering on the edge of self-destruction, time was against me. I had to hurry.

Grandma was already at work, which was the best thing that could happen right now. Because I wouldn't have to explain what I was up to.

I went down to Grandma's storage shed. Built by Grandpa Paul and situated on the far edge of their property-line, the shed had become a mausoleum for all the things Grandma and Grandpa used to do. The wooden doors creaked open. Darkness and spider webs dared me to enter. No telling if I'd find what I needed.

The bare bulb fixed to the center of the ceiling luminated the space when I pulled the string. For some reason, that pull-click sound made by turning on the light reminded me of Grandpa Paul. So did the woody smell from inside. He liked making things and was good at whatever he crafted, from fishing lures to the shelves that now held the remnants of their once-active lifestyle. The sudden ache in my chest had me frozen there, surrounded by sweet memories of the only man I ever fully trusted and loved.

Tears hit the dirt floor as I glanced at the fishing poles, kayaks, canoes, nets, and waders hanging on nails and hooks and lying on shelves. Images of Grandpa fly fishing struck hard. I missed watching him cast his line and the smooth beauty of his motions. And nothing compared to the taste of Grandpa's trout over a campfire.

Spending time in God's country will fix about anything, he used to say.

"I wish I'd loved you better." The words came out like a whisper, breathy and soft. I promised myself I would visit his gravesite.

I pulled myself together before I dissolved into a grieving puddle. Using the flashlight on my phone, since the light was dull, I stepped deeper into the shed and searched for the rope and harnesses once used for rock climbing. Paul and Wanda weren't avid climbers, and I worried the equipment was no longer there, since the hobby didn't last long. Underneath an overturned canoe, sat a pile of ropes, harnesses, latches, and helmets.

A deep, cleansing breath helped clear my head. Or did it? I gathered the equipment and pushed aside the logic—the sound reasoning—that threatened to rattle my nerves and disrupt my shaky plan.

Long before the sinkhole that opened beneath the corvette museum in Bowling Green, Kentucky, an even larger, deeper pit yawned its cavernous appetite on the Fitzmiller farm in Crittenden. Measuring thirty-two feet wide, the hole became famous for its depth and for swallowing Mr. Fitzmiller's tobacco harvester. Locals, geologists, and those who were curious, came from far and wide to get a glimpse of the massive hole.

Proud owners of possibly the largest tobacco farm in the state, the Fitzmillers had worked their 700-acre property for generations. In particular, John and Alva Fitzmiller were known for their hard work, eleven kids, and Ms. Alva's orange marmalade. Donnie and I went to school with several of the grandkids. Once John passed away, though, Alva repeatedly parceled and sold the land. Various changes and sanctions nudged Alva out of the agricultural industry. Along with the fact none of the grandkids showed an interest in running the farm. Now, the area of the sinkhole fell under the guardianship of Grant County, or the Recreation and Park Society, or another entity altogether. Which meant I was trespassing on private property.

I had been here as a kid. If memory served me correctly, I even recalled being there at the farm for a fourth of July celebration one year. Back when people didn't mind a hazardous curiosity. That was back when we were a family—Bill, Mom, Donnie, and me—doing things that families do, in between the dysfunctional episodes at home. The Fitzmillers had erected a yellow barrier fence, the plastic kind that doubled as a snow fence, around the hole's edges. A shudder ripped through me as I recalled standing nearby, peeking through the barrier's rectangles at the giant cavity. Crying, I clung to my mom's bare legs.

"Delilah, what's wrong, baby?" Mom took me into her arms.

"Don't wanna go in!"

"Aww, it's all right, baby. We're safe. Nothing's going to happen to you."

She held me tight and my tears stopped. Peeking through the hair that had fallen over my eyes, and staring at that hole, I was still scared. Scared the hole would come alive and eat me.

To stand there now, near the grass-lipped edge, wearing a harness and loops of rope, that fear revived. Because now I knew it really was a beast. I knew what it had taken from me.

Much of Kentucky sits atop limestone, which is susceptible to erosion. That results in fissures and sinkholes, which are prevalent in the bluegrass state. At least that's what I remembered from 8th grade science class.

I had made more than my share of dumb mistakes in life. Deciding to go into the Fitzmiller sinkhole, in a feeble attempt to search for traces of my mother and her car, was probably a contender for the dumbest. There was a chance the ground was even more brittle and could collapse anywhere I stepped. There was a chance the ropes and harness wouldn't hold. But there was also a chance I could prove Bill had shoved my mother's dead body into that abyss. Wasn't there? Or worse—I'd confirm Donnie's story—and his guilt.

I made sure my helmet was snug, then tugged on the ropes I had tied around the trunk of a bald cypress tree. The lines were sturdy and taught. Wished the same could be said for my courage. Or was it foolishness? I texted Snyder two words: *Fitzmiller Farm.* The last reasonable thing I did before scarfing two deep breaths and working my way down a sloped side of the hole.

Cool air swathed me immediately. Goosebumps pickled my skin. I regretted wearing shorts and a t-shirt, as bugs we anxious to nibble on me for an early afternoon snack. The first fifteen feet down were bedrock. Passed the earthy layers, the chasm opened even wider. Pure darkness engulfed the underground atmosphere. I was afraid to take my hand from the rope but had to reach for the Maglite flashlight I had borrowed from Grandma's. When I clicked it on, the beam did little to counter the inky-black. My nervousness was evident by the light's trembling as I scanned the empty void.

There was nothing. No sign of a license plate or a tire or piece of clothing or whatever fantasy I was grasping for. Nothing but chilled air and pitch-black void. Shining the light downward, more of the same. Just an empty, bottomless black hole.

I chided myself for being so ridiculous. What was I thinking? I turned off the flashlight and slid it back into its holster. I still had an allowance of rope but going deeper was pointless. Since I didn't scale past the bedrock, my feet were still against its surface. I wasn't dangling in mid-air—thank God. I coiled the rope around my arms and carefully worked my way up. Progress came with slow, steady steps—and a refusal to look down.

When I made it up high enough to peek over the edge of the hole, I looked toward the tree I'd secured my lines to. I blinked twice, because I didn't trust what I saw. Sweat trickled down my forehead and into my eyes. I wiped each side of my face against my shoulders and checked again.

A man stood next to the tree, smoking, and staring my way.

Whether it was from the summer haze, a touch of dehydration, or buckets of adrenaline surging through me, I couldn't say, but my vision blurred. I blinked harder, tried to focus. Didn't work.

"Hey!" I called out and strained my neck.

No reply came.

I took a big step, intent on hurling myself out of the hole. Before I could plant my foot down, the other foot lost its hold. I slammed against the dirt and slid back into the abyss. My head thumped against the helmet as it hit the bedrock. Dust and rocks rolled down my face. I was terrified the ropes would snap, that I'd keep falling. Sinking to a certain death. But the ropes caught.

Paralyzed with fear, I held my position as debris tumbled by. With my face in the dry dirt, my arms burned from the skidding ropes. My fingernails dug into my palms from my tightened grip. When the dirt walls stopped crumbling, I looked up. The edge was maybe ten feet away. Relief and anxiousness throbbed through my now-dangling body.

"Hello? Can you hear me?" There was no way to tell if my voice carried out of the pit. No way to know if that man heard me. I waited, hopeful a face would peer over the edge. A face eager to help. But no one came.

I steadied myself, ignoring the discouragement and panic threatening to surface. Deep breaths cleared my head. I took my time, focused on nothing but bracing my feet against the bedrock. As my muscles stretched and strained, I was glad I had pushed myself back in Columbus. My gym held a chin-up competition a month ago. I took third place overall but was the last girl remaining. That familiar burn returned to my arms. Muscle fatigue imminent.

"No!" I gritted my teeth. Channeled every ounce of strength into those ropes. Pulled hard. One hand over the other, like scaling up the rope—bare-handed, legs dangling—at the gym. Ignored the weariness making my arms quake.

Reaching the top, touching solid ground were all I cared about. When I made it to the edge, I crawled out of the pit and onto on the grass. Like a desperate crab, I scampered away from the sinkhole's mouth. All the fear that had mounted inside me erupted. Tears burst forth. I collapsed against the ground, rested my sobbing face in the cool, soft grass.

I'd been so stupid to think I'd find anything relating to Sloan. And what if I did find a license plate? Wouldn't that only prove Donnie's story—and that he had accidentally killed Sloan? Wouldn't that be the worst possible outcome from this exploration?

As my anxiety lessened, I lifted my head and looked toward the tree. No one was there. There was no sign of anyone, anywhere. I couldn't escape the thought—the growing concern inside me—that I was seeing things, and that Sloan's condition had afflicted me as well.

Diagnosing myself was premature—and slightly irresponsible. But it served a purpose, acted as a flimsy band-aid for what was going on inside my head. Had a man really been standing by the tree? Had I been followed out to the Fitzmiller sinkhole? Why? More importantly, why would he leave me there? From his vantage point and for all he knew, I slipped into the abyss. Maybe it was a stretch, but had someone just left me for dead?

CHAPTER FIFTEEN

W ho leaves a person dangling in a pit—or worse, doesn't care if the person fell to her death? The thought chewed at me as I plopped into the driver's seat of my car. My frazzled nerves beginning to settle. Mud and grass ground into my skin. Bloody scrapes streaked my arms. I'd probably never get those tiny, sharp rocks out of my shoes. Aches pulsed through me as I leaned my head against the steering wheel.

Either someone didn't mind seeing me dead, or my mind was starting to slip away. Added to that was my brother telling me he'd accidentally killed our mother. An avalanche of grief wanted to bury me. For a few moments, sitting in my car, I let it.

I wanted to call Mark. He had a knack for making me feel like he could put the world back together. A pinch of disappointment hit when I checked my phone and saw there was no response to the text I sent him. Maybe I wasn't at the forefront of his mind, but I wanted to believe that I—or at least Sloan's case—was currently a priority to him.

On the other hand, I needed Mark to give up on the investigation. At some point he would need to interview Bill. There was no telling what Bill would say, which made me wonder what Bill was waiting on. If Bill was intent on hurting Donnie with the truth about Sloan's death, why had he kept it secret for this long?

Back at the apartment, I took stock of the literal mess I was in. For now, I decided to leave the harness and ropes in the back seat of my car. I couldn't walk back in Grandpa's shed, feeling emotionally raw. Replacing Grandma's flashlight back under the kitchen sink was a must though. Then, I indulged in the longest shower of my life. The cool water stung against my scrapes and soothed me from the summer heat.

Oscar napped in a patch of sunlight on the faded kitchen linoleum.

I texted Donnie to check in, see how he was. He replied that he was watching Emery while Monica worked. Britney had stopped over, he said. Relief and anxiety collided in me. Donnie sounded normal, as best he could in a text message. Normal and occupied. Hopefully shoving aside thoughts of Bill. Anxiety bristled in me because I knew Britney would ask, eventually, why I was worried about Donnie.

I finished getting ready and headed to Donnie's. When I walked in, Emery ran into my arms and squeezed my neck. The perfect dose of affection for my hurting heart.

I joined them for the last remnants of lunch, not realizing until then how hungry I was. If I had to guess, Donnie didn't get any sleep after dropping me off. There was a still-disheveled look about him. One that suggested he was working through a hangover.

"Did Monica notice your head?" A stupid thing for me to ask, maybe, but he couldn't hide it.

"Britney picked her up for me." Donnie and I traded knowing glances. "That way I could...sleep in a bit."

"Yeah, how did you get that bump?" Britney asked. She kept shifting her eyes between me and Donnie, as if she knew we were hiding something.

"Slipped when I got out of the shower. Hit my head on the vanity."

Britney took Donnie by the chin and examined his welt, which had turned bluish-purple. "Klutzy move."

147

"Yeah, yeah. I know." Donnie squirmed from her hold and flashed me a grin. He seemed too proud of his performance. It hit me that he had years of experience at lying and at keeping dark secrets. I wondered what else he hadn't told me.

"And what happened to your arms?" Britney eyed my forearms. "Looks like you were dragged behind a horse."

"Rough day at the gym." Wasn't like I could wear a sweatshirt in this heat to hide the scrapes and scratches, but I hadn't worked on a passable white-lie. "Rope climbing. Slipped a few times."

Donnie stole a glance my way. No doubt he was curious about what I'd been up to.

Desperate to change the subject, I asked Britney how Milt was doing since his minor mishap. She said he was fine and that Tonya had him checked out. Britney also mentioned that business was good at the salvage shop. Three more customers had come and gone the last time she was at the trailer. I said nothing. *They say he's up to no good out there. Heard tell that he's selling drugs.* Grandma's remarks ran through my head.

"Look what I got!" Emery held up four bottles of different colored nail polish. "Britty gave me them."

"Wow! Those are pretty." I bent down to Emery and was glad for the sudden diversion.

"Can't start a girl too young with her beauty supplies," Britney said.

A pang of jealousy stabbed me. I didn't want Emery to love Britney, not more than me anyway. It was selfish and insecure of me, but I kept it under wraps with a convincing smile. What a bunch of pretenders we made.

"Can you do it?" Emery gave me the bottles. "Put it on?"

"I can try. I'm not a professional like Britney though."

Emery ran to the kitchen island and climbed onto a stool. After she wiggled into place, on her knees, she splayed her hands wide on the counter.

"Which one do you want?"

"I want all the colors."

I paused. "You want each finger a different color?"

Her tongue was sandwiched between her lips as she nodded heartily.

My gaze found Donnie's, and I knew we were struck with the same thought: Sloan and her toenails. Donnie turned away. I beat the first bottle of polish against my scraped palm vigorously. A futile effort to fight back tears.

"All the colors…" I don't know why I repeated it. An image rushed through my mind. Feet poking out of a coiled blanket. My mother's feet, with her rainbow-colored toenails.

I couldn't tell Emery that her grandma liked wearing *all the colors* too. No way I would get the words out without dissolving into a sobbing mess. It pained me, not being able to tell my precious niece what she had in common with her grandma.

It felt like being back in the sinkhole. My emotions threatened to crumble in around me, make me slide into a pit of bottomless despair. I had to get a foothold and focus on pulling myself out of that darkness. Right now, I needed to zero-in on Emery's nails and steadily glide on the polish.

"Daddy look!" Emery squealed when we were done. She held her hands up and carefully wiggled her little fingers.

"Wow. Aunt DeDe did a good job."

Gratefulness poured over me in that moment. Seeing that little girl, her face lit with wonder and glee over painted nails, gave me a sliver of peace. And I understood Donnie's determination to do anything to keep Bill away from her. Maybe it wasn't wrong, wanting him dead.

Donnie took Emery into her room. "Come on, Squirt. Mommy sent some clean clothes. Let's put them in your closet and make sure your room's picked up."

"Okay, Daddy." Mindful of her nails, she hopped down from the stool and followed Donnie to her room.

I tightened the lids on the bottles of nail polish. Agony screeched from my hands, still raw and sore from the ropes. Britney took Emery's seat and leaned across the countertop.

"What's up with him, for real?" Britney kept her voice low, even glanced toward the hallway to make sure he couldn't hear her.

Telling Britney the whole truth wasn't an option. Neither was trusting her more than I had to. Donnie had assured me she didn't know the story about Sloan. I had to teeter between telling her enough and protecting Donnie.

"He's had it rough, since Bill got back," I said. "Brings back a lot of memories."

Britney nodded, looked satisfied.

"You think he really got that fat lump on his head from falling in the bathroom?"

"Why wouldn't I?" Heat rushed to my cheeks.

"A friend called me last night and said she saw Donnie drinking at the restaurant. She thought he looked drunk. I was worried about him. Then you texted about coming over today and now he's got a nasty bump." She glanced over her shoulder, as if making sure Donnie hadn't appeared behind her. "If Monica finds out…"

"Yeah, I know. Could be bad for him." The words snapped out of me. Too quickly.

Britney sat back. "You don't seem surprised. Did he call you for help?"

Her tone sounded flabbergasted, maybe even hurt. Like a knife twist in the gut. Was it that hard for her to believe Donnie would turn to me?

"That's why I texted you. I was with him last night. He'd been drinking and didn't need to be alone."

"Why wouldn't he call me?" She said it more to herself than me.

I went to her, put my hand on her shoulder. "He needs you now. He needs both of us. I'm really worried about him."

"Drinking is the worst thing he could do."

"Exactly. So it's best if we keep him occupied…and help make sure he doesn't have too much time on his hands."

"I've got a business to run, D. I'm not on vacation for the summer like you. I can't afford to babysit him." She stood and slid her purse strap over her shoulder.

"He's scared, Britney. He thinks Bill might go after Emery."

The smug expression dissipated from her face. "Are you serious? Has Bill threatened to hurt her?"

"No, no. That's just Donnie. Everything from the past is surfacing for him. He doesn't know how to deal with it. Having Emery to worry about makes it even harder."

Britney stared at the counter, seemed lost in her thoughts. "If Bill ever tried—"

My cell phone interrupted. Grabbing it out of my pocket, I saw Mark Snyder's name light up my screen. I answered without thinking.

"Delilah? Are you all right?"

His deep voice—laced with concern—sent a warm tingle through me.

"Yes, I'm fine."

"What was that text about?"

"Text?"

"Yeah, Fitzmiller farm. Looks like you sent it a couple hours ago. Phone's been charging in my office. Something I should know about?"

"Oh, that. Just wanted to discuss that later maybe…as a possible site to check out or something." Being under Britney's gaze made me too self-conscious. She had perked up when I answered the call and didn't bother to pretend she wasn't listening.

"Hope you ain't got any notions about going out there alone and snooping around. Place ain't safe."

"I know." A lump constricted my throat. Lying to Mark—or misleading him or whatever I was doing—felt weighty and unnatural. There was so much I couldn't tell him.

"Are you coming by this evening?"

Whether that was meant as an invitation or an innocent question, I couldn't tell. I knew what I wanted it to be.

"Um, not sure yet." I turned from Britney. Something told me the effort was in vain. My nervous tone probably gave too much away.

Snyder paused on his end. Maybe he'd picked up that I wasn't alone and couldn't talk freely. "Sure you're okay?"

"Positive."

"Keep me posted then."

I snatched a breath as we ended the call.

"That wasn't Mark Snyder, was it?"

"Yeah. He's been checking in on me, since Bill returned."

Britney nodded slowly. "Is he checking on Donnie too?" She flashed a coy grin.

My stomach knotted. No way I was spilling details to her about my ridiculous infatuation.

"Probably." I tried to sound nonchalant but couldn't look at her as I said it. "It is his job. Plus, he wanted to make sure Donnie and I didn't start any trouble with Bill." *Besides the jab I landed on him.*

"It's been driving my mom crazy." Britney took the bottle of candy-apple-red nail polish and started touching up her manicure.

"What?"

"All of it. You, Bill, worrying about Milt. When Mark talks about you that's when she goes nuts, especially now that you're spending so much time together."

"How does she know about that?" My casual tone started slipping, sounding like a stutter.

Britney shrugged a shoulder, paid no attention to my growing edginess. "Mark said he's reopening the investigation of Sloan's disappearance. Guess he wants to find a way to get Bill sent back to prison. Mom doesn't seem to care about that much. She's always complaining about Mark taking such an interest in you. I think she's worried Mark has a thing for you, crazy as that sounds. Mom gets jealous easily." Britney gave me a dramatic, salacious wink.

"Why would Tonya be jealous of me?"

"She thinks you're moving in on her boyfriend. Duh." She capped the bottle and started blowing on her nails.

"Tonya and Mark Snyder are dating?"

"They live together, at my mom's place. Thought you knew that."

"No." Every ounce of color drained from my face. "I had no idea."

Hearing that Tonya and Mark were involved—*lovers*, living together—made my head reel. My world had already been shaken and disturbed like a snow globe early that morning. Finding out Donnie had shoved our mother down the basement steps was heart-wrenching. That revelation hadn't sunk in yet. I only made the day worse by nearly sliding to my death at the Fitzmiller sinkhole. Now this.

I couldn't let a reaction seep out, not in front of Britney.

When Donnie and Emery returned to the kitchen, I couldn't play family anymore. The build-up of emotions became too much. Escaping the apartment was all I could think about.

I mentioned that I was leaving, as casual as possible. Donnie and Britney seemed surprised but didn't make me feel bad about it. Emery did. She threw her arms around me and didn't want me to go. I promised her I'd see her soon and kissed her forehead. She was about to pout until she caught her dad's eye. I loved those two together.

Outside, the hot and muggy air matched my mood. I felt stifled and burning, in need of a release, but not sure what would fix me. I didn't get a chance to talk to Donnie alone. To hammer home the sentiment of laying off the beers and letting go of his animosity toward Bill. Neither were healthy choices for Donnie.

Since Britney had her own concerns about Donnie brewing, maybe she would scold him. Even mention that a friend noticed he was drunk at work. Maybe a reprimand from Britney carried more weight than concern from me. An idea that felt as comforting as a throat punch.

Back in my car, which smelled like wet grass and now had a layer of dust, I headed home. Grandma was probably back from work, unless she had an event at church. What would I tell her when she asked about my day? When I pulled into the driveway, I didn't feel up to the work of fabricating white lies. I trekked up those rickety stairs, hoping Grandma wouldn't be at my heels minutes later.

Inside the apartment, I froze. The sound of running water greeted me. A quick glance to the kitchen sink confirmed it wasn't on. Was the toilet leaking? Had I left the shower drizzling?

"Oscar?"

He didn't show.

I walked into the bedroom. The bathroom door stood ajar. Steam billowed from the opening. I readied my fist and stole a quick breath. I nudged the door open more, then yanked the shower curtain aside.

"Geez, babe, you scared me!"

There I stood, with a wad of cheap shower curtain in one hand and the other ready to strike, gaping at my nude boyfriend in the shower.

"Jason? What the hell are you doing here?"

CHAPTER SIXTEEN

With one hand over his crotch and one hand stretched out defensively toward me, Jason said, "Babe, are you going to hit me?"

He was right. I let go of the shower curtain and relaxed my fist and stance.

"What are you doing here?" I repeated. My shock had downgraded from horrified to stunned.

Jason turned off the water, then turned to me full-monty style. "I wanted to surprise you."

"Mission accomplished." It came out as a mumble, and at the same time Oscar strutted out from the other side of the shower curtain. I'd forgotten that the cat had a thing for watching Jason in the shower. Weirdo.

"Where's your car?" Would I have even noticed it after today's events?

"Wanda let me park it in the garage." Jason stepped from the shower and wrapped a towel around his middle. Brushed with freckles on crème-colored skin, like a true ginger, Jason was a mix of Prince Harry and Seth Rogan's features. Well over six feet tall, pudgy in places, and crowned with untamable hair that he kept Harry-length. Flirty by nature, he spoiled me with meatless tacos and overlooked my habit of using the bathtub as a laundry bin for sweaty clothes.

"My grandmother knows you're here...naked in her garage apartment?" I returned to feeling horrified.

"Yeah. Well, probably not the naked part, but yeah. She let me in. Thought it was a great way to surprise you."

"She wasn't...upset? I mean, you just show up, a total stranger, claim you're my boyfriend, and she lets you in?" Considering I hadn't shared details about Jason or my love life with Grandma, this disturbed me. Even more so when I thought about the Sally doll and someone watching me today at the sinkhole.

"She's great!" He stopped rubbing his hair. "You don't seem happy I'm here."

He was right. I stood there gaping at him like a startled donkey.

My senses and manners returned. I held him and didn't mind his wet hair dripping on me as we kissed. The warmth of being in his arms poured through me like hot fudge. I had missed him. My body responded, proving it had missed him. But I couldn't ignore the awkwardness.

Guilt wiggled its way in between us and gnawed at me. Harboring an infatuation for Snyder while I was involved with someone else was wrong. Playing games or teasing guys wasn't me. At best I was distant and bumbling when it came to guys. Until Jason. Knowing I might have jeopardized our relationship with my foolishness pained me. Nothing happened with Snyder, but I wouldn't like Jason daydreaming about someone else.

"Hey, your grandma wanted us to have dinner with her. Hope it's okay I told her we would."

I left the steamy bathroom and plopped face down on the bed. Dinner was her means to asking us a zillion questions. *Where'd you two meet? Delilah, how come you didn't mention having a boyfriend? Is it serious between you two, Jason? Think you two will be getting married?* Questions I didn't have answers to.

Jason laughed at my childish reaction. He would probably enjoy the attention from Grandma, along with her cooking. Mostly, he

157

would enjoy watching me squirm under the interrogation, because he wanted certain answers too.

"Aw, man. Is that you?"

I lifted my head to see Jason taking the family portrait from the nightstand.

"That's me."

He chuckled and returned the photo to my bedside. "What's this?" Jason tapped the side of the cardboard box sitting on the end of the bed.

I turned my head to the side. "Box of stuff that belonged to my mom. Bill dumped it off on Grandma when he told her Sloan had left him. His way of making it look like she ran out on him."

When it came to telling Jason about my mom, I had treaded lightly with details. By the time we met, I'd learned that sharing too much family history, too soon was a bad idea. I told him my mom disappeared when I was little, and that I always believed my father was involved.

Jason rifled through the box, because that was him. Ever curious and clueless to boundaries. I kept my face smooshed against the bed and didn't stop him.

"Heh. Haven't seen these in a while."

I peeked and saw Jason holding the blue, oval-shaped pills in his hand. He examined one closely. "These aren't around much anymore."

"What are they?" I sat up.

"Halcion. You didn't recognize them?" He smiled playfully. "We took pharmacology together."

"Yeah, two years ago." I took the pills from him and looked them over. Of course they were Halcion, which explained the LCI lettering still stamped into a couple. "Sleeping pills."

"Yep. So these were your mom's?"

158

"I don't know." I rolled the pills over in my palm. "Would a doctor prescribe sleeping pills for a patient taking antipsychotic meds?"

"Whoa. Where'd that come from?"

I sighed. "Since I've been down here, I found out my mom was diagnosed with schizophrenia."

"Serious? Heck of a thing to find out."

I nodded. "It's explained some aspects of her behavior." I wasn't ready to let him in on the diary yet, filled with scribbles and ramblings about trolls and unicorns. "So assuming she was on, say, Haloperidol, would a doctor give her sleeping pills to go with it?"

Jason shrugged. "Not likely. Whatever she was already taking for her symptoms, Haloperidol or maybe Risperdal, provides a degree of sedation. But who knows? You're talking, what, fifteen years ago? Lot's changed with meds since then. But you're right. A person with schizophrenia usually isn't given a sleep aid."

Grandma had mentioned that Sloan wasn't always consistent with her meds, and that there were times she ran out. I wondered if the Halcion was used as some sort of back-up, maybe during times when they didn't have the money to refill her prescription.

But like Jason said, who knows? Was it just another item to add to the growing list of things I'd never truly know about Sloan? Did it matter anymore? One thing was certain: Sloan didn't die from an overdose.

Jason's phone, which was lying on my bed, buzzed.

"It's your grandma. Probably checking in about dinner."

"What? You gave her your cell number?"

He held up his hand as he answered and turned away from me. *Yeah, she was surprised. Yes, I told her about dinner. Oh, spaghetti? Yes, sounds good.* He moved the phone from his mouth. "She got spinach and mushrooms for you." I nodded as he went back to chatting with Wanda. *Yep, be there soon. Thanks, Grandma.*

"What is going on here?" I felt as though I'd been zapped into an alternate universe. "*'Grandma'*?"

"She insisted. I always obey my elders." He sat on the bed next to me, ran his hand along my thigh. "If you want, I could stay at a hotel, if you're uncomfortable with me being here."

A heavy sigh escaped. "It *is* my grandmother's house, you goof. We're not even engaged or..." I wasn't sure how to finish the thought. *That serious...We don't know if this is going to last.* Maybe that was true. Whether we were destined for each other or not, I couldn't figure it out now. I didn't want Jason to take what I said the wrong way. I had no complaints about our relationship, but I wasn't eager to take it to the next level.

"Let's get through dinner." I patted his hand. "Maybe your new Grandma will insist you stay at her place."

As expected, Grandma punished me with plenty of questions about my relationship with Jason. I returned the favor by reminding her of the perils of trusting a stranger—especially with her cell phone number. When Jason left for the hotel around eleven p.m., I was ready to be alone.

As I crawled into bed, my phone chirped. I figured it was Jason, letting me know he'd made it to his room; he was good about things like that. For a moment, I considered ignoring it but knew that wouldn't be nice. Jason had driven down here to be with me, already missed me after less than a week apart. How could I act callous and indifferent? I reached for the phone. Exhaustion and aches melted away at the sight of a text from Mark Snyder.

Thought you were coming by today. Wanted to see you and make sure you were all right.

I was an idiot. I'd completely forgotten about stopping by the station. Keeping an eye on Donnie and playing host for Jason's sudden arrival had consumed the day.

A jumble of emotions swirled inside me. The infatuation I had swelled when I read the words *wanted to see you*. The concern he conveyed swathed me in inappropriate warmth. Then I reminded myself that he was sleeping with Tonya. Living with her. A thought that hit my libido like a bucket of ice water and made me angry.

Sorry, I replied. *Crazy day. Is tomorrow okay?* Not that I knew what I was going to say to him—or if I'd be able to look him in the eye.

Coming off a night of poor sleep, I gave up and went for the five-thirty a.m. class at the martial arts studio. If nothing else, it felt good to clear my head. After I cleaned up, I headed to the police station.

"Any hits from the press release you sent out?" I tried to sound all business-like with Snyder, as if I hadn't read and re-read his text from yesterday.

"Heard back from a couple precincts. Said they had to check through their property office. Can't say anything sounds promising so far."

I breathed a sigh of relief and hoped nothing would surface that could point to Donnie's guilt. At the same time, it was frustrating knowing Bill got away with disposing of Sloan and had held it over Donnie for years.

Snyder took a seat, laced his fingers, and rested them across his stomach.

"So you wanna tell me what you were doing snooping around the old Fitzmiller place—alone?"

My flesh prickled. Had he been the man by the tree, watching me yesterday? No. There was no way he would've left me out there after I slid back into the hole. At least, I didn't think he would.

"How did you know?" My astonishment was apparent.

He pursed his lips. "I didn't. Until now."

How could I have fallen for such an obvious tactic?

"You know you could'a been killed out there, right? There's a reason all that fencing is up. And the signage."

I couldn't look at him. Shame and guilt battled within me. He'd want an explanation. How was I going to skirt around the truth that Donnie had told me? How long could I keep that from him? I wasn't sure I was the type who could hold family secrets the way Bill and Donnie had. With the right kind of pressure, I'd crack.

"Not to mention, that area's now government property…private property, which means you were trespassing, young lady."

I kept quiet.

Snyder paused, stared at me hard. "What on earth were you doing out there, Delilah? Don't you realize—" He seemed to choke on his own words. Was that a sign of his anger, or did it mean he was struggling with his own feelings towards me?

"It just…came to me. What if Bill had dumped Sloan in there? I wondered if it was possible, and if…anything would be left." My explanation trailed off into a whisper. "And I didn't think about it. I just went there. I had to see it and look at it for myself."

"Was there anything?"

I shook my head. Right then, I wanted to purge the secret and tell him that after all these years, I finally knew what happened to Sloan. That I had to go there and see it. Had to feel and breathe the emptiness of that abyss, knowing what it had taken from me. But telling Snyder the truth meant exposing Donnie as Sloan's killer.

"See, I could'a told you that, before you went off like a chicken without it's head." His voice elevated. He got up, stood inches from me. "That text you sent. That was in case something happened?"

I nodded. Tears stung my eyes, and I wasn't sure why. I couldn't look up at him.

Snyder took me firmly by the arm and lifted me to my feet. "And that text would've been the only thing left...of you. That was stupid, Delilah! Don't ever go off and do something like that again. You hear me?"

He didn't let me respond. Instead, he pulled me into him, buried my face against his chest. His fingers ran into the back of my hair. A hint of pine scent mixed with a manly body wash. He held me. My arms found their way around him. When I recalled how scared I was, sliding back into the hole, terrified the ropes would break, my body returned the fierceness of his embrace.

How long we stood there, pressed against each other, I couldn't say.

"I hope to God Sloan ain't in there." Snyder's lips brushed against my ear. "'Cause if that's what he's done, I don't know how we prove it." His hold relaxed. His hands slid to his sides. Neither of us moved, but we were closer than two casual acquaintances needed to be.

As I made the first move, stepping back, I saw my tear stains on his uniform. My heart pounded so loudly I almost couldn't hear. Too much was happening. Being in his arms. Hearing that concern in his voice. Knowing the truth about Sloan—about Donnie.

I sat again, certain my legs were going to give out.

"I'm not sure we can do this, Mark." Was it the first time I'd called him by his name, in his presence? "It's not going to work. This whole investigation is a waste of time. There isn't a chance of finding any evidence. It doesn't matter if he dumped her in a sinkhole or the Ohio River. We'll never prove anything."

He arched an eyebrow. "Where'd that attitude come from? Barely got the dust off the file and you wanna quit?"

"Yeah, I wanna quit." My words lacked conviction, and we both knew it. I started to feel like a suspect under interrogation, because I knew Snyder wouldn't take this easily. Maybe he wouldn't accept it at all. My acting skills weren't stout enough against his years in law enforcement and dealing with assholes.

"Weren't you the one waltzing in here demanding answers? Now you're done. What changed?"

I couldn't be honest. "We can't be authentic with each other, for one thing."

"What's that supposed to mean?"

"Why didn't you mention that you and Tonya are dating?" I hated the images my head conjured up. The two of them together, laughing and cuddling. Hated the idea of him slipping into bed with her at night. Hated the idea of Tonya making him happy.

Most of all, hated that I was playing games with a man who'd been good to me.

"I think you know why. You already had a hard attitude about me from day one and didn't want to give me a chance."

"That's not true." It was a little true, but I would admit nothing.

"I had ulterior motives here, hoping there was a chance you two could work through old grievances. Talk to each other."

"Yeah? Before or after she shoved Bill in my face?"

Mark's posture sank a notch.

"You just wanted to manipulate me." The chair rumbled as I scooched backward and stood.

Mark stepped in front of me. "That's ridiculous! Can you hear yourself right now?"

I pushed passed him.

"If you walk out of here, Delilah, then you ain't the person I thought."

I faced Lieutenant Snyder. Every muscle in my body taut, intent on getting away. "You don't know me, Lieutenant."

After I left the station, I drove to the grocery store and sat in my car. My body felt awash in emotion. I'd learned when that happened, when I felt overwhelmed, I had to take a minute. Let the tide recede.

I hadn't expected to be at odds with Snyder. Hadn't expected to be clasped in his arms either. I had crafted fantasies in my head of what it would be like to be close to Snyder, feelings running hot between us. When I was finally on that edge of tasting the reality of those dreams, I backed down. Maybe I really didn't want a physical relationship with Snyder. All I knew, as the emotional fog cleared, was that I didn't want him finding out the truth about what Donnie had done. And that was painful—knowing I couldn't separate the truth about Sloan's disappearance from Donnie's involvement.

I checked my phone. Jason had left me a trove of texts and a voicemail, wondering where I was and when he could see me. Naturally, I wanted to bang my head against the steering wheel to relieve the guilt now pumping through me.

I called him and filled him in on my morning. Kept the details about my meeting with Snyder light.

"You've been busy," he said. "Good to hear, because I was starting to think you were avoiding me. Maybe didn't want me here."

That subtle pinch in his voice told me he was still hurt about last night. I had shown no interest in staying with him at the hotel, and Grandma had ribbed me hard about not mentioning Jason. I didn't want to do this right now, rake reassurances over Jason and soothe his wounds. But what choice did I have? None of what was going on was his fault.

"No, it's not that." I reminded myself Jason only had good intentions. "Things have just been crazy since I got here."

"You want to meet for a late breakfast then?"

We agreed on a place and met up. When I saw him, the morning's turmoil slid off me. Jason had a way of making me feel grounded without him even trying. I liked that.

Maybe he sensed the heaviness weighing on me. Jason had a way of letting me come to him, of not pushing me and letting me unload when I was ready. Another trait I liked.

Being raw and vulnerable didn't come easy for me. My past relationships probably suffered and died because I never went deep. Never veered from my labels of student and martial arts competitor. I'd convinced myself a man couldn't love me if he knew where all the emotional scars came from. But Jason hadn't scared easy, and he was here for me now. I wanted to take that step, connect on a greater level, and tell him everything.

Before I could get a word out, my phone buzzed.

I slipped it out of my pocket and saw Lieutenant Snyder's name lit up. I had every reason not to ignore his call. After our meeting and outburst this morning, I figured there was nothing left to say. Curiosity got the best of me though, and I answered.

"Delilah, I know you're upset with me right now," Snyder started, "but I need you to listen. Bill's been stabbed. He's in the hospital and it's looking like he might not make it."

CHAPTER SEVENTEEN

S nyder asked me to meet him at the hospital. Besides which hospital, Snyder didn't have many details. Bill had been stabbed; his condition appeared critical; no suspects were in custody.

As Jason drove us, I gave him a re-cap of recent events involving Bill—his release from prison and return to Venice, neither of which I knew about before I'd decided to come back for the summer. I also told Jason about my two run-ins with Bill, at Tonya's salon and out at Milt's trailer. Jason listened and nodded.

I didn't know how to feel. There was shock, sure. I didn't know anyone who'd been brutally stabbed. But two other thoughts hammered in my head. One was the fact I'd wished my father harm. Maybe not this kind of harm, but I didn't want him to enjoy an easy life, post-prison. The second was the conversation I'd had with Donnie—and his burning desire to get rid of Bill. *We've gotta do something. About Bill...have to make sure Bill never tells anyone what happened that night.* Donnie's words roared through my brain like a runaway train.

And there was one more thought eating away at me: Did Donnie stab Bill?

After we parked at the University of Cincinnati Medical Center, Jason and I quickly found Snyder in the emergency room waiting area.

"Um, Lieutenant Snyder, this is Jason. Friend of mine from back home." There were so many awkward slips in those two sentences, but I couldn't worry about it now. Snyder and Jason traded names and handshakes. The tension between me and Snyder felt thick and palpable. I tried to ignore it. "What happened?"

"Call came in this morning from Bill. Said someone broke into his house and attacked him. When the medics got there, they found him unconscious on his bedroom floor. Blood everywhere. He's in surgery now. I'm waiting to speak to the doctor, see if he pulls through."

A chill shuddered through me. Would this be the end of my father?

"I wanted you here for a couple reasons," Snyder said. "He's got no one, and I figured if the man was dying, you might have something you wanted to say to him. If so, that's up to you, but I wanted you to have that chance. 'Course, no telling if you'll get that chance or if he'll be coherent."

I nodded. It only affirmed what I knew about Mark Snyder—he was a good man. Reasonable, fair, thoughtful to a fault.

"I also put a call in to Tonya and your brother."

My body stiffened at the mention of Tonya's name. Snyder must've picked up on it.

"Don't go getting riled. I told her you were on your way, and that I'd give you first choice over whether you wanted to see him or not. Told her to wait in the cafeteria or her car, that you two causing a ruckus wasn't going to happen. We clear on all that?"

Another nod, then, "Is Donnie coming?"

"Left him a message and haven't heard back."

That made me nervous. A dozen explanations could be conjured for where Donnie was and why he hadn't responded. But I couldn't escape the sinking, deepening possibility that Donnie had been at Bill's. Was the attack on Bill the result of another drunken episode colliding with Donnie's rage toward Bill?

"I stopped out at Milt's," Snyder said, "asked him if he'd seen anything or if he knew what all Bill had been up to since getting released."

"Yeah?"

"Milt couldn't offer much. Just that Bill had been busy running the salvage shop. Said he had customers coming and going a couple times a day, and that he saw Bill on the phone a lot. Any of that seem peculiar to you?"

I held Snyder's gaze. Something told me he already knew the answer to his question. Much like when he asked me about the sinkhole. Again, I had the feeling of being interrogated. Warmth prickled my body. A pit of guilt now camped in my stomach.

"The fact Bill has any freedom at all is peculiar to me. I don't keep tabs on him. Wasn't that your job?"

Snyder looked taken aback. Probably didn't like my smart-aleck tone in front of Jason. Then Snyder shot me a hard glare.

"Mind if we step aside?" To Jason he said, "Excuse us," and added an intentionally-lame grin.

Jason gave a nod as Snyder took me by the arm and led us to an empty nook.

"Who is this guy?"

Now I was taken aback.

"I told you, just a friend."

Snyder stared at Jason, who'd found a seat and was flipping through People magazine.

"When did he show up?"

"You're really that concerned about Jason? We go to school together."

"That's it?"

"Is this really your business?" I could've hammered that point, but I liked the odd feel of the faux lovers' quarrel we were having. No way would I let him talk to me the same way he dealt with criminals though.

My remark must've hit home. He dropped his gaze from Jason. Sighed and rubbed a hand over his face.

"You're right." Snyder cleared his throat. When he looked at me again, his eyes seemed to search mine, as if he was checking to see if we were okay. Like me, maybe he wondered if an apology would help. "You don't have to stay. I just wanted you to know what happened."

"I'm glad you called." My heartrate ramped, and a tingling sensation danced across my skin. "I didn't like how I left things between us this morning." Snyder had a way of leeching emotions out of me that were unfamiliar and sensual. Understanding it was beyond me.

"I'll stay," I said. "I want to be here, but not for Bill." *For you*, but the words wouldn't come. Probably a good thing.

Snyder darted a glare toward Jason. "Any chance you can ditch the new guy?"

I stifled a mild laugh. Seeing Snyder jealous, if that's what it was, gave my heart a strange flutter. I had no idea what was wrong with me.

We went back to Jason, who stood when we approached.

"You know, Jimmy—"

"Jason."

"Pardon me. Jason." Snyder emphasized it. "We could be here a while. You're free to head on out. It's a bit of a private family matter anyway. Delilah can stick with me and I'll give her a ride home."

"I don't mind hanging out, and I won't intrude. Besides," he put his arm around my waist, "I want to be here for her."

Snyder's neck and face colored. "Fine." With that he turned and walked to the nurse's desk.

Conflict boiled inside me, because I wasn't sure which man I wanted by my side.

Mark Snyder busied himself with ignoring me. I didn't care. As I settled in the waiting room beside Jason, I texted Donnie.

At the hospital waiting for news. You coming?

A swift reply didn't come. Neither did news about Bill's condition. The lag in Donnie's response only fueled my suspicions that he was hung over or in hiding. I thought about calling Monica and asking if she'd heard from him lately. That would potentially cause more trouble than what was going on, so I decided against it.

"What's with the cop?" Jason asked. "Seems like he has a thing for you."

Until Mark Snyder pulled me into his arms that morning, I figured I was the only one entertaining mixed, inappropriate feelings. That I was the only one who felt the spark between us. But apparently, my boyfriend had noticed too. Embarrassment hit me like a hot poker to the chest.

"He's a good guy. With all the weird stuff that's happened, he's grown protective of me. If that's what you mean." I felt like I was walking a tightrope and balancing an elephant in each hand.

Jason turned to me. "What kind of weird stuff?"

I sighed. Earlier, when we were alone and enjoying breakfast, I'd been swooning over the idea of growing closer to Jason by telling him everything that had happened since my return to Venice, and its effect on me. Now, while we sat in a hospital, the swoon was gone, except for the intense heart-flutters from Snyder.

I started slow and gauged his reactions. Jason was the kind of guy who believed everything you told him without a lick of skepticism.

That came in handy as I unfolded the story. Viewing the case file on Sloan; Snyder re-opening the investigation; the memory Milt shared and Bill's admission. I even told him about the doll and my snooping at the sinkhole. Through it all, Jason's touch—his hand on my thigh, shoulder, or holding my hand in his—gave me the support and encouragement I didn't know I needed to get through it all.

From time to time, I caught Snyder staring at us. Standing beside corners, sipping from a coffee cup, and glaring at us from the nurses' station. It made me uneasy he didn't just join us, that he held back, focused instead on sending me death-rays of disapproval.

On the other hand, I got a secret thrill, seeing him jealous.

After two hours, Bill's doctor met with me and Snyder.

"He suffered a huge blood loss, but we've managed to repair the damage. He's stable now and with some rest, should have a full recovery."

"Only Bill," I said under my breath. Apparently to the doctor's vexation.

"Is he awake, doc?" Snyder asked. "I need to see if he remembers anything about the attack."

The doctor nodded. "He's come around. Might be groggy though, and I don't know if he'll be able to recall much. You can go in and see."

Snyder looked to me. "You coming?"

Goosebumps popped on my flesh as I nodded.

"You can wait here," Snyder told Jason.

Jason stiffened, which told me he didn't like Snyder's tone. I squeezed his hand, gave him a loving, grateful smile—and over his shoulder caught a glimpse of Snyder's scowl.

Snyder and I didn't talk as we were led to Bill. The flighty, snickering school-girl thoughts dancing in my head over the non-existent love triangle between me, Snyder, and Jason fled. I was about to face Bill. Stomach-cramping tension took over.

When we stepped into Bill's room, his eyes went straight to me.

"Well, if it ain't my girl." The words seemed difficult for him to get out. "Come to check on your ol' man. Always was a sweetheart."

Part of me was disappointed he wasn't in more discomfort. Bill reminded me of Rasputin. A mystic monk shrouded in rumor and legend, he convinced the Russian Tsar's wife that he could heal her son of hemophilia in 1906. Other Russian officials saw him as a threat to the government with his strange ways and plotted his death. Rasputin survived a stab wound to the gut, much like Bill, and tea and cookies laced with cyanide. Three bullets, including a shot to the forehead finally took him down. Supposedly. Why was it that men of a particular evil were immune to destruction?

"Heard you might be dying," I said. "Looks like it was too good to be true." Not that I really wanted Bill dead.

"Bill, you able to tell me what happened?" Snyder asked.

"Woke up in the night with some man in my bedroom. Came at me with a knife, then took off."

"You recognize him?"

Bill shook his head. "Room was dark. He had on all black. Saw he was white. 'Bout all I can tell you."

"Any idea why someone would come after you?"

Bill shook his head. He blinked as if his eyelids were suddenly too heavy. Snyder glanced at me, and we both took it as a sign to leave.

"If you think of anything, holler." Snyder laid his business card on the table in front of Bill. Bill raised his arm, perhaps attempting a wave, but drifted off to sleep. Snyder and I stepped into the hall.

"Heard anything from Donnie?" he asked.

"Not yet." I wished I had an excuse, but there was no need to lie to Mark.

"You okay, seeing Bill like that?"

"It's fine. Amazing how some guys have all the luck. Survive anything."

"He's definitely the cockroach type. Probably walk out of a nuclear blast without a scratch. But you know I gotta job to do, right? It's on me to find out who attacked him. Bill's the victim here."

His words put a sour taste in my mouth, but I nodded.

"You coming by the station later...without Jimmy?"

"Probably not."

Snyder's passive-aggressive game of verbally badgering Jason worsened my feeling of distaste. Not hearing back from Donnie already had me on edge. Keeping my distance from Snyder made the most sense right now.

"I'm gonna go." I didn't know what else to say and wanted to get away.

Snyder touched my arm. "You're leaving?"

"There's no point in staying, and I should tell Wanda what's going on."

"I'm startin' to wonder that myself." He clenched his jaw.

I understood Snyder's reaction. He was frustrated, probably, because I was either crying in his arms and engrossed in the reborn investigation, or I was a blank wall. Void of emotions and seemingly disinterested in Sloan's case. I wasn't a woman who toyed with people and their feelings, but this looked bad.

"I need some time to think." Now I was transitioning into clichés.

He released my arm. "Might not be a bad idea. See if you can work out what's going on in that head of yours."

174

◆ ◆ ◆

I was done muddying my head over Lieutenant Snyder. He could think what he wanted. Feast on his frustrations, for all I cared. Which, right now, I didn't.

Jason and I headed back to Wanda's. On the way, I called and left a voicemail for Donnie and updated him on what I knew about Bill. nger flared in me that my brother had left me in the lurch—and d guilty of a crime while doing it.

I called Donnie's restaurant, thinking I might catch him there. guy on the phone said Donnie had called off for the night. My omach plunged to my toes, because in my mind, that only ratcheted the likelihood that he'd attacked Bill.

"How about we get some food and go back to my hotel? We can just relax." Jason reached over and rubbed the back of my neck. When every joint was sore from Ju Jitsu, when my eyes were bugged out from studying, that's what he did. His gentleness melted me every time. The familiarity of him, of knowing our routine, eased my racing mind.

"I'd like that."

We took care of heavy duty business first—agreed upon a place for food. Jason called in our order while I called Wanda. She hadn't heard about Bill. After filling her in, I casually asked if she'd heard from Donnie. Of course, she hadn't, and said she planned on calling him later, once she checked her garden for fresh tomatoes. She agreed to peek in on Oscar, even though she was convinced he had it in for her.

There was something wildly romantic about eating a fancy dinner out of to-go cartons in a hotel room. At least to me. Maybe it was the air conditioning. After indulging in food and each other, we were in no condition to move.

We lay on the bed head-to-toe, covered by a stark-white, rumpled sheet and afterglow. Dusk began to dim the room.

"I think I've been seeing things."

"Like what?" Jason slid his fingertips along my leg.

I revisited the story about the Sally doll, and told Jason about the orange slices in her undergarment. As I stared at the ceiling, I explained the candy. Its connection to Bill. And the fact she'd disappeared.

I moved on to the sinkhole. Earlier, I'd told him I went there ~~of~~ suspicion, that maybe Bill had used it as a dumping groun~~d~~ Sloan's car and body. I couldn't mention Donnie or Sloan's rain~~bow~~ colored toenails. But I conveyed my fears—that the ropes would snap, and I thought I would plunge to my death. Now, I shared that someone had been watching me, then vanished.

Jason listened, propped up on an elbow, caressing me the whole time. Hearing the words spill out, made the panic and eeriness return. I cringed and wondered if Jason felt my goosebumps.

"You're thinking it's a sign of schizophrenia."

I covered my face with my hands, hating how it all sounded. "What if it's the beginning stages?"

He was silent a moment, then, "Bit of a leap, isn't it?"

That's what I wanted to hear, that I wasn't losing my mind to a ruthless disorder. But what was the explanation otherwise? We searched and scrolled our phones for signs and symptoms of schizophrenia. A total change in mood.

Together, we concluded that symptoms would've appeared earlier, and that what was really going on, possibly, related more to my PTSD from Bill's abuse. Triggered by the stress. And the orange slices.

I sighed and liked the way it sounded. Like something I would tell a patient.

I rolled to my side. Jason moved my way, spooned against me, and put his arm around my waist. He kissed my neck and rested his head on mine.

"See, it's fine. *You're* fine," he said. "If you're still committed to staying here, let's find a therapist. Someone you can really talk to, who can sort it out. Or you can come home with me. We'll get you in to see Dr. Cohen. Whatever you want, babe."

I squeezed his arm, best I could. I didn't want to say I love you. Not for the sake of simply saying something. Not because everything he said was perfect. Because I really did love him. At least what I knew about love. Saying it might ruin the moment. Sure, he'd say it back. But I didn't want a watered-down relationship that worked on autopilot. And I didn't know if he could love the real me. Those secret parts of me that messed up, played flirtatious games with a police officer, had a brother who killed their mother.

I drifted to sleep with Jason against me, satisfied, cool, and dreamily wondering if there would always be something wrong with me.

CHAPTER EIGHTEEN

L eaving Jason's side early the next morning border-lined excruciating, but I managed. Over the last two days, my love for him had been rejuvenated. The mounting issues with Donnie and Snyder—even myself—threatened my soundness. Being with Jason gave me an ease I hadn't felt since leaving Ohio, and the classes at the studio kept my head from imploding. I knew that having a healthy outlet for my aggravations was as important as air and water.

After, I returned to the garage apartment to change and to remind Oscar I still loved him. Not that he cared.

Still nothing from Donnie. What was going on with him that he couldn't even send a text to say he got my messages? Temptation rose in me to contact Britney, but I didn't. If Donnie had reached out to her, confided in her, it would crush me. I didn't want to know. Plus, asking if she'd heard from Donnie would let her know that something was wrong. If she didn't already. No telling what she knew from Tonya or even Snyder.

I decided to leave Donnie alone. Just like when we were kids, and he wouldn't open up. I had done my part. Showed I cared. Time to back off, let him come to me.

I called the hospital for an update on Bill. Mainly to hear he was still there. The nurse informed that he had a rough night but was resting peacefully. She said the doctor would be in soon for morning rounds and thought he might get upgraded from ICU.

The man lived a charmed life, considering what a despicable human being he was.

Right as I hung up, my phone chirped.

Woke up alone. Where you at babe? read the text from Jason. My heart was a bit crestfallen it wasn't Donnie, but I liked that Jason was already missing me.

Before I replied, I had an idea. I called Milt. He had always been an early riser and answered on the second ring. I told him who it was and asked if I could come over and make breakfast for him. Milt said that would be nice.

On my way to the store to pick up groceries, I called Jason. I recapped my morning and told him I was getting ready for breakfast with my grandpa. We skidded into awkward territory when Jason said he wouldn't mind joining us. That gave me pause. My motives for visiting Milt were layered.

"Now's probably not a good time," I said. "He's been sick, and I don't know if he's up for company. Doesn't take much to wear him out." There was truth in that. Absent was the mention of my intended snooping.

The silence from Jason suggested he was hurt. That wasn't my goal. I felt bad about it but would make it up to him later.

"I won't be long," I assured him, maybe too late. "Then the rest of the day is ours."

"Okay, sure."

It seemed better between us before we hung up, but I was reminded how much work relationships demand. Or maybe it was a pin-prick of worry that I was doomed to ruin this, possibly any, relationship I had.

As usual, Milt's smelly dogs barked and hovered around me when I arrived. No way I was letting them in the trailer while I cooked. They probably wouldn't leave my side while stepping on my feet and slapping me with their tails. I squeezed my way in, careful not to spill my bags of groceries.

Inside, Milt didn't budge at the sound of the commotion. I put the bags in the kitchen and went to his side. His skin was feather-white and clammy to the touch. With some nudging, he woke from his nap.

"Are you feeling okay, Grampy?"

"The lawnmower needs fixed."

"Lawnmower?"

Milt had not mowed the lawn, what there was of grass around the place, in at least two decades. Grandkids rode the John Deere in haphazard streaks across the property. It didn't give the place a manicured appearance, but it got the job done.

"Were you trying to run the mower?" I asked.

"Naw." He drew out the word. "Warm in here, ain't it?"

I checked the thermostat, which read seventy-six degrees. From the few visits I'd made, I knew Milt liked it toasty, even on summer days. Seemed as though the temperature was the same, but something was off with Milt.

I made him biscuits and gravy. Some might consider it a cheat that I used Bisquick, but it was Granny's go-to. Growing up, I always saw the bright yellow box with blue lettering in her pantry. Making the fried baloney made me cringe. I chased away the smell by cutting up a cantaloupe and shoving pieces into my mouth. The rest went into a bowl for Milt. When everything was ready, I served him breakfast on a tin tray. He would probably be better off eating the dogs' food, but this was what he wanted.

Milt didn't ask about Bill, which seemed strange. I thought he would fire away questions the moment I walked in. He worked on taking the meds I sprinkled into his palm then settled back into his recliner.

I told him I was going to check on things outside. Milt didn't acknowledge me. Just seemed to slump further in his chair, leaving most of his food untouched.

Outside, the dogs got up and circled me. They followed me to the salvage shop. The gunmetal-gray building was trimmed with burnt-orange rust around its edges. A large sliding door was on the front. When I was little, the door was hard to slide open. Looking at the track, attached above the door, I doubted it opened at all, or would probably crumble to pieces if I tried moving it. I used the side door that led into the office. Luckily, Milt still kept the keys on a rack in the kitchen. The dogs nudged their way in, barking as they went. They sniffed and scrambled into the darkened interior of the warehouse. Maybe they would scare away mice or any other critters hanging out.

No way I was following them in there. Inventory packed the space and made me wonder if anything had been moved or sold or touched since I was a kid. Bedframes, doors, fences, light posts, bicycles, and car frames were just the immediate items I noticed. Who knew what lay deep inside. I would stick to the office.

Papers were scattered across the desk. None with a date less than eight years ago. Thick cobwebs sagged from the ceiling and corners. The phone, covered with a layer of dust, had no dial tone. I had a feeling the rumor Wanda had heard about Bill dealing drugs was true. Because from the looks of the office, he wasn't in the salvage business.

A knock sounded on the office door, and a man walked in.

"Bill," he said, but stopped when he saw me.

I tried to tamp down the surge of fright that hit me. "Who are you?"

Not much taller or older than me, the man looked me over from head to toe. "I'm just looking for Bill. Said he'd be here." His faded blue UK cap was off-center, and his jeans were torn at both knees. A Spanish accent coated his words.

I went with a split-second decision. No telling if I could make it work, or if I was making a worse decision than exploring the sinkhole.

"Bill couldn't make it," I said. "Did you...bring the stuff?" I was on shaky ground here.

He gave me the once-over again, seemed to be calculating his next move. "Bill said to meet him here. Didn't say nothing about a girl."

"Maybe he wants to see if you can handle a last-minute change." I planted my weight on my heels, readied my fighting stance. Not that the guy would notice.

"Maybe you're a cop." He slid his hand into his pants pocket, appeared to fist a knife.

Now I was scared. "Are we gonna do business or not?" I stared at his hand, my way of letting him know I saw the weapon.

"I don't mess with no cops."

A slight smile escaped me. My body tensed, just like it did before a match. I already had three moves in mind for taking him down and landing a throat punch. He wouldn't have a chance to open the knife, because I knew he was underestimating me.

His hand didn't leave the pocket, and he backed toward the door. In a flash the guy was out the door and back in his car. Tires were spitting gravel and kicking up dust when I stepped out. The car must have been left running. I didn't get a glimpse of the license plate.

Back in the warehouse, the dogs barked and came running back to the office. When they joined me outside, they circled me and made a show of barking and sniffing the air.

"Way to go guys. A little late with the security detail."

As the dogs calmed, I wondered if I should call Snyder. There wasn't much I could tell him, just that I suspected Bill was using the shop as a front to deal drugs. I talked myself out of it. Since I didn't find wads of cash or a meth lab in the warehouse, what proof was there? Sure, I could mention that some guy showed up and took off because he thought I was a cop, but it proved nothing. I ran the risk of looking more erratic to Snyder without evidence. Just like I had with the missing doll.

I closed up the shop and started to walk back to the trailer. But stopped. Bill's workspace sat about a hundred yards away. Donnie's words stirred in my head. He said he'd seen Sloan's body, rolled into blankets on the ground. The ground of Bill's work space. Sloan's body had been in there. Besides her car, it was the last physical place she'd been.

How had I not thought of it before? Could there be traces of blood on the floor? My pace quickened and my heart beat like a chased rabbit. Surely the door would be locked. I'd have to break a window. Sweat started slicking my palms at the thought.

Then, the dogs were back to barking. A car was pulling into Milt's lot. I thought it was the UK fan, until I saw Tonya get out.

She whipped her sunglasses off her face and said, "What are you doing here?"

"Checking on Milt."

"Out here?" Her tone haughty and skeptical.

"Some guy just showed up and took off. Thought I'd look around."

She snickered. "I'm surprised you didn't call your boyfriend Mark. He jumps to your rescue every chance he gets."

I couldn't call her out on that snippy tone, since she always talked to me that way. Along with a condescending flare.

It occurred to me at that moment that I hadn't seen Mark Snyder wear anything but his uniform. Maybe the uniform was responsible for making a tangle of my emotions. For the life of me, I couldn't imagine him intentionally spending time with Tonya. Building a relationship with her. She could charm men but neither of her two marriages had lasted beyond a few years.

Maybe Britney was right. Based on Tonya's current attitude, maybe she was jealous of my time with Snyder.

"He has been pretty wonderful. All the time we've been spending together at the station, I've really been getting to know him well. See what an amazing man he is." How I hoped my words dug into her, cut a swath of insecurity into her heart. Cruel, maybe, but I couldn't think of anyone who deserved it more.

"But you should check on Milt," I said, walking toward her. "Something's not right. He seems disoriented and was slurring his words."

Tonya huffed and slammed her car door shut. We both went inside the trailer, the dogs at our heels.

Tonya tossed her purse and keys on the couch. Milt was sleeping. His untouched food had grown cold.

"Daddy, you awake?"

Startled, Milt opened his eyes. Tonya stroked his cheek and assured him everything was all right. I had never heard her voice so smooth. Like Britney, she had a gentle way about her when it came to Milt. Maybe it wasn't the first time ever in my life, but I saw an admirable quality in my aunt.

Tonya got him a drink, then went to check his meds. The dogs had already taken over the couch, and I stood there. Awkwardly.

Tonya came back holding pill bottles.

"These pills are all mixed up. Did you give them to him this morning?"

"Yes, when I made him breakfast."

She sighed. "I better get him to the doctor."

"Let me help."

"No!" She held out her hand as if to stop me from touching him. "You've done enough. I know how to take care of him. Why don't you just get out of here."

For Milt's sake, I didn't argue. Getting away from Tonya was ideal, but I hoped Milt was going to be okay. My stomach clenched at the thought of giving him the wrong medicines. It hadn't crossed my mind to make sure the right drugs were in the proper containers.

I texted Britney when I got in my car and gave her a short version of what happened. I asked her to let me know when she got any news about Milt's condition. *Okay* came her reply, along with a couple confused-faced emojis.

I looked over and stared at the work space. No chance I'd get in there today. It bugged me, being this close and that I didn't think of it earlier. Milt was more important right now. I'd wait and figure something out.

From Milt's, I went straight to Jason's hotel without calling or texting. He was happy to see me.

"How'd it go with your grandpa?"

"He didn't look too good. My aunt showed up and decided to take him to the doctor." Guilt prodded me. I didn't intentionally give Milt the wrong doses, but I should have paid closer attention. Snooping in the warehouse had been a priority.

"Man, getting old seems rough. I say we stay in our 20s."

"Agree," I said. If I told Jason about the mixed-up meds, he'd probably scold me for not noticing. He wouldn't be completely wrong, but I already felt bad enough.

"You know what? If we hurry, we can catch the Reds' game today. Weather promises to be beautiful and should be a good battle between the pitchers."

I nodded. Despite Grandpa Paul's attempts at teaching me the rules, I still knew little about baseball. It wasn't a bad way to spend the afternoon, soaking up some sun while Jason was happy. Few things excited Jason as much as his beloved team, win or lose. But I couldn't imagine being a real fan, not like him.

Was this what marriage was like? Setting aside part of yourself to make the other person happy? Going to a baseball game felt like an easy compromise. But when did it become uncomfortable or asking too much? Jason had no interest in being a vegetarian or in taking up Ju Jitsu. I had no interest in making him do those things, but it bugged me, sometimes, that his health wasn't a priority.

To be fair, he never complained about my spotty sleeping habits or occasional nightmares. Didn't mind my devotion to dietary restrictions or the times I needed to be alone. Did that make us compatible, able to stay together and love each other for life? I didn't know.

We drove to Cincinnati and bought our tickets at the gate. Being with Jason felt easy. Was it because we didn't live together? I wasn't ready to make that change—to commit to doing laundry together and figuring out how we pay bills and who would clean the bathroom. I liked easy.

But what hope does a relationship have, staying in neutral?

In the third inning, Grandma called. She invited me and Jason to dinner later. Said she'd talked to Donnie and he would bring Emery. That came as a surprise, but I didn't let on. I told her we'd be there.

Now I was irked. Donnie hadn't called or texted me since Bill's attack. But he answered when Grandma called. Mostly, I was irritated he didn't let me know he was okay. But was he okay?

I suspected Donnie was involved in Bill's assault. Based on Donnie's behavior that morning in the basement, when he told me how he shoved Sloan down the stairs, his desire to get rid of Bill was flaming. Worrisome. Then Bill ended up in the hospital. In my mind, it wasn't a coincidence.

I also suspected Bill was holding back what he knew. That maybe he did get a glimpse of his attacker. Maybe Bill added that to his repertoire of things to hold over Donnie's head.

Those scenarios wouldn't leave me alone—that Donnie had a part in stabbing Bill, that Bill knew his son tried to kill him. At dinner tonight, I'd talk to Donnie. I needed him to tell me I was wrong.

CHAPTER NINETEEN

A victory for the Reds worked like a dose of adrenalin for Jason. I tried sharing his glee, mainly to hide the turmoil sizzling in my head. My fandom couldn't compare to his though. I told him about Grandma's invite and laid a bit of groundwork about Donnie. Jason knew I was concerned Donnie didn't answer me when we were at the hospital.

"So your brother's doing okay?" he asked.

"Guess we'll find out."

"He ever text you back yesterday?"

I shook my head, tried to act like it wasn't a big deal.

We were the last ones to arrive at Grandma's. Emery ran into my arms and wasted no time launching into a story. As I listened and nodded, I stole peeks at Jason and Donnie. They were easy and friendly with each other, as if they'd been pals for a while. I liked that.

Donnie looked the best I'd seen him in days. Rested and his swollen lump had diminished. Clarity had returned, along with the joy that lit him up when Emery was around.

"I thought you dropped off the earth." A subtle approach had never been my strength.

"Yeah, sorry about that. I…didn't really care about Bill and didn't want to sit around at the hospital."

I nodded. "I get it, but you could've told me that. At least sent a text." I looked him straight in the eyes. "I didn't know what to think."

"Sorry. I didn't mean to upset you."

That was all I was going to get from Donnie. For now anyway. No doubt there was more to it, but he wasn't going to dive deep with Grandma and Emery around. He was here, and he was safe. That was good enough for a family dinner.

Emery told us about her swimming lessons and how she wasn't afraid to go under anymore.

"Where's your phone, Grandma? I wanna picture of my bubble face."

Grandma took out her phone, and Emery climbed onto her lap. "What's a bubble face, honey?"

"That's when I blow bubbles in the water. Watch." Emery puffed up her cheeks like a blowfish and slowly exhaled. "That makes bubbles."

"Oh, I see."

"Now you do it."

They made bubble faces, and Grandma snapped pictures with her phone. We took turns making bubble faces and squishing Emery's cheeks with kisses. I captured some shots on my phone too. Jason and Donnie got in on the fun, puffing their cheeks and crossing their eyes. Emery's giggles were the sweetest sound. So was hearing the mixed laughter of my family. I soaked it up. Grateful we could be together and wanting a thousand more moments just like this.

Swift knocks sounded on the screen door. Mark Snyder and Glenn Rodgers stood on the other side, and Grandma welcomed them in. I was instantly convinced Glenn had a built-in radar for Grandma's cooking, since this made the third time he showed up at an opportune moment. Princess provided her usual greeting, then curled back into her bed.

Snyder's face was stern, all-business. He seemed to look past me, as if we were strangers. A side kick to the ribs would have felt more comforting.

"Evening, all." Snyder removed his sheriff's hat. "Hate to disturb the fine time you're having, but Glenn and I have been talking. He's got a few things he wanted to get off his chest. We thought it best if I accompanied him."

Hairs on the back of my neck wiggled.

"You fellas come right in and sit down." Grandma pulled out two empty chairs from the table.

"Well, it might be best if I stand," Glenn said. The way his eyes darted from each of us and fiddled with his hands, he couldn't have looked more nervous.

Snyder put a hand on his shoulder. "It's all right, Glenn." Snyder turned to Grandma. "A lot's been happening lately, and Glenn wants to clear up a few things. I want you all to listen, give Glenn a chance."

Grandma nodded as Glenn sat. He leaned in, breathed heavily.

"Glenn, you're practically family," Grandma said. "If something's wrong we'll help you."

"It's hard for me to say some of these things," he began, "but I didn't mean to hurt no one." He choked up. "That doll you had," he said to me, "the one with the blond hair."

"My Sally doll, from when I was little."

"Well, yeah. You see, your mom told me about it, how much you loved that doll." He hesitated. "She told me lots of stuff. Stories about Bill...what used to happen."

"Maybe Emery and I should—" Donnie said.

"You should hear this too," Snyder said, then flashed a grin at Emery. "Might be best though if—"

"Hey, I could take Emery outside." Jason popped up. "We can take Princess with us. Do you know how to walk her?" he asked Emery.

"Yeah!" Emery hopped from her chair and got Princess' leash. "Can we Grandma?"

"Don't go too far, and be careful," Grandma said. "Thank you, Jason."

He nodded and shot me a smile before walking out, holding Emery's hand.

"You left the doll?" I asked Glenn. "Is that what you're trying to say?"

"I put it up by your door. Then when you took off screaming, I grabbed it, cause I didn't think that would happen like that, and I ran off."

"You left my childhood toy on my doorstep—along with candy my father used to lick and eat off my skin when he was abusing me—and you didn't think I'd scream my head off?" I was on my feet, yelling in Glenn's face. He held up his hands, afraid I would hit him. His face white with fear.

"Do you have any idea what that did to me, seeing that doll? And...the orange slices?" Tears came, and I fell back into my seat. Snyder put his hands on my shoulders.

"I didn't know exactly...Sloan said Bill had the candy. I thought he used it to calm you down...or something."

No, you idiot! He got off on licking me! Chewing up the candy and licking it all over me! I gagged on the words, couldn't get them out. Which was probably for the best.

Snyder rubbed my shoulders. Grandma clasped my hand.

"But I didn't mean no harm by it," Glenn said. "I was worried, with you being back here and all. I knew you wanted to find out about Sloan and what happened. I didn't want no trouble."

"Trouble?" Donnie asked, irritation evident in that one word. His face was red, and I knew he was reliving those nights with Bill too.

"Yeah, with my wife and kids. I didn't want my wife upset, hearing about my affair with Sloan all over again. Didn't want to put her through none of that. It was a long time ago, but sometimes it's best to keep things in the past. I thought if I left that doll, you'd get scared and leave things alone. That's all."

"That's not quite all." Snyder took a seat beside me, kept a hand on my shoulder. "Got a call at the station the other day. A man said there was a young woman out at the Fitzmiller sinkhole. He was worried that she was stuck, or worse."

"That was you?" My voice elevated.

"Once we got a unit out there," Snyder continued, "no one was around. We suspected it was a prank, since the caller didn't leave his name. Then we traced the call to Glenn's cell."

"I was scared! I didn't know what to do. I'd been following you that day, wanted to try and talk to you a bit. But then you went and had them ropes and everything and got in that hole. I thought for sure you were a goner, doing some thing like that. I saw your face one minute and the next you's gone. I ran back to my truck, but I don't run good no more. So I called the police hoping they'd help. I figured it'd be best if I wasn't around. Might look like my fault or something."

"What on earth were you doing at that sinkhole?" Grandma's words hit the air like a whip crack. "And you went down in it? What possessed you to do such a crazy thing?"

"I…I thought Sloan might be in there." No way I was looking at Donnie. "Bill told Milt that he sunk her body. It made me think of the sinkhole. I wanted to see if…anything was there."

"You went out there, alone?" Donnie asked.

"I just…had to see it for myself."

"You know it's like an abyss," Snyder said. "Ain't no bottom to it."

"It was stupid, I know."

"So when you showed up at the station later that day, that's why I asked you about it, because of that phone call we got. Sounded like a stunt you might pull." Snyder's gaze met mine. "I was furious with you. I knew what could've happened out there." He choked on his words.

"I'm sorry. I didn't think it through."

"I'm sorry too," Glenn said. "When you took off hollerin', I knew I'd done a wrong thing." He hung his head slightly.

I realized directing anger at Glenn was useless. At this point, so many other devastating revelations had come to light, what Glenn had done seemed minor. A pinch of anger still simmered in me when I pictured the Sally doll, relived that burst of panic at seeing her and the orange slices stuffed in her panties. But looking at Glenn, I knew his intent to scare me off wasn't malicious. In fact, I wondered if he had a slight learning disability. Might explain the kink in some of his mannerisms.

Before I said anything, Grandma put her hands on Glenn's shoulders. "You've been awful good to this family through the years. Mistakes happen, and well, I've heard a lot worse."

"She's right." I had to clear my throat a little. "No one's perfect around here, and we understand why you did it."

Glenn glanced at each of us, seemed to absorb the forgiveness in the room. Donnie nodded while Snyder cracked a grin.

"See, Glenn, I told you the best route was to simply come clean. Bet you feel better too."

"Yeah, it's good to have it off my chest...'cept I gotta tell my wife."

"You're on your own with that."

Mild laughter followed Snyder's remark. It felt phony, not at all like our laughter over the bubble faces, but it helped smooth the edges of the sharp revelations.

"Folks, we're gonna step out, let you all enjoy your evening. Just so everything's clear, there won't be any charges filed against Glenn."

"Well, of course not." Grandma patted Glenn on the back. "But you're not leaving without at least taking some lasagna. Made enough for every Wildcat in the state." She whipped out plastic containers and filled one for each of them.

"I stopped by the hospital today. Looks like Bill might be going home in a day or two." Snyder checked our faces but no one said anything.

"Young lady," Snyder said to me, "no more sinkholes, or any other life-threatening activities." He brushed his fingertips along my cheek as I nodded. The sudden glare Donnie sent my way didn't escape my attention.

Glenn left with Snyder, apologizing again on his way out. The kitchen was quiet after the screen door slapped shut. None of us looked at each other.

"I'm gonna have a smoke," Grandma said. "See if I can maybe find Emery and Jason."

One thing about Wanda Baker, she knew how to read me and Donnie. A special radar that beeped when we needed space—or needed a chance to talk alone.

"I can't believe you went out there," Donnie snapped, though barely above a whisper.

"I had to. After you told me about Sloan, I had to go and stand there. Had to prove that nothing was there." I swallowed hard. "Accept that there was no chance of...finding her."

"You shouldn't have gone alone."

Yeah? You weren't in any shape to help big brother. I wanted to yell it in his face. Not just because I was mad at him for compromising his sobriety, but for all the things that changed when he told me the truth. Giving in to my temper wouldn't do any good. I couldn't afford to push my brother away. Not now. He was the one I needed most.

"Yeah, it was stupid." How many times was I going to have to say that?

"And what's with you and Mark Snyder? You two got something going on the side?"

Once again, I could count on my cheeks to make me appear guilty.

"I'm not involved with Snyder. Not outside of Sloan's case. He's just been watching out for me."

"I saw the way he looked at you, touched you. Better not mess around with him, cause he's seeing Tonya."

"I heard. Bet they make a cute couple."

Donnie grinned, evidently detecting the sarcasm in my voice.

"Besides, didn't I introduce you to my *boyfriend*?"

"Nice of you to mention him."

I was surprised it took Donnie that long to toss that in my face, but I was done playing around. I didn't want to squabble about Jason or the fact that Donnie and I were both good at keeping secrets.

"Forget that. I have to know, Donnie. Where were you when Bill was attacked?"

He looked startled by the firmness in my voice.

"Nowhere...here. Working, taking care of Emery."

"Not answering my calls or texts."

"I already told you I didn't want to talk about Bill."

"Did you have something to do with it?"

His expression upgraded to astonished.

"How can you ask me that?"

"You mention wanting rid of Bill, then he ends up in the hospital and almost dies. And no one can get a hold of you. You can't be bothered. What am I supposed to think?"

Donnie snickered. "Like that asshole is ever gonna die."

"Did you do it, Donnie? Did you try killing him?"

Any lightness he had in his face drained away.

"You're looking at me like you think I did."

I said nothing. He seemed to search my face for a sign that I wasn't being serious, that I wasn't really asking him if he'd thrust a knife into our jerk of a father.

He gritted his teeth, stepped close to me. "Is that what you and your sheriff buddy have been talking about? Is he outside, waiting for me to confess? Is that the real reason he came tonight?" Donnie went to the screen door and peeked out. If Snyder and Glenn were still out there, I couldn't tell from where I stood.

My pulse galloped, worried that Grandma or Jason might have heard him.

"I just want to help you and protect you! I can't do that if I don't know the truth."

The spike of his flared anger seemed to crest and fall. "You? Protect me? Since when have you ever been there for me, Delilah? You've always looked out for yourself with no thought about anyone else."

He was right. Maybe there was no way to make up for what I'd done, running away and leaving Donnie here. Leaving him to deal with Bill. Even in prison, Bill had exerted control over Donnie, kept him on edge over whether he'd expose the truth about Sloan's death. I wasn't there for any of it.

"You don't get to stand there and look at me like that. Like you're the only one capable of not making mistakes anymore. Or you're the only one who can make up for what's happened. The last thing I need right now is *anything* from you."

Donnie pushed through the screen door.

I sank to my knees, crippled by the weight of regret crashing into me.

CHAPTER TWENTY

Naked in bed that night, I stared up at the ceiling while playing with Jason's hair. He snored softly, his arm draped over my midsection. Peaceful, as best we could be. Or maybe it was sheer exhaustion, settling in after the flood of tension.

Donnie's outburst had ruined the night—and it was all my fault.

He had every right to say the things he did. Things he probably wanted to say for years. Even though I understood his anger, watching him storm out seared me with rejection and loneliness.

By the time Jason and Grandma rejoined me in the kitchen, after Donnie had scooped up Emery and left, my face was puffed and smeared with tears and an aching helplessness. I didn't know what to tell them. Wasn't like I could cop to my role, admit I'd provoked him. So I rambled through some fluff about how Glenn and Snyder's visit had revived difficult memories. That certain recollections became overwhelming. They bought it, far as I could tell. It enabled Jason and me to make an awkward getaway, because no one wants to talk about or revisit those scarring memories.

Laying in bed now, all I could think about was going home— back to Columbus—in the morning with Jason. He had to get back and had already asked repeatedly if I was coming too in the kidding-not kidding way he had. I'd played it off, but now, I didn't know how I could stay in Venice.

But there was more to it. My future boss from children's services had called. She told me they were going to need me to start sooner than expected. It gave me a valid reason—not an excuse—to put Venice in my rearview mirror. Going back now would mean moving in with Jason. How could I tell him it would be temporary, when he hinted about getting married? I didn't know if I wanted to permanently mix my laundry with his, and I didn't want circumstances deciding for me. But leaving seemed best.

Donnie wanted me gone. He didn't say it, but I felt it. Maybe I'd been wrong, coming back in the first place. Coddling the notion I could make up for past transgressions, past hurts, without having a clue how to go about it. Maybe redemption was only a well-peddled fantasy.

I couldn't help waking Jason when I got up the next morning. He rolled to his side and watched me, his eyes heavy with sleep, as I fiddled with the room's mini coffee-tea maker. My desperation for caffeine had set in.

"You didn't sleep at all."

I gave a half-shrug, not sure how hard he would press the issue of last night and the fallout.

"Do you want me to stay? I could call-in, say I need some more time here."

"That's sweet of you." I sat on the edge of the bed and stroked his cheek. "No, it's fine."

"Not sure I'd go with fine, babe, after last night."

I wondered if that was Jason's way of asking what really happened with me and Donnie. Going full-disclosure with Jason about recent events had enriched our relationship. He knew as much about me now as my own brother, and none of it seemed to have changed his feelings for me. But I couldn't tell him what Donnie had done to our mother. Admitting my suspicions that Donnie might've hurt Bill also wasn't going to happen.

"Why don't you just pack up and come home with me?" Jason put his hand on my thigh. "Get this stuff out of your head. Focus on your new job, on us. Let things cool off here for a while."

"Maybe I should." I left the bed for my piping-hot cup of water, then dipped in the tea bag. "But that's what everyone's expecting—me tucking-tail and running. It's what I've always done when things got heated. But I can't be that girl anymore."

Jason sighed. "I get it, if you want to stay." He rubbed his face and joined me. "We both know you're full of fight."

I grinned to myself. Jason had no idea how true that turned out to be. Considering I had decked both my father and my brother.

"So when are you coming back?" Jason slid his hands around my waist from behind me. Rested his lips on the nape of my neck. I eased into his embrace, let his warmth pour over me.

"Sticking with late August." Truthfully, I didn't know. Wasn't ready to commit one way or the other.

Jason moaned. "I was hoping you couldn't stay away from me that long."

I turned toward him. We pressed against each other and kissed.

"It won't seem long. You'll keep busy."

He pouted, a look that enhanced his boyish features. "And when you do come back, should I clear out space in the closet, make sure the toilet paper roll is hung the right way?"

That's what he really wanted to know. Before I could craft a suitable fib, my phone jingled. My curiosity peaked, seeing Mark Snyder's name.

"Delilah, can you come to the station? There's been a development in Sloan's case."

It seemed strange and natural and fitting of a bizarre love-triangle. Me leaving Jason when Mark called. Sure, I was over-dramatizing the reality. Fabricating a romantic element that didn't exist. All in my head. Maybe there was more of Sloan in me than I realized.

Jason would pack and be on the road in an hour or so. We shared a tender good-bye, with him wanting more of me. I liked that, along with him not knowing what to expect of me. That probably made me a terrible girlfriend.

I shifted all-things-Jason aside, as I joined Mark at the station.

Mark gave me the impression he'd been up for hours, grinding away. No hint of salacious or dreamy desire for me lingered in his eyes. A good thing for now. But his alertness and business-like stride told me I would need another cup of tea to keep up with him. The clock was inching toward ten a.m., and I already worried how last night's lack of sleep was going to push me around for the day.

"I've been working on something. Got a call two days ago from Sergeant Lydia Sands over in Rockport, Indiana. She was calling about the press release I sent out. Said she recalled a strange item from way back. It took some digging, she said, but she tracked it down. Found the item stored in the medical examiner's office. It's been over fifteen years, and it was still there. Know what it was?"

I shook my head, already feeling dizzy from his rapid-fire info.

"A skull. Said she'd never forgotten about it, because it didn't have any teeth."

"What?" I straightened in my chair. Adrenaline suddenly replacing my need for caffeine.

Snyder slipped out a piece of paper from a folder he held. "She emailed a photo. There's no jawbone. Said the skull washed up in October of 2001. Said the medical examiner could tell from looking at it that someone had deliberately pulled out every tooth. There are marks indicating pliers were used." Snyder kept the paper against his chest. "Now, before I show you, are you sure this is something you can handle or even want to take a look at?"

"Lieutenant, I'm about to start a career in children's services. Harsh realities will be my life."

He nodded, pressed his lips together, then handed me the paper. I turned it over and took in the picture of the skull. Its burnt-caramel coloring and spider-vein cracking made my stomach clench. Milt's words echoed in my head. *Ain't no one gonna find her and if they do, they ain't no proving it's her...I know from TV that they need a body and they use the teeth; I took care o' that. Sunk 'em all."*

"No teeth..." It was all I could say.

"Sergeant Sands said they put the information out about the skull when it first came in. Checked local missing person reports, but nothing came of it. They kept it though, all these years." Gingerly, Snyder removed the paper from my hands. "Now, we can't fly off the handle here. We don't know that's Sloan Ramsey."

"Right." *But...it couldn't be Sloan.* I pictured Bill and a younger Donnie, pushing Sloan's car into the sinkhole. Her body rolled in blankets and stuffed into the trunk.

"First thing we gotta do is have a sample of the bone sent for DNA. There's a chance they might not get DNA out of it. Who knows. Next thing we need is Sloan's DNA. Do you know if she was ever in the hospital for a procedure or had surgery?"

My mind was reeling too much for me to think. "I don't know."

"We'll work on it. Check into her medical history, see what we can find. Even if she did have a procedure, could be a chance that the hospital didn't keep her tissue samples, especially since it's been so long. If that's the case, well...let's see how it goes."

Snyder's words flowed like a flooded stream in the spring. Bubbling, energetic, overwhelming. Much of what he said washed over me.

I took a deep breath. "So you think this skull could be my mother?"

Snyder's gaze lingered on the photo of the skull. "I think there's a chance."

I had to get out of there.

Snyder let me go without a fuss. He must have known I was dazed. He said he'd keep me informed of any progress.

It couldn't be true. The skull couldn't be Sloan—because of Donnie's confession. He admitted to shoving her down the stairs; Sloan died from a head injury caused by the fall. Didn't she?

What about her feet, her rainbow-colored toenails that Donnie had seen—touched—as they poked out of the end of the rolled-up blanket?

The skull in the picture showed no damage to the bone above her eye, where her head slammed into the wooden step. Surely it had to be crushed, at least cracked, since she died from the impact. It couldn't be my mother.

But no teeth....

That bothered me. I couldn't get away from that fact. Had Bill killed someone else? Possibly confused her with Sloan? When Bill told Milt that he'd taken care of Sloan, was that just a sick fantasy he played in his head?

Snyder didn't know about the accident. Didn't know the truth. If he followed through with the plan to extract the skull's DNA, at some point it would prove not to be Sloan's. That could take weeks. He was wasting his time. Chasing a unicorn, as Sloan might say.

It was late in the morning, and I ended up knocking on Donnie's door, unannounced. Surprisingly, he flung the door open within minutes. Unlike the other times I surprised him, Donnie was clean shaven and dressed as if he was about to walk out the door.

"You got my messages?"

"What? No, I didn't get any messages." I silenced my phone before meeting Snyder. Only now did I slip it from my pocket and check the screen. Donnie had called and texted several times. "What did I miss?"

"Hey, I'm sorry about last night. I don't know what got into me." He held me by the shoulders. "I'm not mad at you, and I was stupid to say those things, especially the stuff about you not being there for me. Total crap. If you hadn't been there, on the other side of my bedroom door all those times, I don't know if I would've made it through those years with Bill."

I bit my bottom lip, determined not to end up a sobbing mess. Again. "You were right. I focused on me and ran out on people. Maybe I still do. When you told me about the accident and going to see Bill in prison, I know it had to tear you up, keeping all those secrets." I sucked in tears. "But you could've come to me and told me everything. Maybe it would've changed things for us, brought us together, salvaged our last few years with Wanda and Paul. I could've helped you, been there for you."

"It doesn't matter now." He pulled me in and held me, as if sealing our trade of apologies, but only for a moment. "I was ticked at you last night. The way you thought I was involved with hurting Bill, got to me. I didn't know anything could still set me off like that."

"Is this—"

He held up his hands to stop me. "Wait. Let me get through this. You were right to be concerned, even suspicious. Maybe it

203

would've come to that, me acting out, going after Bill. Who knows? After tying one on the other night, I did give it serious thought. Too much thought to be innocent." His eyes locked with mine. "But I didn't go there and stab Bill; I swear to you, I had nothing to do with it."

Relief poured over me like warm bath water.

"But we need to talk about what we should do."

"Okay. About what?"

He sighed, leaned his lower back into the counter. "I didn't sleep much last night, thinking things over. I just want to do what's right." Donnie cast his gaze to the floor, seemed to be considering something. "It's kind of like Glenn. When he came in and told the truth about what he'd done, I envied what that must have felt like. That freedom and release. No more pretending or lying." He paused. "I think it's best if I come clean, tell Snyder about the accident."

"Oh, Donnie, I don't know." Just like that, the relief left. Warm bath water down the drain. "It's not as simple for you as it was for Glenn. You'd be charged with manslaughter, maybe worse. I don't know for sure."

"I can't live with this anymore. Last night proved it. Even if it's the wrong thing to do, I gotta purge this secret out of me. If I don't, I'm not sure what'll happen."

"But…Emery?"

"What kind of dad can I be to her if I keep living this lie? I've got to show her the right thing to do, even if she won't understand for a long time."

He made sense. More sense than I thought he was capable of.

"So, what now? Do we get a lawyer?"

"I want to talk to Snyder, and I want you there with me. He seems to like you, so it couldn't hurt having you around."

I flashed my lame-dog expression, not appreciating what he was implying. "Thanks."

"It's not only that. I need your support. I don't know how I'm going to get through it...reliving it again."

"Should we call people first? I mean, what if Snyder locks you up?"

"I gotta face this and accept the consequences. I trust Snyder. He'll get us through this. Right now, all I care about is becoming a free man."

When Donnie and I walked into the Campbell County Sheriff's Office, Mark Snyder didn't look surprised, but there was a hint of an expression on his face I couldn't pin-point.

"Word travels fast."

Donnie's confusion at Snyder's remark was apparent as he looked to me.

"I'm assuming you told him." Snyder arched an eyebrow at me. "Figured he needs to see it too."

The skull! I hadn't mentioned the discovery to Donnie, hadn't had time to process what Snyder had shared. Had that only been an hour ago? Not even noon and my world had been flipped twice already. At this pace, everything around me would be ashes by dinner.

"I didn't have a chance." My words trailed off.

"See what?" Donnie asked.

My tongue swelled. Felt knotted in my mouth.

"Why don't you two come on back." Snyder led us to the room serving as headquarters for Sloan's case.

Donnie paused at the doorway. Seemed to take it in. Even stared at Sloan's framed picture for a moment. Pride ballooned in me, because now Donnie knew that Lieutenant Snyder had treated

Sloan's case with genuine, renewed interest. But then I wondered if it took a notch out of the courage he needed to confess.

"You guys were serious." Donnie eased into a chair at the table, glanced at the papers strewn on the tabletop.

His reaction made me wonder how long he had suspected Snyder and I were just meeting to flirt. Or whatever he had constructed in his mind. It irked me, Donnie thinking that I hadn't been committed to investigating Sloan's death. But I didn't have enough room inside me now to house another emotion. Not with the thunder of nervousness rumbling through me.

Snyder took his usual seat on the other side, leaned back. "You didn't tell him?"

"No." I avoided his gaze, best I could in the confined space, which suddenly felt as if it was shrinking.

Snyder laid out the photo he had shown me of the skull and gave Donnie the same explanation he had given me earlier. Donnie stared at the picture, then looked to me. I pressed my lips together.

"What am I missing here?" Snyder asked, noting our tacit exchange.

"There's something you should know about Sloan." I stopped there, certain that Donnie needed to tell the story.

Donnie picked up the photo of the skull, handed it to Snyder. "This can't be our mother."

I sat beside Donnie, put a hand on his forearm. Our eyes met again. A hint of reassurance passed between us, even though I was terrified on the inside. I wanted him released from the weight of the secret, just as much as I wanted to run out of the building with him and keep the secret forever. My brother nodded, as if letting me know it was okay; he was ready to expose the truth and swallow the consequences.

Lieutenant Snyder hardly moved, hardly spoke, as Donnie revealed what happened the night of Sloan's death. A few of the details he shared were clearer, probably because he wasn't in a fog of intoxication. He told Snyder the same story he told me. Almost word for word. Everything. He swiped tears from his eyes and squeezed my hand several times. I fought back my own tears.

"Bill told you she was dead, there at the bottom of those steps?"

Donnie nodded. "He checked her pulse, from what I remember. She was bleeding from the top of her forehead." Donnie pointed to the spot on his own head. "She didn't move. Nothing."

Snyder wrote on a notepad. "Rolled her into a blanket, put her in the trunk of her car, shoved it into the sinkhole—and made you help him?"

Donnie glared at Snyder, spoke through gritted teeth. "I was nine years old. He put a gun in my face."

"Easy, Donnie. I just want to know I have this story clear." Snyder had spread out his hands, looked as if he were tamping down Donnie's temper. "Let's go over it again."

The next time through, Snyder took notes and asked questions. Donnie's version of events remained the same. By the end, weariness crept over both of us.

"All right, let's step back, take a break." Snyder stood. "Delilah, mind if I speak with you a minute?"

I followed Snyder out into the hall. Donnie seemed to slouch from exhaustion.

"You knew about this?" Snyder asked sternly, once we were out of Donnie's earshot.

"Not until recently."

Snyder stared at me, seemed to be considering if I was telling the truth.

"Honestly, all this time, I never knew." Hearing the words tumble out, I couldn't blame Snyder for doubting me. Donnie and I only had each other to trust, confide in. It didn't seem plausible that he hadn't told me. "When I got to his place this morning, I meant to tell him about the skull being found. But he was set on coming here, telling you everything. Then all I could think about was him getting arrested and losing Emery."

Snyder sighed, shook his head. "Why's he doing this now?"

"I don't know. He's had some rough patches lately, especially with Bill being released. I think the truth is weighing on him. He wants to do the right thing even though he's terrified."

Snyder took a deep breath and exhaled. "You have any idea what this could mean?"

"Please, Mark, keep him out of prison." Desperation quivered in my voice. I knew I was asking too much. Circumstances were now beyond Snyder's control.

"I'm not sure what I can do yet."

"So the skull...." I fought back a lump in my throat. "You know it can't be Sloan, right?"

That hint of mystery flashed across Snyder's face again. At least, I thought it did. Or maybe I just didn't know the man well enough to understand and decode his facial expressions.

"Let's get through this first."

When Snyder and I returned to the room, with bottled waters and sandwiches, Donnie was leaning against the wall, staring out the window. None of us said much while we ate. After, Snyder reviewed Donnie's story and had him retell it one more time.

Snyder went over his notes, seemed satisfied at last. "I'll have to sit down with the DA and go over this. See how she wants to proceed."

Donnie gave a curt nod, ran a hand over his wearied features. "There's something else…about Bill."

Snyder looked to me. I responded with a blank face.

"He started calling me from prison. After he knew he was getting out. He wanted to make sure he would be set up, able to have a life. He told me I needed to take care of him, get him on his feet. Told me I owed him since he served the time instead of me."

"What?" I spouted. "He tried making you feel guilty that he was in prison—for raping us? That had nothing to do with Sloan."

"Right. It's part of his mind games. Him exercising control. I had to give him money and a cell phone."

"Bill's been blackmailing you, is that it?" Snyder asked.

Donnie nodded. "It's part of the reason I've been working so much and putting in the overtime. I shelled out about five grand."

I gasped.

"But it gets worse." Donnie shifted his glance between me and Snyder. "Day after he was attacked, he called me from the hospital. He said he'd been talking to the police about the attack, said he told him his head was fuzzy, he couldn't remember much. Then he threatened to ID me as the one who stabbed him, unless I came up with more cash." Donnie hung his head. "He said it'd be easy to pin it on me. All he had to do was tell you how crazy I'd been since he got back here. He heard I'd been drinking, and that I'd lost my temper at work. Said based on my history, my anger issues, I already looked guilty. That's when I knew it couldn't go on. That I had to tell you everything."

I sat shell-shocked; Snyder didn't seem phased.

"I don't want to go to prison, Lieutenant, but right now, I'd rather die a thousand deaths than be under Bill's control for another minute."

CHAPTER TWENTY-ONE

Snyder gave us clear, steadfast instructions: *Head home. Both of you. Stay put. I'll be in touch soon.*

That was it.

How was I supposed to rock back on my heels and wait? What did *be in touch soon* really mean, SWAT showing up at Donnie's door to arrest him?

I wanted to accost Donnie with *Why didn't you tell me Bill was squeezing money out of you? Threatening you?* But I let it go. Maybe a weight of shame kept him from confiding in me. Maybe he thought he would find a way to deal with Bill on his own.

Learning about Bill's threats and the extortion explained a few things about Donnie. Including his desperation to get rid of Bill. When I thought of the pressure Donnie had been under, maybe I would've felt the same. Donnie was right—Bill's noose around Donnie's neck would have only tightened.

I didn't fault Donnie for giving in to Bill's demands. Abusive, manipulative parents often held an inexplicable power over their children.

Back at the garage apartment, loneliness greeted me. Sure, Oscar lavished affection until he grew tired of me. The worst part was Jason being gone. I couldn't bury my face in his neck and unload about what a miserable day I'd had. I wasn't the needy type. But hearing that Bill's abuse of Donnie had extended well beyond our childhood worried me. Even frightened me. A lifetime of trauma had shaped my brother. What kind of man was he—could he be—at his core? The rage he had exerted during his youth, justified. But what about now? What was his outlet? What kept him from cracking under the strain? From completely losing it?

Donnie's full-blown confession was a major step for him.

Worrying about what would come next was useless yet inescapable. The perfect diversion? Cleaning. I shrugged off the worry-weight of the unknown. Didn't want to focus on what was going to happen to Donnie. If he'd be handcuffed and in an orange prison jersey by the end of the day.

Oscar amused himself by following me. He made sure to shake himself and sprinkle fur on the table, after I wiped it down. Then left his pawprints along the countertop I swiped clean. I told myself his random, sweet snuggles against my legs made up for it.

Donned in classic yellow rubber gloves and wearing my earbuds, an hour or so ticked by while I scrubbed, then re-scrubbed thanks to Oscar. When I checked my phone, I saw I missed a call from Grandma. She left a message saying she was staying at work later, since two bus loads of senior citizens rolled in. That gave me a snicker, though I had no idea what I'd tell her later about Donnie and today's developments. Grandma didn't know about Donnie's accident with Sloan. What would that do to her, hearing the truth about how she lost her child? How would I even put that into words?

And was it worth mentioning the skull that had been found?

I shook it away. Making Grandma cry, watching that revelation dig into her heart…. I didn't want to think about it.

Texts from Britney also awaited. She updated me on Milt. Said she was sorry for not texting sooner, but he was doing okay. Tonya had taken him to the hospital where they had flushed his system to clean out the drugs. Milt was home and comfortable now—with new bottles of meds.

I surveyed the fridge, which I already knew was empty. Made cleaning it easy. And Oscar didn't nudge his way in. After that, I peeled the gloves off for good and threw them away. The evening stretched before me, and the longing for Jason crept up on me.

As I was on the brink of talking myself into dinner at Cracker Barrel, a knock sounded at the door. With no peephole, I had to open it. Expecting to see Britney or Grandma on the other side, I found Mark Snyder instead. Holding a boxed pizza.

"Have you eaten yet?" He held the box toward me; its aroma wafted into the apartment.

I shook my head. Wrinkled brows and a slack jaw displayed my bafflement. Far as I knew, Snyder hadn't called or texted that he was coming by. Then sheer horror struck me, realizing that I was coated in a light layer of sweat and my hair was in a ratty bun.

"I…uh, no. Haven't eaten."

Snyder made his way inside. "My boys are off to Cumberland Lake with their mom for a few days, which is probably a good thing. These latest developments have consumed me. Can't say I've been much of a father lately. Figured you might be the only other person who could tolerate my bad company." Snyder settled on the couch and placed the pizza box on the coffee table.

"Yeah." What on earth was the man doing in my apartment, bringing me dinner?

"I wasn't sure what you liked, so I went ahead and got most everything on it. Figured that way, you could take off what you didn't want."

I nodded slowly, still working through my astonishment.

"Jason around?" Snyder eyed the small space, as if he expected Jason to pop out from the bedroom.

"He went back to Columbus. Work." I snatched plates from the cabinet and joined him on the couch. Oscar strutted from the bedroom and quickly made nice with Snyder. The lieutenant made kissy noises and talked to Oscar like he a was baby. With my approval, he fed Oscar toppings from the pizza. After a few treats, I shooed Oscar away.

Pizza wasn't a regular thing for me anymore. I was used to getting wedged into situations where I was the odd-one-out with food. Eating organic, non-processed food was equal parts commitment and sacrifice. Making a situation work was easier than always explaining what I did and didn't eat.

"Thanks. It was really thoughtful of you to stop by." That wasn't entirely true. He'd barged in—practically—unannounced. I was grasping for the right thing to say, as if it was my job to make him feel comfortable. And I didn't know why. The easiness between us was gone. At least for me. Snyder was the potential enemy now, since he might be arresting Donnie soon.

Snyder served us, placing a slice on each plate. Ravenous, apparently, he took several bites before he spoke again. "Spent the rest of today with the DA. Gonna take her a few days to sort through Donnie's statement and the case file on Sloan. She'll want to meet with him, hear the story."

Snyder seemed chipper, as though we weren't talking about my brother possibly facing a murder charge. I took a bite of pizza but set it aside, too irritated by Snyder's cheery intrusion to eat. The irony of the scene struck me. When I pictured being alone with Snyder, a pizza between us, nowhere in that fantasy had I imagined being angry with him.

"I can't do this. Can't sit here and pretend things are okay. Not when there's a chance Donnie could go to prison and lose Emery." I rubbed my hands over my face, unable to look at Snyder.

"Let's not get ahead of ourselves." Snyder put his plate down, nudged closer to me. "The DA is considering all the circumstances, taking into account Donnie was a kid at the time, and the fact it was an accident." He gently took my hands from my face. "I think you're missing the bigger picture here." He smiled as our eyes met.

"What are you talking about?"

"Bill. All along, he's the fish I wanted to fry."

"But...he didn't kill Sloan."

Snyder's grin held. "Appears that way, from what Donnie said."

I paused as Snyder went back to his meal. "Is there something you're not telling me?"

He ignored my question, chewed greedily. Then, "Do you trust me, Delilah?"

That drilled into my chest. He was setting me up. But for what? And *did* I trust him? Besides the fact he was seeing my wayward aunt, I couldn't think of a reason not to trust him.

"There's two things I need." Snyder didn't wait for my answer. "Need a DNA swab from you."

"Without an explanation?"

"That's where the trust comes in."

"And the other thing?"

He turned to me. "A DNA swab from Wanda."

I knew what Snyder was up to. At least, I thought I did. He pulled out two boxes that looked similar to the DNA kits people can order online to learn about their ancestry. He opened one and gave me brief instructions on how to swipe the inside of my mouth, then seal the sample. I could show Wanda how to do it, he said. He put the kits on the kitchen counter and left soon after.

Although Snyder hadn't dropped specifics, I suspected he needed to construct a DNA profile for Sloan to compare against the skull. Without an actual sample from Sloan—a tissue, hair root, drop of blood—she could still be identified using mitochondrial DNA, the strain of genetics that's passed from a mother to her children. Mitochondrial DNA from Wanda, Sloan, and me would all match. Of course, thanks to Advanced Biology and Chemistry classes and shows like Forensic Files, I'd known that all along, including the day Snyder had shown me the picture of the skull. But so many earth-shifting things had happened in quick succession, I hadn't mentioned it. Obviously, I didn't need to.

According to Donnie, Sloan's body was dumped into the Fitzmiller sinkhole. The skull couldn't be Sloan's. But I told myself this was proof-positive of Snyder's dedication. He had to be thorough; he had to rule it out one way or the other. Like me, he had to stand at the edge of that sinkhole and see it for himself. He wanted to see if the pieces would fit.

I'd agreed to get Wanda's DNA. That meant telling her everything. Telling her that Donnie had knocked Sloan down the basement steps and was responsible for her death.

No way I could do it on my own.

Not long after Snyder left me with the pizza and the DNA test kits, Grandma made it home. I took the pizza to her place, which she seemed to appreciate. Exhausted from the overtime, she sank into her favorite chair in the living room. Princess piled onto her lap.

I got her a plate and heated up a slice. Even grabbed her a cold Dr. Pepper from the fridge. No judgments. Here I was, serving her the way Snyder had served me, but without the heavy dose of awkwardness. At least, that's what I wanted to believe. Yet here I was, full of secrets and slightly priming her for their revelation.

I glimpsed her hand, noticing the brown spots and wrinkles. There were the lines on her face, creased into her skin by time, stress, and tragedy. I considered those details that defined Wanda Baker: her life-long penchant for matching earrings and necklace; her devotion to White Diamonds perfume; her gold wedding band from Grandpa, which she probably couldn't remove because of her knuckles. The unmistakable aroma of her chocolate chip cookies. That sparkle and gusto in her eyes that embraced and endured what life had given her. I wondered what the truth about Sloan's death would do to her. What mark would it leave on her? Could she take it, hearing that her grandson had pushed her daughter down those basement stairs?

"Know what I was thinking of doing tomorrow?" Grandma chewed greedily.

"Planting something new in the garden?"

"No, but that's not a bad idea." Princess made a weak attempt at snatching Grandma's pizza and got a tap on her nose. "Thought I'd visit Grandpa. You're welcome to come with me, but I understand if you don't want to."

I thought back to when I was in the shed looking for the ropes and harness. Those vivid, tangible memories of Grandpa had surrounded me.

"Sure, I'll go. Would it be okay if Donnie came too?"

Her eyes widened, a surprised alertness replacing her weariness. "That would be nice."

Nice was probably the best word to use. I hadn't talked to Donnie about Grandma, about how we were going to tell her everything. But I thought he should be there. That he should be the one to unload the truth. Morbid as it sounded, maybe a cemetery was the best place for that to happen.

Weeping gray clouds blanketed the morning and set the appropriate tone for the day. I had called Donnie after leaving Grandma's last night, told him the potential plan for today. He didn't say much, other than agreeing that Grandma should hear the truth from him.

Part of me felt bad. Grandma was probably anticipating a pleasant family day. She was old school and thought trips to a gravesite were respectful visits, like checking in on a loved one in a nursing home. On Memorial Day she spent much of the weekend decorating the graves of long-dead relatives. Maybe for her it was a way of staying connected to her past.

I suddenly worried Donnie and I were doing the wrong thing, ambushing Grandma with a horrific revelation at a place she counted as sacred. This ran through my head as I walked to her back door, dodging raindrops as I went. I started to get cold feet about the whole thing and hoped the weather might change Grandma's mind. As I ducked into her kitchen, though, she was shrugging into her raincoat.

"Did you talk to Donnie? Is he coming?"

Her enthusiasm made me pause at first. "Yeah, he said he would meet us there." Doubts gnawed at me. Were we really going to do this to our grandmother? Was knowing the truth best, or should we let her live with whatever her mind had fabricated about Sloan's disappearance?

Grandma shared stories about odd customers she'd dealt with while I drove. Then she transitioned to a few favorite memories about Grandpa. Yes, I did remember when Grandpa caught that eighteen-pound largemouth bass and got his picture in the paper. And the time he played Santa for the VFW and got peed on. The laughs helped sooth my nerves. Until we pulled into the Angelic Arms Memorial Gardens.

Donnie was there waiting at Grandpa's site, flowers in hand. We traded hugs, each of us probably feeling the weight of the somber atmosphere. I had no way to convey my doubts to Donnie. Resignation took over inside me, since I couldn't think of a better alternative.

Grandma polished the granite headstone, its deep gray matching the looming clouds above. Donnie and I knelt beside her as she pulled weeds and chatted. I couldn't look at Donnie. The weightiness in my chest grew heavy, almost toppled me forward.

When Grandma finished, she popped to her feet. Donnie laid his flowers at the base of the stone while I ran my fingertips along and into the engraved letters of Grandpa's name. Two things ran through my head. I ached for Grandpa to still be here, fishing, following the Reds, tending the garden with Grandma, lying in bed next to her at night. Why couldn't they have grown old together, then drifted into that Heavenly sleep one night while holding hands? I wished she wasn't alone.

At the same time, I was grateful. Deeply grateful that Grandpa wouldn't have to hear what Sloan had gone through and what Donnie had done.

"Grandma, we've got something we need to tell you." Donnie's face was already scrunched with painful anticipation.

We went to a nearby stone bench and sat. Grandma in between us. I reached for her hand as Donnie unfolded the story. Grandma listened, gasped, squeezed Donnie's knee with her other hand, and went through an array of emotions. None of us paid any attention to the light rain that fell and mixed with our tears.

When Donnie finished, a deluge of apologies flowing from him, Grandma took him into her arms. By then, Donnie was half-crouched into a ball. Grandma pulled him to her chest, buried her face in the side of his neck. I gently leaned against Grandma's shoulder as heartbreak had its way with us.

"I knew she was dead," Grandma said, a weary sigh in her voice. "The day Bill dropped off that box did it for me. Knew right then he'd killed her. 'Course, couldn't ever prove anything. Just had to live with knowing she was gone. Always hurt that I couldn't lay her to rest. Never had a spot where I could come and sit and miss her. Put out flowers for her birthday and such."

Misery bore into my heart. Grandma would never have her daughter's body to bury. Bill had made sure of that. The three of us, sitting on that hard, stone bench, sharing our sorrow. That would be the closest we'd come to having a funeral for Sloan.

"I'm sorry, Grandma." It felt like Donnie had said it a thousand times.

Grandma cupped his face in her palms. "I know you didn't mean to hurt her, Donnie. It's a terrible thing that happened, but I still love you. Nothing's gonna change that. I'm sorry you've had to live with this pain all these years. I can't get over all the things Bill's done to you."

I thought about Snyder, how desperately he wanted to see Bill locked up for the rest of his life. I also thought of the skull. The picture Snyder showed me flashed through my mind.

"Another thing has come up, Grandma." I swallowed back the lump in my throat. "Lieutenant Snyder called me in to the station yesterday. It's a long story, but a skull was found. Snyder wants to have it tested for DNA. He...he wants to make sure it isn't Sloan."

She hesitated. "It couldn't be...because Donnie said—"

"You're right. That's what I told him, but it's his way of being thorough." I couldn't tell if I was making sense. Actually, nothing made sense anymore. "But to do that, he needs a swab of DNA from both of us." I briefly explained mitochondrial DNA and about the test kits Snyder had left with me. She agreed to do the swab.

"Does Snyder know about the accident?"

I chimed in. "We met with Snyder yesterday."

Grandma gripped Donnie's hand. "Will that mean…"

"We don't know what's going to happen yet. Donnie has to meet with the DA…see what charges they want to file."

"I'll help then, with the fees. Do whatever I can. Take a mortgage out on the house, if I need to."

We huddled together tightly, still perched on that bench, damp from the sprinkling rain. Maybe it should've been one of the worst moments of my life. It was. My micro-sized family, clenched to each other, ripe with worry, fearful of what lay ahead. For whatever reason, I had never felt such a bond of love, nourished by the strength we exuded. Bonded in love and mired in the loss of Sloan. I had never loved two people more. For whatever reason, that gave me an inexplicable hope, even though uncertainties loomed ahead.

CHAPTER TWENTY-TWO

Grandma wasn't a nap person but needed to lie down when we got home. I helped her settle in with a dose of Advil and Princess curled at her feet. Never had I seen my grandma so pale. Had we done the right thing by telling her the truth about Sloan?

Donnie left. Said he had to get ready for work. He looked bland, as though he had been scrubbed free of emotion. I hugged him around the neck before he went. It felt like there were a dozen things I wanted to say, but they were all stuck. Nothing that came to mind would make Donnie feel better. Me either.

I made myself a cup of tea and sat on Grandma's front porch. Memories of her and Grandpa watching me learn to jump rope surfaced. They took turns counting the number of skips I made as I sang *Down in the Valley*. A bricked flower bed lined the skirt of the porch and had once been my favorite spot to capture and play with caterpillars. The thought of touching bugs and having them creep along my skin gave me the willies now. Pink geraniums, blooming proudly and speckled from the rain, filled the dirt box now.

As I was half-tipped over the side of my chair, checking to make sure no creepy-crawlers were getting close, Glenn Rodgers pulled into the driveway. He was in his truck and towing his mower. I tensed at the sight of him, until I remembered that he took care of Grandma's yard. Stealing a quick glance at the lawn, I saw it needed tending.

I gripped my mug and forced a smile. "Hi, Glenn."

"Afternoon there, Delilah." With wet grass clippings stuck on his shoes and the ankle of his pants, he tipped his cap. "Didn't know if the rain was gonna let up."

"Guess you caught a break." Gray clouds hung heavy in the sky, made the day look moody and robbed of its summertime glory.

"Yeah, I reckon." Glenn put his hands in his pants pockets, scoped the yard. "She needs a-cuttin'."

The awkwardness between us felt as thick and muddled as the clouds. There hadn't been time to process and dwell upon what Glenn had done. I could still picture the Sally doll, her panties full of orange slices. And Glenn, standing by the tree while I slid into the sinkhole. Maybe it was best, not thinking about how Glenn had watched me, stalked me. Knew how to rattle me.

"About the other day and all—"

I held up a hand to stop him. "It's fine, Glenn, really."

He scrunched his face. "When we's over here, I didn't get to say the one thing on my mind."

My heart trembled. There was more? What else had this man done? I thought of Grandma resting inside. How I didn't want to burst into her house sobbing or yelling or whatever to escape Glenn. If it came to that.

"I followed you, that day when you went out to the Fitzmiller's place. Ain't been out there in, gosh, ages, I s'ppose. Anyhow, I was following you cause I wanted to know something." He shifted his gaze my way, stepped toward the porch. "I ain't never said nothing about it to no one, but you might be the only person who could help me. You see, I spent an awful lot of time with your mother. We's fond of each other for a while, and well, I don't know, but I was wondering if you knowed, if there was any chance you could be my...my daughter."

His words hung in the air. I thought my brain shut down.

"You think you're my father? My real, biological father?" I don't know where that came from. "What makes you think that?"

"Don't know." He flopped his arms forward, his hands still in his pockets. "Just one a-them things that always nagged at me."

I studied Glenn's face without looking like I was studying his face. Were there similarities between us? Physical traits we shared? What would it mean if he was truly my father? That I'd been raped and abused by my stepdad...while my real dad knew what was going on but played helpless? In my mind, that only heaped upon the damage done to me.

Did this explain why Glenn hung out on the peripheral edges of my childhood? Why he was still around, taking care of things for Grandma?

"I never heard or found anything that indicated..." I couldn't finish the sentence. Most everything I'd learned about Sloan had been in the last two weeks. Until I'd cradled that dusty box from the closest of the garage apartment, I didn't own anything belonging to Sloan. Didn't even have a picture of her. I also didn't come across anything suggesting Bill wasn't my father, but how did one really know?

"Well, I know a gal over at the clinic there in Kerton County. She told me all it'd take was a blood test and we'd find out. Don't have to go together or nothing like that neither."

I nodded slowly. Did this explain Glenn's odd behavior? Maybe some. Sitting in the folding chair with Glenn staring at me, I felt vulnerable. Rattled. Maybe more rattled than when I found the doll. Glenn had suggested that we might be related—and that the only family I'd known, might not be my family.

"I can give you the name and number and all." Glenn rubbed the back of his neck. "You...you think you'd go in?"

"It's the only way to know the truth."

Glenn shrugged. "If it's all right with you and all, I don't want no one else to know about it. Especially if it's true and all."

Funny, I had that same menacing feeling.

Glenn took to Grandma's yard, and I took off to Kerton County. Now was as good a time as any. Plus, I wanted to get it done. I peeked in on Grandma before leaving. She and Princess didn't stir, even when Glenn passed by outside on his mower.

At the clinic, I found Shirley, Glenn's cousin that he referred me to. Shirley didn't ask questions and was done taking my blood in about five minutes. Couldn't have asked for better, under the odd circumstances.

When I got back to Grandma's, Glenn was gone. The scent of fresh-cut grass lingered in the damp air. I was glad he wasn't around. Glancing at the pinprick in my arm, I hoped—hard, the way a kid pinches a penny and wishes before tossing it into a fountain—hoped he wouldn't prove to be my father.

In Grandma's kitchen, I found her zipping around like a fly. Loretta sang from the CD player and Princess barked her usual greeting. Grandma looked frazzled but focused as she assembled ingredients onto the table. I was worried a bad dream had startled her awake—or feared that Glenn had mentioned the paternity testing.

"I clean forgot about the spaghetti dinner at the firehouse tonight. I promised to bring two pies for the dessert auction."

"Can I help?"

"Sure you can. As long as you can still roll out a pie crust." She smiled and looked more like her usual self.

"It's been a while." I hadn't attempted to bake since I'd lived in Grandma's house. For one thing, it was no use. My creations never compared in taste or appearance to Grandma's pies. Once I got my life together and got into a seriously healthy lifestyle, well, pie was out.

Grandma and I worked side by side. I mirrored her actions, best I could, and she saved me when my technique showed its lack of finesse. We reminisced about when the fire fighters used to host Bingo on Friday nights. In the summertime, we walked over. Four of us, until it dwindled to three, because Donnie preferred being with his friends. Then came my issues. But we recalled the few times we won the pot, something like twenty-five dollars, and how Wilma Jennings seemed to win every week. Most of us were convinced she cheated, but nothing became of it. Bullfrogs and crickets often serenaded us as we briskly headed home, swatting off mosquitoes the whole way.

Grandma and I laughed light-heartedly and got the apple and peach pies ready for the oven. I figured it was best not to bring up Sloan and Donnie's admission about the accident. If Grandma wanted to talk about it, that was fine. I didn't know how Grandma dealt with her feelings. Donnie and I went to therapy after Bill's arrest. It lasted through the school year and proved helpful. Had we stayed in therapy, maybe our teen years would've been less volatile. But what did Grandma have to see her through? Grandpa had been her rock. I was a poor substitute for Grandpa, but I wanted to do what I could. I just didn't know what Grandma needed.

We both changed, and since Grandma didn't want to risk us tripping and dropping a pie, we drove to the fire station. The evening sun was warmer than it had been all day.

After greeting several fire fighters and volunteers, Grandma took off to help with set-up. I found a private spot and called Donnie.

"You doing okay?"

"Teaching Emery how to play Connect Four." He let her have the phone, after she pleaded to talk to Aunt DeDe. My heart soared. She told me how fun it was, beating Daddy at the new game. I heard the sound of the red and black chips falling, which made Emery giggle. She eventually gave the phone back to her dad. "How's Grandma doing?"

I told him about the pies and our plans for the evening.

"I wasn't sure if…she wanted me to call."

"She seems okay. Maybe a little distant."

"It's a lot to take in."

Donnie was right. Not only had Grandma learned the truth about her missing daughter, but she'd also learned her grandson was responsible. Then there was the issue of the skull and comparing the DNA. Was it too much? I wondered if Grandma was in a state of emotional shock. Unable to process it all, she decided to keep busy, focus on the here and now.

"Did we do the right thing, Donnie?" I hated asking with Emery there.

He hesitated. "There wasn't much choice. It's all gonna come out."

When he said it, I felt like someone reached inside my chest and squeezed my heart. Soon, Venice would be buzzing with the news about Sloan. Rumors would no longer tell her tale. The truth and closure would prevail, but my brother was bound to pay the price by losing his freedom.

Had circumstances been different, I would've teased Grandma about the two gentlemen vying for her attention at the spaghetti dinner. As it was, she seemed oblivious to their flirting, which fed my suspicion she was on autopilot. After the spaghetti dinner and Bingo wrapped up, Grandma was eager to get home.

I worried about her as we parted ways for the night and wondered if I should stay in the house.

"Grandma, are you feeling okay? Is there anything I can do?" I wrung my hands and hated feeling helpless.

"No, doll, I'm fine. Just ready to hit the bed."

"I'm sorry about today and everything. We can talk about it if you want to. I was confused and upset when he told me..." I shut my rambling mouth.

Suddenly, Grandma lit up. "Why, I didn't even think about that. Bet that was terrible, hearing what your mom went through." She pulled me in for an embrace. "It's hard...knowing, and after all these years. Guess you got what you came for, Delilah."

Her words hit me like a hot poker. Not that she sounded accusatory, but there was a painful truth in what she said.

"I didn't mean for Donnie's life to be ruined."

"Of course not! We've got to hope and pray it doesn't come to that. There's been enough tragedy for this family."

I held her tighter. "I hope so, Grandma." Not for a second did I put any trust into those words.

We went through the next couple days in a fog. Our gusto for life muted. A break in the catatonic haze came when Donnie and I took Emery to the Cincinnati Zoo. Emery's delight over Fiona, the baby hippo, proved contagious. The warmth and glory of the summer sun perpetuated the belief that everything would be all right. Even though we knew Donnie's meeting with the DA was imminent.

Back in my apartment, after spending most of the day at the zoo, I stretched out on the bed. Sleep was on the verge of taking me away when my phone vibrated. A text from Britney, asking if I wanted to meet for dinner. Part of me groaned. Had the rumor mill reached Britney? Was the invite a ruse to talk about what she'd heard? Or were her intentions pure, and I was simply a jerk for thinking the worst?

Only one way to find out.

We met up later that evening.

"You look frazzled," I said to Britney, after we were seated. It was a departure from my usual conversation starters, but I wasn't used to seeing her with her hair up and minimal make-up.

"I'm so stressed. You have no idea. Everything is so weird right now, I don't even know. My mom is making Bill stay at the trailer with Milt. She's looking after both of them and said that way it was easier on her. But she has me stopping over there all the time. She doesn't want them to be alone too much."

"Poor Milt." In his already frail condition, Milt was probably miserable sharing his home again with Bill.

"No kidding. I told her it was a dumb idea, especially since she thinks Bill was the one who mixed up Grampy's meds."

"Really? Like Bill did it on purpose?"

"Yeah." She rolled her eyes at me, as if that fact wasn't obvious. "At first she thought maybe it was you, since you were there the day Grampy got sick, but she said you probably weren't smart enough to know how to mix up the medicines."

A little jab I probably deserved. Had I paid better attention, I would've noticed the switch.

Britney took a shot of her drink. "Mom didn't tell Grampy that she suspects Bill. It's already been hard on Grampy, since he's so afraid of Bill."

I didn't understand Tonya's logic. Why would she put Bill and Milt together like that, knowing it would stress Milt? If Bill had rearranged the pills, was he trying to kill Milt and make it look like an accidental overdose? Like Milt had confused the pills? If that were true, Bill had added attempted murderer to his lengthy list of poor qualities.

Surely, Tonya had shared her suspicions with Snyder. I wasn't going to risk another snide comment from Britney by asking.

"Did your mom switch the deed to Bill's name?"

Britney shook her head. "She's not that stupid. Bill keeps asking her about it, but she keeps telling him she's been too busy. She's been acting super weird since Bill got released. It's like she's waiting on something to happen. Things are just a mess right now."

I thought about the messes in my own life. All the things I was worried about and thought Britney had heard about, she didn't have a clue. The truth about Sloan. Bill extorting money from Donnie. The paternity test.

The paternity test. I'd put it out of my mind for a while, focusing on Grandma and Donnie instead. As I sat there with Britney, it occurred to me that she might not be my cousin after all. If the test proved Glenn was my biological father, then I wouldn't be related to Grampy or Tonya either. It felt strange even considering it. Sure, they weren't much of a family, but the thought of having that dysfunctional clan taken from my family tree felt odd. Sad even. How would Britney feel about me, if we weren't related?

Britney shifted gears and didn't notice I was lost in thought. She talked about her salon and the latest in hand-tied hair extensions. I let her ramble, nodded when needed, and eased her off having a third drink. I was glad she didn't meet Jason.

Back at Grandma's house, later that evening, I thought about going in and checking on her but didn't. That's the thing about not being there for people or running out on them when times are tough—they learn not to need you. Then, when times are tough again, they don't know how to need you, how to lean on you.

I texted Grandma from the garage apartment, letting her know I was home safe. She sent back *Goodnight* with an emoji blowing a kiss.

She didn't need me.

After my early morning kickboxing class, and mandatory shower, I took breakfast to Donnie's apartment. I liked popping in on him, and quietly making sure he was sticking to his promise of not drinking.

"Can't you call or something first?"

"And spoil the surprise?"

I unpacked the small breakfast bounty, complete with coffee for Donnie, tea for me. Donnie slumped on his stool and rubbed the sleep from his eyes. Today, he included an audible yawn.

"I meet with the DA later today."

"Why didn't you tell me?"

"Yeah, I just got the call a little while ago. Can you still come along?"

I nodded and nervously chewed a mouthful of food before asking, "Have you told Monica about any of this yet?"

Donnie sighed. "No. I wanted to wait as long as possible...see how this goes."

See if I'm going to prison soon was what he didn't say. I couldn't imagine how wrecked he was feeling.

Just like last night when I was with Britney, my mind detoured to the paternity test again. *Donnie!* Was he only my half-brother? A rush of anger shot through me. Of all things on this earth, I wanted Donnie to be my brother, to be all mine. He was the only one who knew what I'd been through. Who survived being in that house with me. Who knew Sloan the way I did. I'd never forgive Glenn if that test showed I was his daughter.

But did such a thing matter at this point in our lives? Maybe it would to Donnie. He was the one who had endured more physical and mental abuse from Bill, had still been suffering, thanks to the extortion. If Bill wasn't my father, would that widen the divide between us?

That was it. No way I would mention the paternity test to Donnie.

"What's up with you?"

Donnie must have read the distress on my face.

"Just...wish all this could be over." All of it. The doubts. The knowing. The not knowing. I wanted to crumple all of it into a ball and hurl it into space. But Grandma was wrong when she said I got what I came for, because I was on the verge of possibly losing what little I thought I had.

"One way or another, little sister, it's going to be."

CHAPTER TWENTY-THREE

District Attorney Kristen Stafford proved to be amiable, professional, and much younger than I expected. She didn't treat Donnie as though she was put off by him, disgusted by what he had done. While she was straightforward and focused, she also came across as friendly. Caring even. Call me crazy, but if Donnie had met Kristen under different circumstances, I think he would've asked her out. It was awkward, sitting there as Donnie retold the tragic tale of Sloan's final moments—which I now knew by heart—and picturing the two of them in a more romantic setting. I snapped myself out of it.

Kristen was attentive and sensitive toward both of us. She was also tight-lipped on what we should expect, stating, "We want to have all the facts, every detail we can before making the next step." She left us in the dark about what that step would be, but said she'd be in touch.

Afterward, we picked up Emery from Monica's. Emery was probably a baby the last time I'd seen Monica. Even so, she was pleasant and seemed happy that we had a brief chance to talk. I had always liked her and remembered being mad at Donnie for ruining their relationship with his drinking. Despite those hard times, Monica wasn't a woman who held grudges or became infected with bitterness. That elevated my admiration for her, and I was thankful she was such a good mom to Emery. Naturally, all this zipped through my mind—

along with the meeting at the prosecutor's office—as we stood chatting outside Monica's apartment.

Emery grew restless among the adults and started moaning about being hungry. We made a polite getaway and headed to McDonald's.

"My favorite! I want chocolate milk!" She downed her chocolate milk and took bites of her apple slices and cheeseburger.

My stomach was still too roiled from earlier. Not that there was a chance of me eating at McDonald's anyway.

Donnie and I talked about Grandma while Emery climbed through the playscape. I told him Grandma seemed fine, that she hadn't mentioned our morning at the cemetery.

"She probably doesn't want me around."

Hearing Donnie say that felt like a knee thrust to my stomach. I couldn't argue. Not really. Grandma had kept her emotions to herself. Maybe she was upset with Donnie. Or maybe the blame she carried, thinking she could've done something to save Sloan, had only deepened.

"She's still processing. On one hand, she knows Sloan didn't run away and leave her children. But knowing what really happened can't be easy either."

Emery came bouncing back to our table. She told us she made a friend on the playscape. Donnie encouraged a few more bites of her apples.

"Daddy, you know what I want for Christmas?" Emery's eyes lit up.

"What, sweetie?"

"I want a doll! The kind that looks like me."

Donnie knew which one she was talking about; I didn't but liked hearing them talk about the features it would have. My chest tightened though. What if there were no more Christmas mornings for Donnie and Emery? Christmas was a little over five months away. By

n, Donnie's freedom could be long gone. So could his time with
ery. I squinted my eyes shut for a second to chase the thought
y.

♦ ♦ ♦

/lcDonald's, Donnie took Emery home to his apartment. I figured
eeded daddy-daughter time. We talked about getting together
ier, but Donnie had to check on the restaurant first.
I felt restless. Being alone with my thoughts probably wasn't
t idea. Sitting and baking inside the garage apartment didn't
ppealing, so I went to the car wash. It was needed anyway.
ıss, and rocks still littered my floorboards from my sinkhole
ə.
s I worked hard to get the vacuum into the crevices, I ran
ıe meeting with the DA. Every time Donnie relived the tale,
əd over me when he talked about being in the workspace
ˉhat's where Donnie saw Sloan rolled in the blankets, her
ıg out. Why had Bill bothered to cover Sloan up like that?
care about her, and probably didn't care about Donnie
ın's dead, cold face again. So why wrap her in blankets?
ade me wonder if the workspace should be searched. The
ding anything were probably as good as they were with
the sinkhole—slim to none. But that didn't settle my
ıanted to get in there and look around.
ıldn't show up at Milt's, though, and freely search the
Not if Bill was parked in the trailer, next to his father,
ı his stab wound. Tonya might also be around to chase

the car wash and went for a drive. It had been years since
rough the beautiful hillside. With the windows down, I

235

welcomed the aroma of the woods and breathed it in deeply. Few things could refresh my soul like the raw forestry of Kentucky. The only thing that could enhance the perfect sunlight spilling through the Kelly-green foliage would be a sip of freshly distilled moonshine. Not that I'd had any since I was a teen. Instead of a still site, I came across a roadside food stand. Always a sucker for corn and watermelon, I was chatting with the farmers and paying for my bounty when Grandma called.

"Delilah, honey, can you get home?"

"Yeah. Are you all right?"

"Everything's fine, but I need you to come home."

When I got to Grandma's, already jacked up on anxiety from her call my adrenalin kicked up another notch. A Campbell County Sheriff' cruiser sat in the driveway. So did Donnie's car. Bursting into th kitchen, I found Grandma, Donnie, and Snyder standing around.

"What's going on?" I couldn't read any of their faces.

"Delilah, I asked Wanda to give you a call, because I thought was important for all of you to be here together for the news." Snyd came to me and gently touched my shoulder.

"News?"

He held a folder and removed a sheet of paper. "Results car back for the DNA tests. The one you and Wanda submitted sampl for."

"For the skull?"

Snyder nodded, then looked at each of us. "We got a mat The skull. It belongs to Sloan Ramsey."

I looked to Donnie. Skeptical disbelief marked our faces.

"But...that can't be." I felt like my body had been infused with pop-rocks. Every part of my skin pinged and sparked. "Donnie helped pushed the car...with her body."

"Yeah." Snyder pulled out chairs from the table. Grandma and I sat. "There's something I didn't tell you about the skull. When Sergeant Sands called me from Rockport, she said the skull had a bullet hole in the back. Looked like a .22 caliber."

"Wait." Donnie held up his hands as if the information was coming at him too fast. "You're saying there's proof that a skull that washed up in the Ohio River is my mom—and that she was shot in the back of the head?"

Snyder nodded again. "Delilah told me about the conversation between Bill and Milt. The one where Bill said he got rid of Sloan. Sunk 'em, teeth and all. Those words rolled through my head when Sergeant Sands described what she had. A skull, found by the river with no teeth. In fact, the teeth were missing because each one had been pulled out. She also mentioned the bullet wound. I figured Bill had shot Sloan, removed her teeth, thinking she couldn't be identified, and put her body in the river."

Grandma, Donnie, and I traded stares but said nothing.

"When I told Delilah about the skull," Snyder continued, "showed her the picture I had, she didn't seem too moved. Didn't get upset or have much of a reaction. I couldn't figure out why. Then the two of you show up at the station, and I get the story about the accident with Sloan. What complicates it for me is the fact that you saw Sloan's body," he said to Donnie, "helped Bill put it in the trunk of the car, shoved it into the sinkhole. Right?"

Donnie nodded.

"So it's gone. There's no chance of finding that car or Sloan. But here's the thing. Since the skull was found and turned out to be Sloan, there's only one explanation that I can think of." Snyder cleared his throat and looked as though he didn't want to say what he was about to say. "Bill must have cut off her head."

The air left the room. Time stood still. I don't know how long it took the three of us to absorb what Mark Snyder had said.

"Hear me out."

Our shell-shocked faces focused on him.

"I been thinking hard on this, and I need y'all to stay with me. I've got this theory about what must have happened. Donnie was upset with his mother. Had a burst of anger and pushed Sloan down the stairs…

CHAPTER TWENTY-FOUR

Bill

Venice, Kentucky

Summer 2001

B ill couldn't believe his stupid good luck. All that time and effort he'd spent, working to get rid of Sloan, and here his kid went and did it for him. So it seemed.

He knew he had to get Donnie out of there quick. Sent him to his room. Bill chuckled to himself, recalling how the kid blazed a trail out of that basement. Old wooden steps be damned.

Sloan still had a pulse when he checked on her. She wasn't dead. Least not yet. Bill figured the fall busted her up good. A solid smack to the head like that was sure to cause internal bleeding. A few minutes, maybe an hour, she'd be dead. He just had to wait it out.

But that meant he had a body to get rid of. Wasn't the way he planned it. No, he was expecting to find her dead in bed one morning, call the authorities and have them haul her away. Whole thing would look like an accident—or maybe like Sloan had committed suicide with the pills. He'd get off scot-free, move Rita right in.

He looked down at Sloan now. Disdain filling his veins. The nerve of that crazy-headed woman, stepping out on him with that loser Glenn. Bill regretted not thinking of a way to make him pay too.

Important thing now was dumping the body.

First thing he did was call Rita from the phone in the kitchen. Made sure she didn't come over. Told her he'd had a fight with Sloan. It was best she stayed away for a bit. Rita didn't ask questions.

He snagged a beer from the fridge and took a long pull. He sat at the table. His head already buzzed from the drinks he'd had earlier. Needed to think. Best thing to do, he figured, was to dump her into the river. Water made the best grave. But then he thought of movies and TV shows where the body came floating to the surface, even though it was weighted down. He couldn't risk it.

But he needed rid of his dead wife. Where then?

Agitated when nothing came to mind, Bill made his way to his bedroom. Doors to the kids' rooms were shut. Bill was noisy, a sure-fire way to make those kids hunker down, fear he was coming for them. He liked the idea of Donnie and Delilah scared. Best way for a man to run his house. Took what he wanted, when he wanted it; answered to no one.

In his bedroom, he took his gun from the top shelf of the closet. Wasn't his really. Milt had given it to him a while back, and it was still registered in Milt's name. Bill figured that was a good thing.

He made sure it was loaded, but his eyes didn't want to focus. Too much alcohol slushed through him. He went back to the kitchen, plopped down at the table again. The belch he exhaled brought no relief. He leaned forward, rested his head on the table. Never intended to doze off.

Bill heard something. Thought he did anyway. He fought through the fog of drunken sleep and raised his pounding head. It took several minutes for him to remember what had happened. Sloan's fall. Telling

Donnie she was dead. Getting the gun, jamming it into the waistband of his jeans. The beers. All the beers.

He rubbed his face. Wished his head was clearer. The window above the kitchen sink told him that evening had moved in. He didn't know how long he'd been out but figured a couple hours. His stomach hurt from the gun wedged between his gut and his jeans.

The noise again. A shuffling sound and a moan. It came from the basement. Bill noticed the door to downstairs had been left open. Stupid on his part. He wondered if the kids had come out of their rooms and snooped around.

Just as he stood, he turned and saw Sloan standing at the top of the stairs. Dried blood streaked part of her forehead and face.

"What did you do to me?" Her voice came out as a whisper. She blinked heavily, looked as if she had as much to drink as Bill.

"I ain't done nothing to you. Stupid woman. Don't know what I ever saw in you."

"Where's the children?" Sloan braced herself against the edge of the kitchen counter, held a hand against her head.

"What do you care? All you do is run around with Glenn. You ain't no fit mother."

"Taking my children away from you." She closed her eyes as she ran a hand over the side of her face that wasn't lined with blood.

"You ain't taking nothing out of this house, you whore. I'm through with you. Go tailin' after Glenn. Bet he won't take you in."

"Donnie!" Her voice was dry, ragged.

"Hush your mouth! He ain't coming to you. I told you to get out." Bill turned her toward the back door, gave her a shove.

"Not leaving my children."

"Yeah, you are." Bill pulled the gun from his jeans, held it upward.

Sloan backed into the door.

"Start walkin', woman."

Sloan fumbled with the knob until it gave. She stepped outside. "Gonna call the police…get my family."

Bill went to the open door and stood at the threshold.

"Never letting you near them again." Sloan spat the words at Bill, turned her back on him.

Bill grinned, whispered to himself. "That's what you think."

He squeezed the trigger.

Sloan collapsed to the ground.

"Dead now. Serves you right!"

Bill dragged Sloan's body to her car, then dropped her into the trunk. He looked around furiously, checked the windows of the house for curious eyes. Milt and Ginny probably heard the shot. Not unusual for the area. Their house sat too far off for them to see anything.

He checked his hands, which were dirty now. The front of his shirt was smeared with blood. Had even dripped onto the back of the car.

Won't matter, he told himself.

Bill had to admit, he was worried for a minute. Seeing Sloan come up those stairs after thinking she was dead. He'd never forget that rush of shock. That look on her bloodied face. He knew right then she was serious about leaving him. For good.

He couldn't let that happen. Wasn't that he cared much about the marriage. Or the kids. But no woman—no cheating woman—was going to walk out on him.

But he loved Sloan. Ever since that first time he saw her outside the Marathon station. Flashing hazel eyes at him. Smiling behind the straw of her Slurpee. All he could think about was sucking the cherry stain off her lips. She was barely sixteen, wasn't nothing like the women he'd been with. Found out later a lot of that had to do with her mental issues. Didn't seem like a big deal. He made sure she got pregnant, making it easy for them to get married right off. Bill had her all to himself. The good feelings wore away after a few years. Constant money problems, stress of another baby, Sloan needing monitored by a doctor, medications. It added up to plenty of misery.

Bill couldn't think about that now. He had to get busy. Had things to do. For one, he had to make sure that face of hers would never be recognized again.

Bill's family had always hunted. Always had a growing collection of knives. So picking out one that could cut through flesh and remove Sloan's head from her body wasn't a problem. He knew he was doing it for spite, but he wanted her to know, even in death, even as she rotted in two graves—in pieces—how much he hated her.

She shamed him, carrying on with Glenn. And when that wasn't going on, she was acting like a lunatic with all the imaginary stuff she saw. Everyone in Venice talked about Sloan Ramsey. The way she wasn't right in the head. The way she made love with Glenn Rodgers in Bill's house. Bill boiled, just thinking about it. Made plucking and yanking out all those teeth easy. Gave him a means to work out his wrath, cussing at her, calling her names as he went.

When he was finished, his shirt was soaked a dark maroon. He took it off, tossed it over Sloan's gaping, toothless face.

Bill had made more work for himself, doing it this way, but he didn't care. He had to get his revenge for what she'd done. No one would ever see it or know what he'd done to her. But he would.

At the same time, Bill had to keep up the ruse that Donnie had been responsible for Sloan's death. Had to play up the part that a nine-year-old had pushed his mommy to her death. Had to root it into his mind. Best way to do that, Bill figured, was to make sure Donnie saw the body. Part of it anyway.

He put those frayed, scratchy blankets in the car and drove over to his workspace. Milt and Ginny, from what Bill could tell, were sound asleep. Not much could rattle those two awake, from his experience. He laid the blankets on the dirt floor of the workspace, then placed Sloan's headless body near an edge and rolled her like one of them God-awful sushi rolls he'd seen at the store. When it was done, he looked it over, extra satisfied her feet were poking out of one end. He smiled and patted the blankets.

"You wait here, baby. 'Bout time for me to get your little boy."

Bill found Delilah sleeping beside Donnie's closed bedroom door. He wondered what it meant but didn't care enough to linger. After he put her in her own bed, Bill found Donnie asleep on his bedroom floor. He tapped him awake with his foot, and said, "Better get up, boy. We got work to do."

CHAPTER TWENTY-FIVE

When Mark Snyder finished sharing his theory, disbelief marred our faces. His scenario played through my mind. I could see it. All of those terrible details. It made sense, and it took my breath away.

"You think that's what happened?" The words were dry in my mouth. "That the fall didn't kill Sloan?"

"Exactly." Snyder wore an earnest expression. "Your mother was unconscious. Probably could've died, but the impact wasn't severe enough. Bill didn't know that till she woke up.

"Think about Donnie's story. There are scraps and pieces that don't make sense." He looked to Donnie. "You said you heard voices, like two people having an argument. If Sloan came out of the basement and surprised Bill, there would've been a confrontation. Some yelling, accusations getting thrown around. That would account for the arguing you heard. Then there's the gun. You mentioned a firecracker noise, which was probably Bill taking that fatal shot. Sloan was trying to get away from him, maybe get help, Bill shot her from behind. That gives us the skull with the bullet hole in the back of her head. It's a small caliber. So when you looked out your window and you saw her face up on the ground, you couldn't see the bullet hole."

We each squirmed. Thinking of what Sloan's last moments were like probably disturbed us all.

"Yeah." Donnie paired it with a nod.

"Bill did all he could to make you believe Sloan's death was your fault, your doing," Snyder continued. "You were a kid. He could make you believe whatever he told you. And he knew he could hold it over you, use it against you, which he did for fifteen years."

"But why would he..." My hands went to the base of my neck. I couldn't finish the thought. Couldn't shut out the images of Bill sawing, cutting, tearing through my mother's flesh.

"Because he's pure evil." Snyder seemed to realize his tone was too gruff and exhaled. "The truth is, we probably won't know everything that happened that night. Only if Bill provides a full confession, and I don't expect that to happen." He put a firm hand on Donnie's shoulder. "Right now, the important thing to know is that we've got a skull with a DNA match and a bullet hole. That proves you didn't kill your mother."

I didn't hate Bill Ramsey for raping me and stealing my innocence and wrecking my childhood; I hated him for what he had put my brother through his entire life. I'd been lucky in comparison, worked through a lot of my issues, especially in recent years with Dr. Cohen. Donnie had carried the blame of Sloan's death since he was little, coupled with Bill's physical abuse and threats of exposing him as Sloan's killer. No doubt, Donnie would need time for the truth of Sloan's demise to sink it. For those shackles of guilt to disintegrate. For the new reality to take hold—that he didn't kill our mother.

As he sat at Grandma's kitchen table, Donnie had trouble breathing. Grandma consoled him. I felt on the periphery, for some reason, like I belonged on the outside. Maybe I did. More consequence of having separated myself from my family for so long.

Snyder made ready to leave and said we would hear from the DA soon. He wanted assurances that we were all okay. Looking at my brother and grandma, both haggard and ashen with grief, I nodded for all of us.

"I'll walk you out." I needed out of that room, and I was convinced Grandma and Donnie needed a minute alone.

Stepping into the sunshine was equally glorious and awful. How could the sun show off its radiance on such a day? Then again, what else could ease the burden of sadness, make my shoulders feel a little less heavy?

"Why didn't you tell me about the skull having a bullet hole?" It nagged at me, hearing Snyder share information he hadn't told me first.

"It's my job to protect the investigation."

"What else are you holding back?"

"No need to have that tone with me, young lady."

He was right, but I didn't like being scolded. For some reason, it reminded me of the age gap between us. It also reminded me of the drawn lines separating us: Snyder was a cop with a duty; I was a girl with a dead mother and abusive father. In his eyes, I was probably nothing more than damaged goods. He had the satisfaction of solving a cold case, which made me feel a bit used.

"But you're right." Snyder sighed, as though he had held it in the whole time we were in Grandma's kitchen. "There is something I haven't mentioned. Not sure it affects you, but maybe you should know. Tonya and I made a clean break of things."

Heat tinted my cheeks, and I looked away as I asked, "Meaning what exactly?"

"I moved back into my place, and we both decided it wasn't working out anymore. Truth is, my boys never got along with her, and I think I spent too much time overlooking things that bothered me. When Bill came back to town, that was the beginning of the end for me. Watching her support him, stand by him, none of that sat right with me."

"Sorry to hear that." I wasn't but it was the right thing to say. "Must be hard on you."

"Nah. We were convenient for each other, and that was about it. Wasn't meant to last. Not forever."

Is that what you're looking for, Mark? Someone to share forever with? I couldn't say it, obviously.

"I should probably get back to my family."

Snyder nodded. "Don't worry, Delilah. I'm doing everything I can to bring closure on this case. You just gotta keep trusting me."

Walking back into Grandma's was hard. I knew I'd be interrupting her and Donnie. It made sense that the two of them shared a closer bond. Donnie had never left Venice. He'd been there for the anniversary of Sloan's disappearance, every time her birthday came around, and when the letters came from the parole board, warning of Bill's release.

But I wondered how Donnie's guilt had injured their relationship. Were there times when Donnie skipped out on Thanksgiving because he was too wrecked, thinking about what he'd done to Sloan? Times when a phone call from Bill had made Donnie's emotions bare and raw? Had Donnie retreated from Grandma and whittled down their interactions?

When I walked back inside, they broke from their embrace. Tears were fresh on their faces. I ignored my feelings of raging inadequacies. It was better to focus on how good they both must have felt, having a better grasp of the truth.

They stood and reached for me. We huddled together. Apologies poured from me. I was sorry for leaving them, for not being there when Grandpa died, for the fact they had been forced to deal with so much, that I hadn't been there to lean on. They poured their love and forgiveness on me. Our cheeks pressed against one another's. Our tears dripped and ran together.

I didn't think it was possible, but finding out the truth about Sloan's death had brought the broken pieces of my family together. Exposing our weaknesses—Donnie's vulnerability to Bill, my constant running away, Grandma feeling helpless—was exactly what we needed to destroy those strongholds in our lives. Maybe it sounded cheesy, or like therapist-speak—but I was proud of us. And hopeful about the family we could become.

Life has a way of getting in the way. Donnie's phone rang. The assistant manager was calling from the restaurant, asking him to come in earlier for the evening shift. Donnie said he'd be there. I wasn't sure how he had the frame of mind to go to work after the cascade of emotions, but maybe work was a good thing. Maybe we needed those normal functions to help balance the crushing sadness.

Donnie had to go. I headed back to the apartment to clean myself up and check on Oscar. I texted Grandma that I would pick up something for dinner, after my face recovered. She appreciated the gesture.

I hunched over my bathroom sink and splashed about a gallon of cold water over myself, then I stretched out on my bed. Oscar joined me, pawed my stomach.

So many thoughts were steaming through my head. I wondered what else Snyder knew that he wasn't telling me. A sting of resentment throbbed inside, hearing his words echo in my brain: *It's my job to protect the investigation.* I was a means to an end, and my complicated feelings for him felt misplaced.

Jason also occupied my mind. I owed him a long phone call but shoved that aside, not wanting to replay and rehash the emotions. Part of me didn't feel like talking to him, which sounded callous but wasn't. I just wanted more time.

Letting Snyder and Jason go, my brain switched gears again. I lied there, staring up at the yellowing popcorn ceiling, and crafted a contrary stunt. My lips ticked into a grin, appreciating my brilliance. I checked my phone for the time and convinced myself I could pick up dinner for me and Grandma, and easily execute my plan.

With an armload of groceries, I tapped on the trailer door before letting myself in. Bill was on the couch with his feet propped up. His eyes popped open wide and his jaw fell a little when he saw me. Milt seemed to be napping in his chair, the dogs at his side.

"Well, if it ain't my girl. Come to check on your daddy."

His dramatic tone fell flat for me. The menacing schtick he oozed wouldn't work on me anymore. But I had to admit, seeing him shirtless gave me pause. My mind darted back to those warm nights, his sweaty skin against mine, and how I held my breath as long as I could, hating the ripe smell of him.

He sat there now with a well-fed gut and graying chest hairs. His stitched stab wound was bare, puffy, looked glossy, as if slathered with ointment. And pink. The color reminded me of a tube of lipstick I had when I was little. Came with one of those kiddie make-up kits that weren't really make-up. More like clown-face paints. And to me, Bill's remark was childish and clownish at best.

"You'd like to think that." I rolled my eyes at him—and hoped he didn't notice my tightened hold on the bag of groceries. I kept moving toward the kitchen. Milt didn't stir as I walked by, making me think his nap was medicine-induced. His chest rose and fell in a steady rhythm, an assurance he was okay. The dogs perked up and watched me but had no interest in leaving Milt. Quietly and quickly, I tucked away the groceries. Bill grunted and edged his way off the couch, then joined me.

He peeked inside the last bag. "Slim Jims?"

"They're Milt's favorite." I skipped on buying beer and went for vitamin water instead. Who knew if Tonya would let him have it, or if he would even drink it. Worth a try though.

Bill puffed out his saggy pecs and ran a hand down his chest. The cowlicks on the back of his head suggested he had spent plenty of time on that couch. The funky body odor he gave off crawled up my nose. I didn't let a reaction slip on my face, because that's where Bill found his satisfaction, in repulsing others.

"I wanted to make sure Milt was okay. Can't imagine you're easy to put up with."

Bill glanced back at Milt, who still hadn't moved. "He ain't got a thing to complain about."

"Just forced to play roommates with a killer."

Bill squinted an eye and looked caught between being amused and uncertain. He took one of the Slim Jims and tore off the wrapper with his teeth. "What's that supposed to mean?"

I crossed my arms over my stiff chest. "I know what really happened to Sloan, and after all these years, it's finally going to come out—and I'm going to enjoy watching you go to prison for the rest of your miserable life."

He chewed his bite while eyeing me and waited a beat before he spoke. "You taking after your mother now, imagining things? Guess that was bound to catch up with you."

I wanted to throw the evidence in his face—the skull, the DNA match, the bullet hole—how it pieced together what he had done to

Sloan. How it proved Donnie was innocent—and now forever free of Bill's manipulation.

But I kept it together, answered Bill with only a smile. A big, knowing grin. His days as a free man were numbered. I liked knowing something he didn't. I could already picture his face as Snyder showed up and slapped handcuffs on him once again. It wouldn't be like last time, when I was little. Clinging to the door frame, quivering with fear as tears spilled onto my Powerpuff Girls shirt, with Bill getting the last word. *Daddy's gonna be back for his pretty girl.*

Bill would be blindsided when he heard that part of Sloan had been found—the only part he hadn't shoved into the sinkhole. His need to tear her apart would be his undoing, and I couldn't wait.

I leveled a stare at him. "There's nothing you can say or do to hurt me anymore."

His creepy yellowed grin appeared. "Oh, sweet girl, that's what you think."

I left Milt's, trying not to let Bill's words get under my skin. Who was I kidding? Everything about Bill got under my skin. Standing in Milt's cramped kitchen and giving Bill a hint of his impending doom was premature. I didn't know when he would be arrested, or how the DA would move forward, but I had to get in that jab before the news was released. I'd cherish that look of cluelessness on his face.

As I slid inside my car and got out of there, a feeling of regret pinched me. Because I wondered if I had provoked Bill. Were the wheels turning in his head now? Was he cooking up a way to get back at me or Donnie? What if he found a way to kidnap me and throw me—and Donnie—into the sinkhole?

"Stop." I thumped my head against the back of my seat.

I wasn't a child anymore. There was no need to run away with paranoid thoughts. Bill no longer had strength and force on his side. He barely made it off the couch. Being afraid of him was ridiculous, made no logical sense.

"He can't hurt me." I needed to hear myself say it. I repeated it, screamed it inside my car, and ignored the shivers streaming down my back.

When I got back to Grandma's, with Chinese take-out per her request, I didn't mention my pit stop at Milt's. Donnie had checked on both of us via text. I liked that, and I liked how Grandma seemed lighter than she had in days, twirling in the kitchen with Princess at her heels as she joined Loretta on *You're Lookin' at Country*.

After we ate and cleaned up the kitchen, Grandma wanted to sit on the porch. Twilight was settling in and the folding patio chairs we eased into gave a strained squeak as we sat. Grandma lit into a cigarette while Princess helped herself to Grandma's lap.

"We should have a memorial for Sloan," she said. "Now that we know everything, and we have something of her." She paused a moment, swallowed hard. "Just something small for the family."

"I think that would be nice."

Sloan's remains deserved a proper burial. When the time was right, I hoped the local newspaper would do a feature story. The people of Venice should know what Bill had done—and that Sloan Ramsey had not abandoned her children. Weeks ago, I couldn't have dreamed of such an outcome. Now, emotional healing and closure felt within reach. Was a degree of peace on the horizon for my family?

The next morning, after hitting the gym hard, a pang of guilt hit hard too. I still had to call Jason. He had sent various messages, checking in. I hadn't much effort or information into my replies. But with the clean-slate feel of a new day, along with the germination of optimism about my family relations, my resolve to call him became steadfast.

Until I checked my phone. It showed that I had missed a call and received a voicemail from an unknown number. When I played the message, my heart sank a little.

Um, hello. Delilah. This here's Glenn Rodgers. I's wondering if you could stop out at the house here today. I got them results back, and well, thought the best thing would be to read it together. It's sealed up and everything, and I didn't want to open it till you could be here too. Gimme a holler. Thank you.

Dread socked my stomach. I wasn't crazy about the idea of going to Glenn's house. Maybe it was the thought of being alone with him. No one there to buffer. But I didn't have a choice.

I hadn't devoted much thought to being Glenn's daughter. If he was in fact my biological father, it didn't make Bill any less of a monster. Nothing about my past changed. It only meant that going forward, my life would be complicated. Would we share holidays together? Would we *mean* something to each other? I didn't know the first thing about building a relationship with Glenn. Or if I wanted to.

I texted him and said I could stop by; he gave me a time and sent his address.

When I pulled up to his house that afternoon, my body felt swathed in anxiety. Like a boa constrictor was coiled around me, squeezing mercilessly. Despite this, I made it to Glenn's front porch and knocked on his door.

"I appreciate you coming. Rest of the family's out for a while." He stepped aside, and I went in.

"Sure." This topped my list of most awkward moments. I rubbed my sweaty palms against the back of my shorts.

Glenn handed me an envelope. "Might be best if you's the one to open it, see what it says."

I nodded and ripped the end off, having no interest in prolonging this un-Hallmark scene. My eyes scanned over the jargon, until I read the one word I was after.

"Negative."

We both let out a breath, which made me wonder what Glenn had hoped for. Or feared.

"Well." Glenn put his hands on his hips. "That takes a load off my mind, I reckon."

I wasn't sure what to say so only nodded.

"I know I ain't done right by you. If there's a way to make up for them things, I would."

"Thanks, Glenn. It's probably best if we put all this behind us." I didn't know if he'd told his wife about tormenting me with the Sally doll, or his suspicion that he could be my father. My guess was that he'd said nothing on either topic.

But that sounded harsh. Unforgiving. Glenn could've left the matter alone. He could've gone on wondering his whole life, not taken the risk of what it would do to his family to find out he'd fathered another child. But Glenn cared enough to know for sure. Maybe I had been too dismissive, too insensitive towards Glenn's feelings. Because when it came to Sloan and their relationship, maybe he still had his own healing to do.

"I can walk you out."

Since it was more of a statement than an offer, I headed to the door and out to my car with Glenn close behind. With each step, I struggled inwardly with what to say to him. Did I owe him an apology? A hug? Those concerns dissolved as a Campbell County Sheriff's car pulled up in front of Glenn's. Accompanying him were two white vans.

"Delilah, what are you doing here?" Mark Snyder asked as he got out of his cruiser.

"It's a long story. How about you?"

Several men and women emptied from the vans. They wore Tyvek suits, similar to the kind hazmat specialists wore. Gloved and toting what looked like stainless-steel suitcases, they poured out over Glenn's yard and house like a jar of ants released at a picnic.

Snyder looked to Glenn. "I've got a search warrant for your property, Glenn. An anonymous call came in yesterday. Told us we could find remains out by your barn."

"Remains of what?" I asked, after waiting for Glenn to say something. He stood frozen and speechless.

Snyder darted a look from me to Glenn. "Sloan Ramsey."

Glenn had what most would call a nice spread. Although his house was quaint, it sat on several acres his family had handed down to him. He had a barn that once housed horses, a pond, a two-tiered deck off the back of the house, and a sizable, detached garage that he used for his landscaping equipment.

Most of the men and women from the white vans headed for the barn. A few started scanning the perimeter of Glenn's house with metal detectors.

I almost gave myself whiplash, taking in the buzz of activity.

Snyder suggested we head out back. Once we were on the porch, he explained that the search was limited to barn, garage, and outside areas. He apologized for the abrupt approach but said he wanted the search done by the book, especially considering the sensitivity of the case. He handed Glenn a copy of the warrant.

"Let me get this straight." I waited until Snyder had finished. Glenn still hadn't spoken. "You got a tip that said something of Sloan's could be found here?"

"The caller specifically said there were remains inside the barn. We're not sure what that might mean, not until we find something—if we find something." He gave Glenn a look of resignation, one that was bound to duty.

Glenn's face had paled. Was it anguish from the ambush of crime scene techs crawling over his property—or was guilt taking hold of him?

Remains. What remains could possibly be in Glenn's barn?

"Lieutenant," called one of the techs from the opened barn door, "you might wanna come see this."

Snyder glanced from me to Glenn. "Wait here."

"Not a chance." I leapt from the porch and kept in step with Snyder. We made it halfway across the yard before he stopped and took me by the arms.

"Delilah, I'm not sure what this could be, and after yesterday..." He pressed his lips together. "Might be best if you went back to the house."

"I have to see it, Mark." My voice betrayed me, revealed my trepidation with its trembling. I was truly afraid. Seeing a picture of my dead mother's skull was one thing. Coming face-to-face with—*what*—what was in that barn? The anticipation threatened to be more than I could handle. Even so, I had to get in there.

Snyder looked worried, as if letting me be there was against his better judgment. "Hang back, Delilah."

I promised nothing.

Inside the barn was sparse. Various parts, probably to riding mowers, lined two tiers of shelves. The scent of flaky rust and motor oil danced in the air. Much like the salvage shop. A distinct difference was the hint of fresh-tilled dirt.

Two crime scene techs knelt beside a hole, an aura of dust surrounding them. Their flashlights were aimed on a small object. The tech who had called for Snyder reached in the hole and brought out the item. He gently rolled his gloved fingers over the top to crumble away the dirt. When he stopped, he held out his palm to the others. Faded purple fabric with paisley designs and an eroded brass clasp were illuminated by the light.

"What is it?" Snyder asked.

The tech shrugged. "My guess would be a coin purse."

At that moment, my mind reeled. A memory of Sloan flashed before me. I saw her with the coin purse, sliding it out of her handbag and dribbling coins into it from her hand.

"Isn't it pretty? It used to belong to my mom, and even her mom a long time ago." Sloan ran a hand over the silky purple fabric. "Purple is special. Brings good luck." She smiled at me.

When I gasped, the techs and Snyder looked to me.

"It was Sloan's."

"You sure about that?" Snyder arched an eyebrow, clearly skeptical.

"Yeah, I always thought it was beautiful...and I used to play with it." There were times I had snuck it out of Sloan's handbag, because it was one of my favorite pieces for dress-up. It was also one of the few items I associated with my mother. "Sloan told me it used to belong to Wanda and Wanda's mother."

"An heirloom." The tech added a sympathetic smile with his observation.

"All right. Let's open it."

Upon Snyder's command, the tech pinched open the crusty clasp. He held out his other hand as he shook the coin purse. Yellow-brown bits sprinkled onto his palm.

"What's that?" Snyder moved in closer and squinted.

I lifted my head, found his gaze. "Like what?"

"Not here. Probably best if we get you back to Wanda's for now."

I felt my body turn green. How would I tell Grandma about the teeth? She'd already been through enough. The shock had brought me to my knees. What would this kind of news do to her? How much more could she take? And what did it mean, Sloan's teeth buried in her old coin purse in Glenn's barn? Too many thoughts vied in my head. Coherence escaped me.

I gave up trying to make sense of it.

Snyder spoke to another officer, then led me to his cruiser. I let him take care of me. Or maybe I was too numb to function. Sitting in the police car, I looked out the window and realized Glenn was staring at me from his front porch. He looked anxious and weathered.

Was Glenn a victim in this latest development—or had he played a part in Sloan's death?

I had to pull myself together before we got to Grandma's. She couldn't see me like this, catatonic and disoriented. As a teen, my angst had ruled over me. The scars from Bill—and Sloan's disappearance— stayed raw and swollen for ages. As far as I was concerned, others were obligated to bear my misery. That led to an unstable life, and a lot of emotionally scorched earth behind me.

Now, Grandma would need me to be strong.

"What were you doing at Glenn's?" Snyder asked.

My answer about the paternity test and results surprised him. I hadn't planned to tell anyone about it, especially since Glenn and I were in the clear. A somewhat embarrassing episode I wanted to keep to myself.

"Did he really think he was your father?"

"I don't know."

My snarky reply conveyed my agitation, as Snyder changed the subject. He said he'd get my car home if I gave him the keys. I dug them out of my shorts pocket as we pulled into Grandma's drive. When I moved to drop the keys into a cup holder, Snyder reached for my hand. He didn't say anything or look at me, just held that part of me for a moment.

I forgave him, a little, as I left the cruiser without a word and didn't look back.

Snyder followed me in without warning. I let him take the lead and tell Grandma what had happened at Glenn's property. She absorbed the news about Sloan. She took a sharp breath in and covered her mouth. I had expected an abundance of tears, but she kept her composure. Maybe she had nothing left to cry. The agony bore so deeply into her that it evoked bafflement.

Although I was perturbed at him, I was glad Snyder was there. Grandma was too. Before he left, she held him tight and rested her head on his chest. I stayed at the other end of the kitchen and didn't make a move toward him.

"I'll make sure your car gets back, Delilah."

I slid my hand along Princess's curly-topped back and didn't look at him. "Thanks."

Alone in the garage apartment that evening, I called Jason and told him everything. It was exhausting, especially since Grandma and I had spent an hour on the phone with Donnie, catching him up to speed. Jason's questions and concerns matched Donnie's. He offered to come down, but I told him I didn't need him. That wasn't how I said it, of course. Something softer. Truth was, after all that had happened, I didn't mind being alone.

That night, I slept solid for a change. Neither the slightly muggy temperature of the space nor Oscar nesting in my hair bothered me.

After an early morning at the gym, I called Snyder. Maybe it was cruel, calling before the work day had kicked off, but at least I didn't have to worry about my call waking up Tonya.

Snyder croaked out a hello.

"I know it's early, but I needed to talk to you about Bill."

"Delilah?" Grogginess racked his voice.

I guessed he hadn't checked his screen before answering. He grunted. I waited a few beats. "Sorry if I woke you, but I want to know where you're at with the case and when you're arresting Bill."

"That's not up to me. I work with the DA to build a case. Takes time, Delilah. Believe me, it never moves as fast as you want it to. I'll keep you posted, but for now, you should focus on your family."

"Is it because of Glenn? Do you think he was involved?" I tapped my foot in the floorboard of my car, needing a release for my rising frustration.

"Off the record? No, I don't think Glenn had a part in what happened to Sloan. But yesterday was one of those curve balls I didn't expect."

You and me both.

"Delilah, there's one thing you should know."

I held my breath.

"The media's got a hold of the story. Some reporters might be calling and showing up at Wanda's. You better let Donnie know too."

I sighed as I imagined a mob of microphones and cameras and hyena-like reporters invading Granma's lawn. "It was bound to happen."

"Yeah, but it's best for now if none of you said much. It's still an on-going investigation, and we want to protect the evidence we've got so far."

For some reason, Britney came to mind. I could picture her asking me tons of questions, like she was deeply concerned about me and my family and everything that had gone on. Only to find out later she became a source for a TV interview and online articles.

"I'll tell them."

We ended the call soon after. Disappointment niggled. I'd wanted assurances. Wanted to hear that it wouldn't be much longer before Snyder was tossing Bill into the back of that cruiser.

When my phone buzzed in my hand, I thought it had to be Snyder, but it wasn't.

"Britney?" I answered, weirdly struck by some psychic vibe since I'd just been thinking about her.

"Can you come to the hospital?" She said it through sobs and over the whirring sound of a siren.

"What's going on? Where are you?"

"In an ambulance with my mom. I think she might be dead."

When I dashed into the emergency room at the University of Cincinnati Medical Center, I felt as frantic as Britney had sounded. I found her at the nurses' station, shoulders rolled forward, and her face wrinkled with anguish.

but leaving them didn't feel right either. I drove them to Tonya's house and helped Britney get her mother settled. Once Tonya eased into her bed, she fell asleep instantly.

Britney and I left her and padded our way back to the kitchen.

Then it hit me. "Oh, no, what about Milt?"

Britney's weary-worn eyes went wide. "I forgot all about Grampy! You think he's okay?"

I knew where this was headed. Me, going over to make sure Milt hadn't mixed up his meds and that he and Bill were stagnant but alive. A phone call wasn't sufficient; we needed to see that Milt was all right.

"I can't leave Mom."

There it was. The reason it had to be me.

"Yeah, she probably shouldn't be alone." Although I doubted Tonya would move for the next twelve hours, she deserved to have someone near after what she'd been through.

"You don't mind going over there, do you?" Britney wrung her hands. Was it because she knew I didn't want to see Bill? Or because she didn't want to do it? I couldn't say.

"It's fine. I'll go."

What choice did I have?

I drove slowly up to the trailer, trying to minimize the crunch and pop of gravel under my tires. A sure-fire announcement of my arrival. It was evening but still light out. Not like I could sneak up on the place anyway, but I tried. From the outside, things looked calm. No one appeared in any of the windows. No bellowing of the dogs. The salvage shop stood silent under the glow of a single bulb. Only the cricket chirps cheered me on.

A deep breath in and I was out of the car and entering Milt's trailer. The dogs barked and came over to me. I figured they were desperate for a potty break and let them out. Bill wasn't on the couch, which surprised me.

Milt added to my disbelief.

"DeDe? What are you going here?" With effort, he rose from his chair.

"I just came by to check on you, since Tonya couldn't make it today." My voice trailed off. I figured Britney should be the one to tell him about Tonya.

"Yeah, that's not like her. She's pretty good about showing up once or twice a day."

I nodded. "Maybe tomorrow." That was probably a lie. Good time to change the subject. "Where's Bill?" Not that mentioning Bill lessened the awkwardness.

"He ain't been around. Which is fine by me. Matter of fact, haven't seen him for a day or two."

I didn't know what to make of that. Was he better and back at the house? Was he up to something else?

I followed Milt into the kitchen. He took his evening meds and said he felt like having a pot pie for dinner. I heated one up for him in the microwave and took care of the dishes in the sink. After, I sat with him in the living room and watched tv for a while.

Milt was alert, maybe even more so than during my first visit. He answered several questions correctly on *Jeopardy!,* laughed at a commercial for a sitcom, and took an interest in me. Where I was staying, how long I'd be in Venice, had I tried the fried green tomatoes at Al's Diner. This was how I imagined a visit with my grandpa should be. When I thought of my childhood memories of Milt, I was afraid of him. Maybe I associated him too closely with Bill. But now, I could separate the two, and simply enjoy time with my grandpa.

Later, on my way out, I let the dogs scramble back inside. Hearing Milt talk to them as I closed the door made me smile. With the sun and humidity down for the night, the air felt pleasant. As I was planning to drive home with the windows down, I was struck in the back of the head.

Pain shot through me. I sank to my knees. Then pressure hit my calf muscle. A foot. Someone was standing on the back of my leg. I cried out. Someone snatched a handful of hair from the top of my head. Tugged hard. Pulled me back into an awkward arch. Then twisted my right arm behind me. Pain clouded my vision. A stench of body odor and beer hit my nostrils.

"Where's them fancy moves at now?"

I blinked voraciously, until Bill's face formed. He grinned when recognition dawned on my face, then pressed our cheeks together. "I got a few moves too. Prison does that." His raunchy breath mixed with my desperate panting. "If I wanted to, I could end you right here, sweet girl. You know that, don't you? But I'm going to tell you this one time, so listen real good. You best keep the police away from me. I don't want no one knocking on my door anymore about Sloan Ramsey. You hear me? 'Cause next time, I might not be so forgiving. You got that?"

He let off my calf muscle. Before he released the handful of my hair, Bill licked the side of my face. Letting go of my arm, he shoved me face down to the pebbly ground. Something like a chuckle-grunt belched from him as he walked away.

CHAPTER TWENTY-SEVEN

There on my knees, my palms against the gravel, pain pulsed through my body, as the night crept in around me. I didn't waste time on tears. I scrambled into my car and peeled out of there. Shame began to trump the pain. How could I have been so stupid to let down my guard?

Back in the apartment, I hugged Oscar so tight he wiggled his way out of my grasp. Sitting on the couch, I let Bill's words stream through my head. *You best keep the police away from me.* Was the Campbell County Sherriff's Department putting pressure on him? Were they closing in, preparing to arrest that jerk? If so, it couldn't happen fast enough.

I texted Britney that Milt was fine and asked about Tonya. Right now, I didn't want anyone to know that Bill had ambushed me. *I could end you right here.* After Britney replied that she was glad Milt was okay and that Tonya was still sleeping, I hit the shower. Not before I slid the couch in front of my apartment door.

Then I cried.

If I were honest, it was more from a sore pride than actual aches. I had endured worse from sparring and competitions than what Bill dished out. But that was his main intent—take me down a peg, prove that he could come after me, have his way, if he wanted.

I jumped a little when my phone vibrated.

A text from Snyder. *You able to meet at my place in an hour?*

Hearing from him couldn't have come at a stranger time. I told him I would be there, and he sent his address. Part of me wasn't sure if I had any business going to Snyder's home. The other part felt like that was exactly where I wanted to be.

He lived closer to Grandma than I expected. Not shocking, considering Venice, Kentucky's size. Shocking came with the tidiness of Snyder's home, combined with the overpowering scent of Febreeze-like cleaners. Those distractions quickly faded away.

"Thanks for coming on short notice." He reached in the fridge for a beer and offered me one. I took a bottled water instead.

"Did you hear about Tonya?" Not the smoothest segway.

He sat on the couch, then nodded with indifference, as if the news was the same as hearing his favorite burger place was closing.

"Yeah, I read the report, called the hospital. I haven't talked to her yet. Imagine she's out of it right now. I'll head over there later."

I couldn't say why exactly, but his lack of urgency bugged me. Hours ago jealous notions had pricked me, thinking he was going to lavish Tonya with attention and concern. Instead, he had invited me over to his house. And we were alone.

He twisted the cap off his beer and took a drink. A heavy sigh followed. "We've got problems, Delilah."

I sat beside him, feeling a shift in his emotions.

"First off, we put a rush on the DNA test for the teeth we found at Glenn's. It matched the skull."

"Yeah." Just like I knew it would.

Snyder took another pull on his beer, seemed to collect his thoughts. "I thought finding those remains would be a good thing, help build the case against Bill. Until today."

Snyder wasn't looking at me. A sure sign I wouldn't like what he had to share.

"Spent most of the day at the courthouse," he continued, "The DA and I had a long, long talk with Bill."

This time, the mention of Bill made a shudder run through me. I slid a hand up to my still-aching neck but made sure no reaction escaped me. Maybe I should've blurted it out right there—that Bill had attacked me, threatened me. But I was back to being a little girl, keeping Bill's dirty little secrets.

"Pains me to say it, but I haven't given him enough credit." A sneer flashed on Snyder's face. "The DA asked him to come down for an interview, told him there was new info on his wife's disappearance. Bill gave her the run-around on the phone, didn't really say if he'd show up or not. But he did, with his lawyer. Stafford and I know him. He's got a reputation for being expensive and mouthy.

"Stafford showed Bill a picture of the skull, told him we matched it Sloan. She pointed out the bullet hole, which proved Sloan was murdered. Bill sat there. Didn't flinch. I told him we had a detailed account of what happened to Sloan and how she died at his hand, that we knew he dumped her body and car in the sinkhole…and what he'd done to her head. We told him about the anonymous phone call that led us to the teeth on Glenn's property."

Snyder needed another drink. It worried me, made me think he was working hard to numb the stress from the day.

"And then, it all started to crumble. Duncan Wheeler chimed in. We call him the wheeler-dealer—not because we like him. He looked at us with that cat-that-ate-the-canary-grin and told us we don't have a case against his client. He said there was no physical evidence tying Bill to Sloan's death—and that he could easily sway a jury to believe that Glenn had killed her."

"What! That's ridiculous! Donnie's testimony proves everything—"

"Wheeler promised he'd bring in a parade of experts to refute the eye-witness testimony of a child, that it was just Donnie's way of getting back at his father for the abuse."

"But the extortion…"

"Donnie paid him in cash, and Bill doesn't have a bank account. There's no proof."

"I can't believe this!"

"We can't arrest Bill with what we've got. Wheeler is right. A jury might acquit Bill, might think there's enough reasonable doubt. Wheeler is the kind of guy who could confuse a jury and put a spin on the evidence."

"You think a jury won't see through that guy and his tactics?"

Snyder held his palms open. "It's a gamble. Then there's Glenn. He'd never survive on the witness stand, not with Wheeler coming after him, painting him as a jealous lover who got tired of waiting for Sloan to leave Bill. It wouldn't take much for the guy to confuse Glenn. Hell, Wheeler might get Glenn so confused he confesses while he's on the stand. Sloan's diary won't help matters. Neither will the fact that Glenn has a .22 registered in his name. Bill doesn't, never has."

If a truckload of bricks was dumped into my lap, it would've had a more comforting effect than what Snyder was telling me.

"So all things considered at the moment, Stafford doesn't want to press charges."

"Basically, we're right back where we started, Delilah."

Snyder turned to me. His burdened gaze met mine, and he gave me a solemn nod.

I left Snyder's soon after. Dismay or heartbreak or whatever obscure emotion it was pounded through me. Snyder didn't try to stop me from leaving. Didn't comfort me or sheath me in the security I craved. I went there thinking he wanted me. That we would reward the ripe attraction between us. Irrational and stupid, I know.

Because I wanted to feel good. Wanted to think about anything besides Bill. Wanted to block out the feel of his hands on me—his skin against mine. Instead of getting lost in an imaginary love affair with Snyder, I got the news that he and the DA were practically giving up the case against Bill.

I knew Donnie was working and drove to the restaurant. Being on the later end of the evening, the crowd was thin. I sat at the bar and probably looked like an idiot ordering water. When Donnie saw me and came over, I wasn't sure what to tell him first. I started with Tonya. Donnie had already heard, thanks to Britney. We both agreed the situation could've been worse.

I moved on to the DNA results from Sloan's teeth. Like me, he wasn't surprised. But hearing about Bill's day-long interrogation with Snyder and the DA, and how one cocky lawyer had poked holes in the evidence, dazed him.

"Are you telling me Bill's going to get away with it?"

I shrugged. "He's gotten away with it for fifteen years. Plus, he seems to have a cloak of invincibility. Nothing touches the scumbag."

As Donnie digested the news, I teetered on whether or not to tell him about Bill attacking me. It was hard to say which was better—forgetting it even happened or solidifying the fact it happened by telling him. My greater concern was Bill doing the same thing to Donnie. Ambushing him, bringing him to his knees, getting his message across. I couldn't let my brother be blindsided.

"I saw Bill earlier. Out at Milt's. He…uh, wasn't happy with being questioned."

"What does that mean?"

I glanced away, wishing there was a way to get through this without Donnie losing his temper.

"He came at me from behind. Hit me with something. Then stepped on the back of my leg, grabbed my hair, twisted my arm."

"Bill attacked you?" He raised his voice, but not enough to draw attention from the diners.

"That's one way you could put it."

"Tell me you turned it around and beat the shit out of him?"

"No. He definitely got the best of me. He did it to try and prove he's smarter and stronger than me. He also told me to get the police to back off from investigating him. He wasn't too happy, spending the day with Snyder and your new friend at the DA's office."

"Have you told Snyder what happened?"

"No." Was it possible to self-combust from embarrassment? Almost there.

Donnie said nothing for a few minutes. He understood my inner turmoil. Knew better than anyone what it felt like to be imprisoned by fear. Even when it was unreasonable and only gave the monster more power over you.

"We can't let Bill keep doing this to us," he said. "It's time he was held accountable for everything he's done."

"Donnie, if you're thinking of—"

"Calm down, little sister." He held up his hands. "I'm not going near him. Somebody else already has it out for him." He stepped close and plopped his arm on top of my shoulders. "We just have to stick together and see this through. It won't be for nothing, I can feel it."

I relaxed under the weight of his arm and returned a smile. Nothing could give me greater hope at the moment than seeing my brother truly free from the guilt and shame he'd carried. If he believed there would be justice for Sloan, I could too.

I resisted Donnie's nudging to call Snyder. I couldn't. Not until I was ready. Donnie said waiting would only make it worse. No argument there. But if Snyder couldn't run out and arrest Bill for assaulting me— due to a lack of evidence or something—I didn't want to face another disappointment. Didn't want another small victory for Bill.

Before leaving the restaurant, I hugged Donnie tight. Was there a better healing balm than a brother's embrace?

I texted Britney for an update on Tonya. She said Mark was there now and staying the night. My heart ached for him. No way it was easy for him to see her battered. Plus, with Sloan's case at the forefront of his mind, I wondered if he felt on the inside the same way Tonya looked on the outside. Britney then asked if I could meet her at Tonya's salon in the morning and help her with clean up. I said I would be there.

Back at the house, I chatted with Grandma, giving her the latest on Tonya. I couldn't tell her what Snyder said about the case against Bill. Couldn't tell her that Sloan's remains might end up meaning nothing.

That morsel of hope I coddled earlier with Donnie had crumbled away. Although I was thankful the bullet hole in the skull prove Donnie was innocent of murder, it was frustrating to hear how Bill's lawyer would dispute the evidence.

When I crawled into bed that night, I held Sloan's diary to my chest.

"Please, God, find a way...make him pay for what he's done."

It was my turn to bring the morning drinks for Britney and me. She'd been thoughtful, my first morning back in Venice, making sure I had a pick-me-up on our way to visit Milt. Now, she needed the favor returned, but in a bigger way.

Britney had jumped in, done everything to take care of her mother since the assault. Maybe that's how a family worked—or was supposed to work—when times were difficult. But Britney's nature tended to be selfish. Seeing her shed that skin, even if it was temporary, made me want to help her and be there for her.

When I got to Tonya's salon, Britney was already there. Stepping over the threshold, drinks in hand, I paused. Britney was sweeping up the pieces from a broken mirror. I looked at the floor and saw where Tonya must have been when Britney found her. Blood stained the laminate.

My eyes met Britney's, and my breath caught.

"I'm sorry. That had to be terrible for you, finding her the way you did."

Britney glanced at the stain, then back to me. "I thought she was dead."

I could see why. Not only was one of the mirrors broken, but furniture in the waiting area was overturned and a shelving unit of hair products knocked down. Chills ran through me as I pictured what Tonya must have gone through as some thug beat her and wrecked her business.

"I can't believe someone came in here and…did that."

Venice was fortunate enough to remain a small town still insulated in innocence. If there was such a thing. Violent crimes didn't happen here. Sloan's case being the exception.

"How's your mom doing?" I handed Britney her mocha. We both sat in the comfy salon chairs.

Britney sipped and shrugged. "Better, I guess. Having Mark there made a difference."

I wasn't positive but detected a pinch of resentment in her remark.

"Mark's supposed to look after her this morning. He might stay again tonight. Kinda wondering if this will bring them back together."

I made a point not to choke on my tea. She could be right. An incident like this could cause a change of heart. It sickened me a little to think about it. "Any word on the police nabbing the guy who did it?"

"No. They said they would check security footage from nearby shops and see if it captured his picture. Mom gave them a description, but it was pretty vague. There's not much they can do if the security cameras didn't catch him."

The evil imp inside me wanted to ask her how she liked it, seeing her mother suffer and having no promise of justice. I knew it wouldn't cross her mind, the thin parallels between Tonya's assault and Sloan's death. But it wasn't lost on me.

To be fair, it was obvious Britney had a rough time, seeing her mother hurt. Her light make-up wasn't enough to hide the fact she probably hadn't slept well. Her hair in a bun and loose-fitting clothing told me she didn't care how she looked—and Britney had always cared about how she looked.

"I blame Bill." Britney said it absent-mindedly, as if she wasn't expecting me to hear her.

"You think he had something to do with the attack on your mom?"

"No, not directly. It just that ever since Mom said he was getting released and coming back here, things have been falling apart. She's done nothing but worry about what he might do to Milt or even her. She and Mark broke up. She's had to do everything Bill wanted. Grampy ends up in the hospital, getting his meds mixed up. Now this."

If she only knew…

"I think Bill and trouble go to together." Trouble and dumb luck, at least.

"I've always hated him. Even when we were little, I couldn't stand being around him. He...he always looked at me a certain way. He called me pretty girl all the time and used to touch my hair." Britney shivered at the memory.

"Yeah. His creep-factor is off the charts."

"And there were those times...."

I noticed Britney's hands were trembling.

"He would catch me alone. Either in the salvage shop or in that patch of woods between your old house and Grampy's. *Well, there's my pretty girl. Out here all alone.*" She covered her eyes as the tears came.

I knew what came next, what she was trying to tell me. "He raped you too?"

With her hand over her eyes, she nodded. Sobs followed. I embraced her. How could I have been so stupid all those years? Never realized that Britney's hot-cold temperament with me was because of Bill and what he'd been doing to her.

"Did you tell anyone?"

"My mom, but not until she told me he was coming back. I thought he was going to stay in prison a lot longer, or maybe never get out. It's not fair!"

I squeezed her tighter, wishing I could ease her pain.

Britney went through the inventory of her encounters with Bill. How he sometimes snuck her out of Grampy and Granny's trailer during our sleepovers with cousins and took her to the shop or the workspace. The times in the woods, fallen pine cones and twigs digging into her back. Even in the basement of our old house. And how he always made a point to run his fingers through her hair. Slide strands through his mouth, leaving it wet with his saliva.

It angered me, the opportunities and sexual stamina that man had.

Britney said Bill threatened to kill her if she ever told. She tried telling Tonya, but each time Tonya seemed to shut her down or played flippant. Until she told Tonya everything a month before Bill's release. Tonya was devastated and apologized for not doing anything. For not listening to Britney when she was younger.

After hours of letting it all out, Britney apologized to me for the harsh ways she treated me over the years. She said it was her way of not being able to separate me from Bill, even though he had hurt me too.

I understood. I understood so much.

CHAPTER TWENTY-EIGHT

When we left the Beauty Bar Salon, Britney looked radiant. Her eyes were puffy and still had smeared traces of make-up, but she reminded me of Donnie. He wore that same expression—hopeful and refreshed, most importantly *freed* from an unjust burden—after sharing his account of Sloan's last day with Snyder and again after our meeting with the DA.

"I'm going to check on Grampy," she said, then shrugged a shoulder. "I still have to tell him what happened to my mom."

"How 'bout I go with you?" No way I could stand the idea of her going to the trailer and running into Bill, especially after our morning together.

"Yeah?" Her tilted head and bashful half-grin reminded me of when we were little, repairing the ground of our friendship after a childish squabble. Back then, neither of us knew the weight of what the other carried.

"Yeah."

As we piled into her car, I felt a genuine connection between us for the first time. It had always been there, I supposed, but now I recognized what truly bonded us. Resilience. A trait that undoubtedly ran thick in our blood.

Britney called Tonya, on speaker, during the drive. She sounded awake and functioning, but I imagined her body told a different story. Britney let her know we were on our way to Milt's. I squeaked out the obligatory well-wishes and wondered if my relationship with my aunt had any hope of becoming more than surface-level exchanges. Rome wasn't built in a day, I reminded myself.

Britney and Tonya began to chat about the salon and I reverted to checking my phone. A passable ruse as my mind ventured to the developments in Sloan's case. In particular, I was bothered by the anonymous phone call the sheriff's department had received about the remains on Glenn's property. The discovery of Sloan's teeth had been a triple punch of thrill, horror, and detriment. Like the skull, the teeth proved Sloan hadn't abandoned me and Donnie, but they also spoke of the gruesome death she suffered. Worst of all, they clouded the waters of Bill's involvement with reasonable doubt to a potential jury.

Who had suddenly reached out with the precise location of Sloan's remains? And after all these years, why now?

My mental ramblings took a backseat when we turned onto the gravel drive and noticed several vehicles on the lot. Déjà vu struck too. White vans and people in hazmat suits dotted the area, just like they had two days ago at Glenn's.

"What's going on?" Britney asked, wide-eyed as she parked and cut the engine.

"Looks like a heavy-duty search."

"For what? These guys look like they're from outer space."

My insides twisted. *Now what?* "Only one way to find out."

Before heading inside the trailer, we saw Snyder's cruiser. The dogs greeted us with agitated barks but settled at Milt's command. He seemed alert but distressed, seated in his chair. Britney went to his side.

"Afternoon, ladies," Snyder said from his seat on the couch.

"Another tip come in?" I twirled a finger in reference to the search team outside.

"No, more like a follow-up search after what went down at Glenn's place." Snyder patted one of the dogs. "That discovery of remains gave us the probable cause we needed to put the wheels in motion for a thorough search here. Got a judge to sign off before the dirt was off that coin purse. Team's been at it since early this morning. Combed over the old house, trailer, the workspace, the shop, woods, everything."

"Wait." Britney held up her palms. "Remains? What are we talking about?"

I had no idea what Britney knew about Sloan's case and if Donnie had told her anything. In my opinion, now wasn't the time to catch her up.

"It's a long story." I hoped the over-used cliché placated her for now.

"Delilah," Snyder said as he stood, "how 'bout we step outside?" Then to Grampy, "You've been good company, Milt. Appreciate your patience and cooperation today."

"That's all right." Milt held up a hand.

Snyder followed my lead outside, where a handful of techs were scattered.

Flushed by a degree of humiliation, I asked, "You couldn't have sent me a text, let me know you were pouncing on Milt?"

"Slick back your ruffled feathers. I didn't want you on the alert or intervening with that well-meaning but not-so-helpful way you have."

My flush deepened.

"And I've been with Milt most of the morning. Didn't want him shook with all the action. You seem to forget we're on the same side here but we ain't exactly equals in this hunt."

I swallowed. Snyder was right. I'd coddled the impression we were working together, but he had a job to do. A sworn duty to uphold. "Did you find anything?"

"We bagged dozens of items, but I think we hit the jackpot in the workspace, least that's my hope. Found some work boots, tools, and knives that tested positive for the presence of blood. That included a pair of pliers. It's possible Bill used them...for dismembering Sloan...and taking out her teeth."

A shudder ran over my body.

Snyder turned, seemed to survey the activity. "Doesn't look it now, but we had the place covered. Called in deputies from surrounding counties for extra manpower. I'm right proud. There ain't an inch we didn't go over. All we need is one thing—one drop of blood—that we can link to Bill." Snyder cast his gaze downward, shook his head. "Praying to God we find it."

"You did all this right under Bill's nose? Did he come out on the porch and sip iced tea while the techs combed through the house?"

Snyder grinned. "We should head to the station. Got a few surprises for you."

We popped inside the trailer and quickly told Milt and Britney we were leaving. Snyder tried soothing their anxious expressions by assuring them the techs would clear out soon. I couldn't tell if it worked, but my guess was they didn't know what to make of the whole thing. I told Britney I'd touch base later, kissed Grampy, and we left.

On the ride to the station, tension built within me. I hated surprises. Snyder fielded a few calls and seemed unaware of my restlessness.

"I saw Tonya," he said, after finishing a call. "Stayed at her place last night."

"Yeah, Britney told me. Must've been hard, seeing Tonya like that." I shrank in my seat a little, the needles of jealousy poking me. If they got back together I wouldn't be shocked. Tragedy worked like that at times, and I worried that announcement might spring from the so-called surprises he had in store.

"It's a poor excuse of a man that lays his hands on a woman. I've seen worse though. She got off lucky."

I nodded, waited for more, but Snyder only focused on driving.

Once we arrived, Snyder led us into an office lined with desks, computers, and monitors. Officer Dalton sat staring at a set of screens, clicking a mouse. He swiveled and greeted us. Since I'd been around, Dalton and I had become better, less prickly acquaintances.

"Does she know?" Dalton asked Snyder.

"The fun's about to begin."

Fun? What kind of fun? Good fun? Bad fun? My eyes darted between them as my muscles stiffened.

Snyder offered me a chair, then sat between me and Dalton.

"Before I show you this," Snyder said, "I gotta let you in on a little something. Dalton, why don't you get that footage ready."

Dalton busied himself with typing and clicking.

Snyder continued. "Tonya was deeply concerned about Bill returning to Venice. She was near hysterical at the idea of him living near Milt. Feared that he would hurt him. So before Bill was released, we set up hidden cameras inside the trailer, the shop, and around Milt's property. Had Milt's permission for everything, since he's the rightful owner. It was a chore, keeping up with the footage, but worth it. Caught Bill mashing up pills and putting it into drinks he served Milt." He pointed to a screen.

Bill appeared. He stood in Milt's kitchen, his back to Milt and bottles of pills in front of him on the counter. With a spoon, he pressed and smashed pills into crumbs, then wiped them into a drink. A few stirs and he handed the cup to Milt, who downed several pills with the drink before setting it aside.

I shook my head. "Bill's been a perfect asshole to everyone he's ever known."

"We charged Bill with attempted murder this morning when we got to Milt's. He's sitting in a cell, getting used to the idea of being behind bars again."

"He's here? Locked up?"

Snyder and Dalton nodded proudly as goosebumps popped on my skin.

Joy and relief overwhelmed me. My hands covered my gaping mouth. Bill was in jail. Maybe it was premature, but hope flooded my soul—hope that this time Bill would never know life outside those iron bars. Hope that Donnie and I could finally heal. Build lives without Bill casting a shadow over us.

"It was a good thing Tonya got Milt to the doctor," Snyder said. "They ran a tox screen on his blood, which showed an elevated level from the drugs. Also caught Bill swapping pills into different bottles. Ain't no lawyer out there who can argue Bill wasn't trying to kill his father."

"You nailed him." I leaned against the ergonomic chair. "I just can't believe it." *Wait till Donnie finds out.*

"Now don't go planning a parade or nothing. Next couple a days we gotta lay low, wait for the test results on the stuff we found at Milt's. And that ain't all." He sighed. "The media got wind about the investigation being reopened. They can be relentless when it comes to something like this. A cold case with new developments stirs them up, especially in a town like Venice. I want you and Donnie and Wanda to prepare yourselves."

"What does that mean?"

"Treat it like a tornado warning. Trouble's been spotted. Seek shelter. Hunker down. I'd add, stick to people you know. Some of those tabloid reporters will try anything to get a story or reaction out of you. Look out for each other. That sorta thing."

"You're thinking reporters are going to be staked out in front of Grandma's house?"

Snyder nodded. "There's a fair chance this story could explode. Might even go national."

I pictured flashes of my family's tragedy swiping across internet news feeds. Dread swelled inside me when I thought of Emery—and what such an intrusion could do to my family. A focused cleansing breath eased the tingle of anxiety.

"They're always lookin' for the next big thing to latch on to," Snyder added. "We've kept plenty of facts under wraps, because I've gotta do my job and protect the case. So keep mum when they go poking a microphone in your face or answer with 'no comment' and move along."

"Easy enough."

Snyder and Dalton traded glances and Snyder paired an eyebrow twitch with a slight movement of his head. Taking the cue it seemed, Dalton got up and excused himself. When we were alone, Snyder laced his fingers and laid them across his chest.

"I wanna circle back and talk about those cameras we hid at Milt's. They caught a bunch of stuff." Snyder turned to me, gave me a stare that told me I had some explaining to do.

At first I worried I'd done something wrong—or been running around naked—but I knew what Snyder was pushing for.

"Are you referring to an episode inside the salvage shop? Involved a guy wearing a UK hat."

He nodded. "That'd be one event. Any idea who the guy was?"

"No, but Wanda had heard rumors that Bill was using the shop as a front for selling drugs. So I tried acting like I was supposed to be there. Like Bill had sent me in his place, and I was there for the latest delivery. It was stupid, I know. Didn't work. The guy thought it was a set-up and ran."

"First you're dipping into a sinkhole, then you're trying to play gangster. You might need counseling for that death wish you got."

I held up my hands, defenseless.

"You and Wanda wouldn't be wrong about the drugs. We were able to find out who the guy was. Name's Ricardo Diaz. According to his arrest record, he and Bill did time together at Blackburn. Could be they met and decided to start their own little empire once they were both on the outside. We've got an APB out for him but haven't tracked him down yet."

I couldn't say why, but I breathed a sigh of relief. Maybe it was knowing that Ricardo had a name, and that the police were on to him.

"There was another moment I was concerned about."

"Outside Milt's trailer?" *Where I was on my hands and knees with gravel digging into my palms?* Donnie was right. I should've told Snyder after it happened. Having him find out like this was embarrassing.

"Want to tell me about it?"

Not really. But I did. I explained how Bill got a thrill out of attacking me and making sure I knew he could end me anytime he wanted. I told him about the pictures Donnie and I took of my bruises too.

"Guess I shoulda paid better attention when I saw you last night. You seemed on edge, but I chalked it up to all that's happened these last few weeks."

"I should've said something, but I feel like I'm always crying to you about one thing or another."

288

"That's not true, young lady, and you know it. One thing's certain. Bill won't be leaving that cell anytime soon. If the DNA tests come back positive on those pliers or work boots, I'm gonna be there to make sure he gets the maximum sentence. Been a long road for you and your brother."

I was determined not to cry. So many emotions toiled inside me. Anger. Relief. A feeling that my mom would finally get the justice she deserved. My chest felt overloaded. I stood so I could get a deep breath. Snyder stood too and embraced me. Taking in the aroma of his dry-cleaned uniform and that hint of woodsy cologne he wore, I felt safe. Relaxed. He rested his chin against my forehead.

We stayed like that. Maybe longer than acquaintances were supposed to. That's when it happened. When my desires and hunger for Mark Snyder welled-up. They took over as I lifted my head and looked into his eyes. I couldn't read what he was thinking. But I inched toward his lips.

He stepped back but didn't let go of me.

"Delilah, you know this can't happen between us. I've been over it a hundred times in my head. I know I may have sent some wrong signals, but I just don't think this is the right move for us. Might be nice for a while, but I'm not gonna use you like that, knowing there's not a long-term future ahead."

Before I melted to the floor from utter disgrace, Snyder pulled me close again.

"I care about you too much to end up hurting you."

As I stood there, my arms limp at my sides, the dreaminess of Mark Snyder slowly dissipating, I knew he was right. Was I ready to be a stepmom and embark on a relationship—rocky or genial—with Mark's ex-wife? No. Those were just two of the issues we'd face at the forefront. Probably not the best foundation for a lasting commitment.

Not that I knew anything about a lasting commitment. I still had plenty to figure out about me. Plenty of emotions and hurdles to face before my past was laid to rest, and I knew the direction I wanted my future to take.

CHAPTER TWENTY-NINE

Days later, when the DNA test results came back as a match for Sloan Ramsey on Bill's pliers and work boots and knives, Snyder's prediction about the media came true. A full-blown storm hit Venice and took Sloan's case to national exposure. Reporters set up tents and lights outside of Grandma's house and spoke into the cameras around the clock. The neighbors were hounded, along with anyone we had known while growing up. Most of them had long suspected that Bill Ramsey had killed his wife, and most didn't have a kind thing to say about him.

It probably didn't help him any when the coroner released a report and stated that the pliers matched up to marks left on Sloan's skull.

My family became a feature on every media outlet. We kept interviews to a minimum and usually had Snyder present when we spoke to anyone. Grandma and Donnie largely shied away from the attention. For me, I saw an opportunity to broadcast encouragement to kids who were being abused or who had lived through it. I told them to speak up and tell a relative or teacher or doctor—and that there was no shame in going to therapy and getting the help they needed.

Snyder predicted the trial wouldn't start until late spring or summer of next year.

"You think you'll be around?" Snyder asked me over a coffee-tea break at Panera.

Since our embrace, we had kept things platonic. Our friendship became easier and more comfortable. My romantic notions had fizzled. I was thankful Snyder had confronted the issue, had the foresight to know what was best, even though I didn't say it.

"Actually, I've decided to come back to Venice."

"Permanently?"

I nodded. Snyder didn't respond with the glee I expected.

"What about your boyfriend?"

"Jason's going to come down on weekends, when he can. I haven't asked him to move here, so we'll see." That was as deep as I wanted to get. Not because of Snyder, but because it was still a topic of the unknown for me. How did two people know when they were meant to be? I was still trying to figure it out. In the meantime, I was content with the weekend visits and Jason staying in the garage apartment while I stayed at Grandma's. Oscar was happy about it too.

"Got any job prospects?"

"A few. One good thing about being on TV, it's also doubled as interview material. Had a couple places tell me they liked how I handle myself. The sad part about it is the need. There's no lack of abused kids."

"It's a shame, but just think how much better off they'll be having you as a role model."

I hadn't thought of it like that. *Role model* didn't fit me. Felt like an itchy wool sweater. A role model was someone who had everything figured out, had the right answers to every problem. I wasn't there. Maybe I never would be. It didn't matter at the moment.

"There's something else I need to bring up." Snyder downed the last of his coffee. "Tonya."

A lump formed in my throat. Was he about to tell me they were back together? "How is she?" I hadn't seen her since I drove her and Britney home from the hospital, which was almost two weeks ago.

"Better, as far as the injuries go, but we picked up a friend of hers yesterday. You might remember Ricardo Diaz."

"The guy I had the run-in with at the salvage shop? UK hat guy?"

"That's the one. When we started questioning him about his working relationship with Bill, he added a few surprises for us. Told us how Bill said he would soon be the owner of the shop and the land, and that he knew Bill's sister Tonya. We got to talking, as we do in interviews, and come to find out, Tonya hired Ricardo to stab Bill."

Had my eyes gone any wider, my eyeballs could've rolled out of my head.

"According to Ricardo, Tonya was often around whenever he stopped in," Snyder continued, "and apparently, she got comfortable around the guy. Enough to where she told him how scared she was that Bill was gonna kill Milt. So she hired Ricardo to sneak into the house. Told him how to shimmy the lock open on the back door, where Bill's room was at upstairs. Said no one would suspect a thing, that Bill had a lot of enemies. Ricardo believed her, said he knew what kind of guy Bill was. Only, when it came down to it, Ricardo said he chickened out at the last second. He was set to run, forget the whole thing, but he was already standing in Bill's bedroom. Bill woke up, two of 'em struggled until Bill got stabbed. Then, Ricardo took off."

"That might explain why Bill's injury wasn't fatal."

"I think so. Ricardo hides out, couple days later, he's hurting for money. He showed up at the shop to steal what he could and sell it. Said he was hoping to find Bill's stash of cash or drugs, but that he ran into some chick. He bolts from the shop feeling desperate, not knowing what to do now that someone's seen him on the property. 'Course, he didn't know about the cameras we had set up.

"Couple days later, he decides to pay Tonya a visit at the salon. He shows up before she opens, tells her he wants the money she promised him for stabbing Bill. Tonya refused, said he messed up, that Bill was gonna be fine and she wasn't paying for that. Ricardo lost it. Tore up the salon, attacked Tonya, and stole what he could."

"So Tonya knew the guy who attacked her but didn't give him up, because she knew he would reveal that she was responsible for Bill's stabbing. Whoa." I gave the revelation a few beats to sink in. "Have you talked to her?"

Snyder nodded. "Heard pretty much the same thing, same details from her. She cried her way through it, kept saying she didn't know what to do, that she was only looking out for Milt."

I believed it. Despite the way she treated me, I knew both Tonya and Britney loved Milt deeply. I also knew that Tonya had another reason for wanting Bill dead. I doubted it was my place to tell Snyder about the abuse Britney had endured, if he didn't already know. That alone would be enough to enrage a parent, especially one who felt she didn't do all she could to protect her child.

"What's going to happen to her?"

Snyder hesitated. I wondered if the feelings he had for her resurged. Along with a sense of helplessness. "She'll be charged with conspiracy. If she gets a good lawyer, maybe they can plea bargain it down. Too early to say. I'll do what I can to help her. But Diaz? Well, he and Bill might want to pick out decorations. They could end up together for an awfully long time. Can't think of two cons who deserve each other more."

I resisted hollering *Amen!* Since I doubted Diaz was half the snake Bill had been.

"You ready for the bonus round?"

I waited.

"We got Bill's burner phones when we arrested him. Finally traced one of the numbers to that anonymous call about the coin purse in Glenn's barn."

"That puts Glenn in the clear then. Proves that Bill planted the coin purse there after he killed Sloan."

"Bingo. It's good news for Glenn. I had a feeling all along he was being used." Snyder kicked back the last of his coffee. "Nothing beats finding out the truth."

I met Britney at Milt's trailer later that afternoon. She greeted me on the door stoop with a half-smile and a tight hug.

"How are you holding up?" I asked.

"Looks like I'm going to be running both salons. Not sure if you've heard—"

"I just talked to Mark a while ago. He filled me in on some things."

Britney nodded. I thought I'd save her the angst of pouring out the details about Tonya's involvement with Bill's stabbing.

"She's probably going to end up in prison. Can you just imagine my mom, in prison? She's not made for that."

Picturing Tonya in orange prison fatigues and shiny handcuffs was a stretch for my imagination. So was picturing her with Diaz while they plotted Bill's death.

"Hopefully she'll get a light sentence." Okay, I clearly needed to work on what to say in an oh-sorry-to-hear-your-mother's-committed-a-felony situation.

Britney glazed over my comment. "You know what's really not fair? The fact she didn't do anything wrong. I mean, not really. She got someone else to do it. It's really Bill's fault. He's the one who messed up people's lives, and now my mom's going to pay for it. So unfair."

There were bits of her logic I probably agreed with, but it worried me that she viewed her mom as innocent. Even so, I wasn't there to argue with Britney and it wasn't my job to set her straight on legal issues. She was lashing out and hurting. That, I could relate to.

"Your mom is a tough lady. You'll both get through this." I wondered if Britney would be called to testify against Bill and share the nitty-gritty about what he'd done to her. No way she was ready for that, but I vowed in my heart to be there for her when the time came.

We headed inside Milt's, worked our way through the barking dogs, and got to Milt. Just like the last time I saw him, he was awake, sitting a bit straighter, and called us both by our names as we kissed his peachy cheeks.

"What's the latest?" he asked. "They firing up the electric chair for Bill?"

His tone was too giddy for me.

"Geez, Grampy, isn't it weird to want your own son dead?"

Kudos to Britney for saying what I was thinking. It was absurd, but so was the fact we'd all been victimized by Bill. And here we were, together and strong, and looking like a church-basement survivor's group. I laughed. Hard. Because most people couldn't understand what we'd been through, and fewer would find an ounce of humor in the situation like I did. We were definitely scarred. Scarred but persevering.

"No one believed me for the longest time." Milt shook an opened hand toward Heaven. "I kept saying Bill had done it. He'd killed Sloan. No one would listen."

I recalled the morning when Milt told me about his Fourth of July celebration with Bill. How Bill had confessed—or bragged—over kamikazes about what he'd done. If it hadn't been for that morning, I wondered if I would've entered the Campbell County Sheriff's Office with such conviction and determination to solve the mystery of Sloan's disappearance.

"You were right," I said. "Took a long time, but it finally caught up with him."

The peace that washed over me from saying those words felt incredible.

A positive aspect of the media frenzy, was reconnecting with people I hadn't seen or talked to in years. As hard as it was to have my mother's death turned into entertainment for some, most people treated the graphic details of the case with sensitivity. I was often met with sad, apologetic faces and hand squeezes and caresses, almost like I belonged to the public. That was okay for now. I knew it wouldn't last. That another family was destined for tragedy, and their story would become the newest obsession.

When I walked in to Cracker Barrel in the middle of the afternoon, I couldn't shake my nerves. Grandma had made the arrangements for the two of us to meet. I told myself it would be fine, once we sat down in front of each other. Getting over that hump and breaking the ice after years of no contact, that was the hard part. That's what I told myself.

Grandma met me at the hostess stand. "She's already here. I figured the back corner was best. Give you two some privacy. She told me she's nervous, so do your best to make her comfortable."

I forced a smile and nodded. It had been a while since Grandma had talked to me like a child, which made me think she was anxious too. I followed her back to the small table.

Rita stood as I approached.

"Delilah! You sure grew up to be a beautiful girl."

"Thanks, Rita."

We sat and tried catching up, best we could. I was amazed how easy our conversation took off. We talked about Wanda and Paul, and how sorry Rita was to hear about Grandpa's passing. She told me about her life in Bowling Green, that she'd gotten married twelve years ago and had a slew of step-grandchildren. Rita had turned down all media requests for an interview, since the story broke, not wanting to re-live the worst times in her life.

"Them days with Bill," she nodded as she spoke and stared into her coffee mug, "They were hard. I don't know why I ever fell for him or moved in. I suppose it was because of you kids. He never was good to me. Worse, I knew how he treated your mother."

"What happened the night Sloan died?" Was it cruel, shifting so effortlessly to such a tragic event? Sure, I could've used more tact, acted more like the trained therapist I was now. Instead, I bulldozed through and sat tensely on the edge of my chair.

"He called me that night, told me not to come over. He said things got heated between him and Sloan, that he'd have to call me later. Well, it wasn't until the next day, and he told me Sloan was gone, had left him for good. Was never coming back. I didn't know what to think at first. I figured they just had a fight and she left. But then Bill told me to bring my stuff and move in. He needed help with you kids.

"Well, I was surprised. I knew Sloan had her issues and all but never dreamed she'd leave you kids with him. I guess y'all were the reason I did move in with him. You needed me all right, and I wanted to know what was really going on. Bill wasn't much of a talker, and he didn't say another word about Sloan. When I opened the closet and saw it was empty, well, I had the chills go through me. A bad feeling right then that something was wrong. I had my own issues back then. Drank too much, did other things I probably shouldn't've. Those things probably kept me around. Bill accepted me, and we all know what a wreck he was."

Grandma checked on us, topped off Rita's coffee.

Rita looked at me. "He never told me what he done to Sloan, or that he made Donnie help him. Reading about that in the paper, made my heart ache for that boy. I...I caught Bill, doing what he done to him." Her eyes glistened with tears.

I put my hand on top of hers. "You were a big part of getting Bill arrested. If you and Donnie's teachers hadn't gone to the police, he would've abused us for years to come. We're both grateful you were there."

She gave me a pressed-lip smile and patted my hand. "Y'all deserved so much better in life. It's good you went with your grandparents. They always was fine people."

We took a moment. Sat back against our chairs, both dabbed our eyes with our napkins.

"You know, there's one thing you should know about." Rita took a swig of her coffee. "It might not mean nothing now, but it's one of them things that stuck with me. One night, Bill smacked me around something awful. We were both drunk, of course, and to be honest, I don't remember most of it, which is maybe a good thing. But Bill got that look in his eyes, and he said he might as well start putting them pills in my drink and kill me too."

"Pills?"

"Yep, he had a bottle of little blue pills. I found it one day. Didn't have no label, so I asked him about it. He took it from me and laughed. *That's what I tried killing Sloan with*, he said. Didn't work though. Only made her sleep and extra loopy."

The Halcion pills!

"Bill was trying to overdose Sloan on sleeping pills?"

Rita nodded. "That's what he told me. He said he tried mixi up those medications she had to take, and he used to mash up th pills and put 'em in her drinks. He got 'em from his doctor. Told hi had trouble sleeping."

Rita's explanation made perfect sense. I could pictur face as he watched Sloan drift to sleep, hopeful that he'd drug to death. He probably expected one of two things to happe would appear to have committed suicide, either intent accidentally. Wouldn't have mattered which, not to Bill.

look like Sloan had messed up taking her medications and had taken too much of the wrong kind, even though she wasn't prescribed the Halcion. Bill would've ended up with a dead wife and could've put any spin on it he wanted. The toxicology report would put him in the clear, or so he imagined. Bill probably thought the sleeping pills were strong and would interfere with Sloan's medications. I wondered how long he had been trying to drug my mother.

Thankfully, his attempt to kill Milt with the same method had also failed.

"I'm glad you got away from him, Rita, and I'm glad nothing happened to you."

"Me too. I know if Bill had his way, I'd be in the same grave. And I'm sorry about your mother. I know now she was a good woman, and I got no doubt she was a good mother."

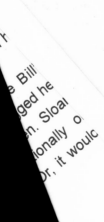

EPILOGUE

With the media attention in a lull, we held Sloan's memorial service in November. Overcast skies and cold, drizzling rain matched our emotions. Sloan's remains had been returned to us, even though the trial wouldn't start for another six months or so. We rented a mausoleum vault just in case forensics or the DA needed access again.

Grandma treated our gathering like a grand occasion. Grandma, Donnie, and me had dressed up. Grandma had also insisted on having a big meal ready for when we got home, further commemorating the best worst day of our lives. Neighbors and friends from Grandma's work offered to take care of the food. A sweet gesture that spoke of the goodness of Venice's people. Glenn also contributed with a generous display of flowers.

Only having the three of us at the service felt awkward and appropriate. Grandma sat with the box of Sloan's remains in her lap, never taking her hands off the specially-made container. That might seem morbid to some, but it showed me how much Grandma still missed Sloan, and that having part of her—any part of her—made her feel closer to her daughter again.

From our phones, we each played a song that reminded us of her. Grandma went first with Dolly Parton's *Jolene*. I followed with *Hello, Darlin'* by Conway Twitty, and Donnie had us laughing with the SpongeBob SquarePants theme song.

"We should share a memory. Maybe one that we each don't know about."

"Oh, got one," Donnie said. "I think I was around seven. She had put me in this little suit she'd just bought, and I hated it. Seems like it was for Easter, because it didn't fit very well. Was too tight in some places and the pants were too long. She said it could work for one day and it was the last one in the store. I ran out of the house and straight for that spot near the back door that was always muddy. Even days after it rained, that patch took forever to dry up. I went over and started rolling around. Mud went everywhere! Sloan came out yelling and trying not to get splattered, but it ended up on her legs and the bottom of her skirt. I stopped when I saw the brown speckles on her legs. I thought for sure she was going to let me have it, but she burst out laughing. She came down on her knees and started patting the ground with her hands. Mud got in her hair, all over her face, and then she rolled over and grabbed me and kissed me on the cheek. She laid on her back and just kept laughing. Pretty sure we missed church that day."

"I can see that happening." For Sloan, it was easier to make light of a situation than to yield to the expectations of convention. "I don't have a lot of memories of her. But she used to read to me as we sat on the porch swing. My legs were too short for my feet to reach the ground. She'd go slow, rock back and forth on her bare heels. One of my favorite stories was this little book called, *Davy Deer's Red Scarf*, I think. It had this cute little deer that looked like Rudolph. His mom had knitted him a scarf, and as he went through the forest, showing it off to his friends, it came unraveled. He went home and cried to his mother that the scarf was gone, but she wasn't upset. She told him all he had to do was go back through the forest and collect the string. She'd knit him a new scarf." I had never told anyone about that story, and how it made me think of my mother. How I wished that every problem was that easy to solve. How Davy's mother was there for him when life seemed unraveled.

My life had unraveled many times, since Sloan's death. Losing her meant losing a part of me I would never know. Sloan and I didn't have enough time together. I couldn't remember what her voice sounded like or if she kissed me goodnight at every bedtime. It did me no good to think about what I didn't have and the milestones we wouldn't share. The best I could do was honor her memory and focus on the future.

A big part of that meant recognizing the gift I had in my grandma. In my family. Even with all our family secrets unearthed, Venice was home. Where I belonged. Where I planned to constantly become a better woman, one who made my mother proud. I'd share our story with brutal honesty, and along the way, hoped to rescue as many kids as possible from the monsters in their rooms.

ACKNOWLEDGEMENTS
& AUTHOR'S NOTES

This story is a work of fiction but combines elements from two real-life cases. Both women were victimized--and dismembered--by the fathers of their children. Both men were eventually arrested and imprisoned for their crimes. What drew me to fictionalize and write about these cases was the resilience of the victims' families. I haven't had contact with anyone related to either case, but in researching these events, it was heartbreaking to know that these two women didn't get to raise their children. Justice prevailed, providing comfort, but the loss these families suffered is immeasurable.

I owe unending thanks to Eileen Curley Hammond, who helped strengthen this story and graciously took on more than she bargained for with getting this book to market. A generous lady, with a no-holds-barred approach to feedback that I truly appreciate!

Every writer should have a critique partner as insightful and talented as Alicia Anthony. The writing trenches can be a disheartening place, so it means everything to share the journey with the best writing pal out there. I couldn't be more grateful for her dear friendship, our fun travels, and epic lunches.

Special thanks to friend Ric Black. Although Ric has worn the hats of many careers, he's dedicated most of his life to helping abused children. Ric also tolerated my myriad of questions concerning medications and the evolution of pills over the years. Any errors or misrepresentations are mine.

My forever favorite beta reader, Twila. When she's not red-penning her way through the pile of 300+ pages I send her way, she's a sister of my heart. *Fé always*.

Buckeye Crime Writers has been a lifeline of inspiration and support. Thanks to Patrick Stuart for launching and commandeering the accountability group, though we don't speak of the Wet Noodle enforcements that accompany said group. BCW and our local writing community are a well-spring of creativity and comradery. We are fortunate to be surrounded by a collection of talented people, an incredible library system, and fabulous independent bookstores.

As always, I'm thankful for the people I get to call Home. Nothing means more than your love and support.

ABOUT THE AUTHOR

MERCEDES KING is a Columbus, Ohio, native and founding member of Buckeye Crime Writers. With a degree in Criminology from Capital University and a passion for writing, she enjoys exploring the depth of criminal behaviors through her stories. Mixing fact with fiction is her specialty, as is setting her tales in not-so-distant decades, which she's dubbed Modern Historicals. In 2016 and 2017, Mercedes was a finalist for the Claymore Award. When she's not elbow-deep in research, reading, or enjoying the local bike path, she might be at Wrigley Field or sinking her toes into the sand somewhere along Florida's coastline. Join her mailing list at MercedesKing.com

Every Little Secret follows Kyle Reed, a young college student determined to unravel family secrets entangled around the unsolved murder of her father's mistress.

Columbus Noir features Mercedes' short story, "An Agreeable Wife for a Suitable Husband", set in Columbus' gritty South Side during the 1970s.

A Dream Called Marilyn (novella) focuses on a psychiatrist who is hired to treat and subdue actress Marilyn Monroe, no matter what it takes.

Plantation Nation, follows the journey of Emma Cartwright, a 16 year old Southern girl who disguises herself as a young man and joins the Union Army.

You can connect with her on Facebook, Twitter, and Instagram.